I0577425

CHRISTMAS CONFESSIONS
Copyright © 2025 by Calla Cross

ISBN: 979-8-9932613-1-7

Cover Design by Haya In Designs

Edited and Formatted by Represent Publishing

CHRISTMAS CONFESSIONS

CHRISTMAS CONFESSIONS

CALLA CROSS

RP Represent
Publishing

DEDICATION

For the readers who cracked open this book and stepped into this story with me—thank you for believing in a world that lived in my head long before it lived on the page. And for my editor, who held my hand through every messy draft, every panic spiral, and every "wait, what if we change the entire thing?" Your patience and guidance made this possible.

AUTHOR'S NOTE

I grew up watching Hallmark movies like they were oxygen —soft lights, snow-dusted towns, people finding their way back to themselves and each other. Even as a kid, I knew I wanted to write stories that felt like that: warm, hopeful, a little magical, and full of the kind of romance that sneaks up on you and refuses to let go.

This book is that childhood dream made real. If you've ever chased a dream long past the point where it made sense . . . if you've ever loved stories for the comfort they bring . . . if holiday movies were your emotional support TV the way they were mine—this book is my love letter to you.

Thank you for letting me share it.

PROLOGUE

FROST HARBOR, VERMONT
MIA

Christmas Eve
Six years ago, 21 years old

The moment Frost Harbor's iced breath hit my lungs, I should've known what kind of night waited for me.

Not home. Not comfort. Just a trap dressed in tinsel.

Cinnamon. Pine. Scorched sugar. The air's so heavy it turns every inhale into a confession.

I shove open Riley's Taproom door. Heat blasts out, making me hesitate on the threshold.

Same drooping string lights. Same Christmas tree listing left like it's plotting an escape.

The jukebox is still stuck in 2016. So am I.

Behind the bar, a cheap cardboard Advent calendar hangs with half its doors unopened. Not the felt one from our kitchen—the *real* one—but close enough. I catch myself counting the doors anyway, like numbers can pretend to offer control.

"Snowden!" My best friend Harper lifts a shot glass in mock salute. "You were five minutes from becoming a missing-person report."

I shrug off my coat, still chilled, still here. Still doing my best impression of someone this town can't bruise.

She slides a cinnamon-spiked cider toward me. "Drink. We're on a schedule."

I huff. "We're still doing that?"

"Classic Tradition."

Tradition—same as pretending I'm fine.

I cradle the mug, letting its heat chew at the numbness. "God, what was wrong with us?"

"You," Harper fires back with a wicked grin. "You cooked this up as a teen, remember? One truth, one dare, one confession. Your own personal chaos menu."

A real smile tugs at my mouth. I've missed her—the razor humor, the way she refuses to let me disappear into myself.

Music hums low, filling the space between our laughter and the quiet ache underneath it.

Then my gaze drifts to the door.

"Don't even try it." Harper leans in. "You're pale, twitchy —watching that door like it owes you money."

"Seasonal ambush." I sip my cider that tastes of nostalgia and burns. "This town weaponizes memory, and I came under-armored."

Her eyes narrow. "Sure. And it has absolutely nothing to do with a certain Carter, right?"

I roll my eyes. "Please."

But my pulse misfires anyway. Three years. He's probably long gone—or worse, still here, living a life that never made room for me.

"Ah, there she is," Harper declares. "My favorite over-articulate Grinch."

"Don't start."

But my attention keeps snagging on the entrance. If he walks in, every lie I told myself walks in with him.

Harper taps her glass. "Truth, dare, or confession. Pick."

I stall. Say anything but the thing that still tastes like him. "I regret . . . not kissing the person I actually wanted to in high school."

Her brows lift. "Scandal. Who?"

Jake. The name rings through me, quiet but unmistakable.

He promised letters from every country . . . proof he was still alive out there. Instead: three years of static on my side of the ocean.

"I'm allowed one secret." I hide behind old rules, acting as if they still matter.

"You're deflecting, which means I'm right."

"About what?"

"That this has everything to do with him. He's back, by the way," she says. "Been home a week."

The words strike like sleet.

"He's . . . home?"

"Mm-hmm. Helping at the tree farm. And no, I haven't seen him with anyone."

Relief and panic twist through me. Jake Carter, back under his father's roof. Back in the place he once swore he'd escape for good.

"Do you think he forgot me?" The question slips out before I can stop it.

"Not possible."

"Harp—"

"I'm serious. You're not forgettable."

People forget easier things when it hurts enough.

The door opens. Winter air sweeps in, carrying snow and a shiver of memory.

Harper's voice drops. "Well. Speak of the ghost."

I turn—already knowing.

The consequence I never stopped imagining.

His boots hit the floorboards, each thud a low drum under my ribs. Light skims over his dog tags as he moves—broader, steadier, the boy I knew sharpened into something danger-ously defined.

He laughs near the bar, a sound roughened by cold and distance, familiar enough to tilt the room.

My mind says, *Look away.*

My heart says, *Don't you dare.*

My body votes for neither.

I look. *Hard.*

My eyes—greedy, shameless—take him in because they've waited years. Heat flares low climbing its way to my throat.

"Mia." Harper's voice is half warning, half prayer.

Too late. The past is already unfurling inside me like a fuse.

"Oh my God," she whispers. "Are you drooling?"

"I am not—"

"Don't lie, Snowden. That was a full-on gape."

I glare at her, cheeks warming.

She slaps her palm on the table. "One confession!" Too loud, of course. "I've absolutely imagined slapping Ava with a stocking full of coal."

A laugh escapes me, guilt fizzing where it shouldn't.

"She's my sister."

"Twin," Harper corrects. "You got the soul; she got the spreadsheets."

She's not wrong. Ava and I used to share everything—birthdays, clothes, late-night secrets whispered through the wall. Then at some point she became the version of us people found easier to love. Easier to choose.

"You okay?" Harper asks, voice softening.

I nod. "It's fine."

It isn't. Not even close.

Harper's on her feet in a blink, flagging Rein for another round. Rein—short for Reindeer, because Frost Harbor leans into its own nonsense—shoots us a grin from behind the bar, patron saint of bad ideas.

When she returns, she's carrying two shots and that look —the one that always means trouble is about to find me first.

"Dare," she pronounces, like a spell she can't wait to cast.

I open my mouth to protest, but she nudges the shot closer. "Now, Snowden. Before you alphabetize your excuses."

Fire hits first when the whiskey goes down; courage follows.

Harper flicks her hand, bossy as ever. "Shoo. Before I drag you."

A restless thrum awakens at the base of my spine as I move through the crowd.

"Mia." His voice crackles through the noise, unmistakable.

He stands by the pool table, forearms bare, cue resting loosely between his hands. Older. Quieter. Grounded in a way that wasn't there before.

I forget how to keep my lungs steady.

"Jake." His name barely makes it out.

He tilts his head, a faint smile appearing. "Still claiming the best booth, I see."

"It's called territorial nostalgia."

"Grad-school diction," he murmurs. "Missed that."

He studies me—focused, unhurried. "You stayed away a while, Mouse."

The nickname breaches the walls I rebuilt.

I came home whenever I could; he was always gone, folded into deployments and places I only knew from headlines. That's why the letters mattered—they were the tether.

And then they stopped.

"I wasn't planning on running into anyone," I manage.

Not a complete lie.

Every year, I swore I didn't care . . . yet some part of me waited to be shown wrong.

"You always plan too much."

"And you never did."

He huffs a breath, rueful. "Guess I needed friction. Something to figure out what I was made of."

Chalk dust ghosts his knuckle as he turns the cue. "I'm back at the tree farm. Christmas miracles."

I almost smile. "Didn't think you and your dad were—"

"On speaking terms? We're . . . trying." A shrug. "Chopping spruce is cheaper than therapy."

For a beat, we're quiet, the room thick with things neither of us touch.

"You look good," he says softly.

"So do you." I fix on the chalk smear instead of his eyes. "Didn't think you'd ever come home."

"Didn't think I could." His voice roughens. "Turns out the town keeps breathing even when you don't."

We test whatever's left between us, seeing if it still fits.

"Do you still have it?" I ask. "The telescope?"

His mouth tilts—not quite a smile. "Yeah. In my truck."

The answer stings more than it should.

I see it: the dented tube, the chipped tripod, the nights we dragged it into snowbanks because the stars looked sharper here.

He always said Frost Harbor skies made the world honest.

"Germany. Italy. Poland." He says it like he's carrying the weight, not reciting it.

Three years, three countries. Maybe he's naming the ones that left the deepest dents.

"But that always stayed."

A truth knocks offbeat inside me.

Because what he isn't saying—and what neither of us will —is that I stayed too.

Just not anywhere he could find me.

His hand finds mine.

"I didn't forget you, Mia." His voice is worn down, scraped close to truth. "You were the one thing that cut through the noise sometimes."

He doesn't look at me, and that somehow hurts worse.

"I'd close my eyes," he murmurs, "and if I could still hear your laugh, I hadn't lost everything good."

His eyes lift to mine, gray and bright as a lake right before it freezes.

I should say something clever. Or safe.

Instead: "I used to imagine my twenty-first birthday with you," I admit softly. "Us sneaking off like always. You dragging out that beat-up telescope, swearing the stars looked clearer here."

His mouth lifts—old muscle memory. "You never let me name any constellations."

"Because yours were boring."

"Boring? Europa Rising was poetic as hell."

"You were obsessed with Europa."

"And you loved pretending it annoyed you."

For a second, it's us again—before deployments, before silence.

Without thinking, I step closer, forehead brushing his.

We stay there, one shared breath, a fragile warmth in winter air. His hand slides to the back of my neck, thumb sweeping once along my cheek.

"God . . . I missed this," he whispers—meaning everything between the touches.

Something loosens in me—half hope, half warning.

A horn blares.

Rein yells, "Fire drill!" and half the bar erupts—laughter, cider, chaos.

Jake's hand finds mine again before thought can protest.

"I hate this tradition." I pout as he threads us through the crowd.

He glances back, mischief flickering. "No, you don't."

He's right. I don't.

I never hated it—just the part after, when the night ended and he wasn't mine to follow.

Frost Harbor's "fire drill" tradition kicks in—every Christmas Eve, everyone bolts outside with whatever they're holding. Rein cooked it up years ago after a real alarm, and the rules haven't changed:

- Run.
- Take something that won't survive snow.
- Trade it before you're allowed back in.
- Kisses count.

Jake and I did it every year in high school—me handing him doodled napkins, him giving me half-melted candy canes like they were tiny promises.

Now the memory surges back—sharp, immediate, the way a heartbeat remembers its rhythm.

We weave through tables as people grab whatever's closest and race for the door.

I glance at the booth through the swirl of bodies. Harper catches my eye and winks—Don't think, just go.

We burst into the alley, breathless, the cold biting at our lungs, snow spinning like sparks around us.

His hand is still laced with mine.

"Did Harper put you up to that?" he asks finally.

"To what?"

"The staring. The walk over. The part where I thought you might actually talk to me."

I pull my hand back, fold my arms to steady them. He steps in anyway, like gravity has its own plan.

"Truth. Dare. Confession," he says. "Which one brought you to me tonight?"

My heartbeat jerks. "Does it matter?"

"Yeah." His tone drops. "It does."

Snow hangs between us, waiting.

"I've imagined this a thousand times," I admit. "Not exactly like this—just . . . versions. Sometimes I said everything right. Sometimes you did. But it always ended the same —I woke up wishing it hadn't."

His mouth tugs, bittersweet. "So which version is this?"

"The one I didn't plan for."

His eyes flare. "Those were always the best kind with you."

He studies me, tracking every tell. "You're doing it again."

"Doing what?"

"Thinking your feelings to death." His hand hovers near

my jaw. "Wrapping everything in words so you don't have to risk anything real."

Heat climbs my neck. "Some people survive by naming things."

His fingers slip to the back of my neck, thumb brushing my cheek like instinct. "Mia. Stop pretending none of it mattered."

"I'm not—"

The lie collapses.

"Truth?" he murmurs. "I missed every damn part of you. The way you see the world. The way your voice changes when you let yourself feel."

His thumb grazes my lower lip. "Confession: I've replayed that night so many times it almost stopped being a memory. Every version ends the same—with me wishing I'd reached for you."

"And now?"

"Now," he closes the last inch, "I'm reaching."

I could step back. I don't.

His hand cradles my neck.

"Mia," he breathes.

That's the only warning before his mouth hits mine—hungry, unhesitating, like this has been simmering under his ribs for years.

I gasp; he swallows the sound, deepening the kiss. One hand clamps at my waist like letting go isn't an option.

The cold drops away. The noise. Everything but him.

He only breaks when air becomes necessary, keeping his forehead pressed to mine.

"Tell me you felt that," he pants.

My fingers are still knotted in his jacket. "I've wanted to do that for so long."

"Didn't expect it to feel like losing my mind," he says

with a dazed laugh. "The second you leaned in . . . it was over for me."

"Over?"

"Yeah. Done. Ruined."

He tucks a piece of hair behind my ear, thumb skimming my pulse. "Still trying to figure out how one kiss turned into that."

"You're ridiculous," I mutter, pushing at his chest.

He catches my wrist, lips brushing the inside like it matters. "I'm dying to kiss you again."

He proves it—drawn out, intent threading through every pull of his mouth, like he's imprinting me.

When he finally pulls back, his forehead rests against mine, our breaths tangled.

"We should—"

"Go," I finish. I know what he means; hearing it would hurt.

The walk to his truck is a blur of cold air and too-warm hands. The windows fog before we touch them.

Outside my parents' house, he kills the engine. Neither of us moves.

"If we walk inside," he says quietly, "we're not pretending anymore."

"I know."

His gaze searches my face. "Tell me to leave."

And I should—every instinct says I should—but wanting him has outrun every warning I've ever taught myself.

"I can't."

"Didn't really want you to, anyway."

He reaches across the console, hand sliding to my waist, pulling me onto his lap.

Not rough. Not rushed. *Just inevitable.*

"Been wanting you close like this for so long," he murmurs. "Didn't know how bad until tonight."

He kisses me with a heavier kind of want, paced like he's intent on making the moment last.

By the time we stumble inside, we're half-laughing, half-shaking. Boots thud onto the mat. Coats trail behind us. Pine and cinnamon linger in the doorway.

"Still you," he says against my mouth. "Always you."

I curl my fingers into his hair. "Then don't forget again."

Something tightens in his eyes—regret, warning, both. Then he kisses me like there's nothing left to hold back.

Just want.

Just surrender.

Christmas Morning

Early sunlight filters through the curtains, winter-pale, almost blue. It glides across the sheets, across the empty pillow beside me.

For a beat, my half-asleep brain tries to fill the space: the weight of him, the warmth of his breath, the slow sync of shared air.

But there's nothing. Just cold silence.

The bed is still warm where he slept.

I sit up slowly, body humming with the aftershocks of last night. My fingers brush the dent his head left in the pillow.

No footsteps. No Jake.

Just a faint ring from his coffee cup on the nightstand and a folded scrap of paper with my name on it.

For one ridiculous second, my chest lifts. A note. An explanation. A promise.

I open it.

Inside: *nothing.*

But the page isn't untouched. There's a faint gray smear at the top, like he started a sentence and dragged his thumb across it until the ink vanished. A half-pressed pen dent beneath it—three or four letters, maybe, before the line cut out.

The bottom corner is creased sharply, as if he folded it once, changed his mind, folded it again.

A message that wanted to exist . . . and didn't.

A goodbye he couldn't write or couldn't finish.

Or wouldn't.

Maybe that's worse.

I press my palm to the mattress. This is what silence feels like when it stops pretending.

I tell myself he's gone for good. But four weeks later, when the nausea hits before the coffee's even brewed, I learn something else about silence: It doesn't just echo. *It multiplies.*

Truth: *I'm not done with him.*

Dare: *I'm going to pretend I am.*

Confession: *We made a person, and I'm the only one who knows.*

1

WHAT WE PRETEND NOT TO KNOW

MIA

Five Christmases out of Frost Harbor, and winter still tastes counterfeit. Silence posing as peace.

Luca's backpack lies on its side, defeated. The microwave is shrieking for attention, and my coffee tastes like scorched disappointment. We're late—again—and single motherhood is basically combat without the courtesy of armor.

"Mom! My dino folder!"

Of course. "Teeth or stickers?" I call, attempting to juggle keys, grad-school chaos, and the last scrap of optimism I haven't misplaced yet.

He slides in—literal socks-on-tile chaos. "Both."

Naturally.

I fish the folder out from under the couch, along with a granola bar old enough to vote, and hand it over.

"Shoes, Luca. Matching ones."

He grins. "Gotta confuse my enemies."

That grin. God help me. It settles with the weight of a

name I've kept locked behind my teeth for five years—a name that still feels like a detonator whenever I get close to saying it.

I shove my laptop into my tote, check the clock, and wonder whether my professor will appreciate the irony of a thesis on defense mechanisms written by someone demonstrating all of them before breakfast.

Behind me, Luca climbs onto a stool to finish his waffles, humming as he drags syrup across the counter with the casual artistry of a child unafraid of consequences. I wipe the mess with a towel and nudge him toward the door. "Buddy—shoes. Now."

My phone lights up. *Mom.*

Her name cuts through the kitchen louder than the microwave's wail.

Every nerve draws tight.

It's not that I don't love her. It's that love in our family is folded so many times no one remembers where truth ends and performance begins.

I pick it up.

"Mia, sweetheart!" Her voice pours sunshine. "Let me see my boy!"

I angle the phone. Luca waves a syrup-slick fork like a victorious banner.

"He's getting so big! And his hair—darling, trim it. It's curling like your father's."

I swallow a sigh. Same script; fresh tinsel.

"I like it long," I reply. "So does he."

"Well," she soothes, "I can't wait to see him in person."

Here comes the trapdoor.

"We just miss you. This time of year isn't the same without you."

"Mom . . . things are complicated."

My catchall for: Don't push or I'll disappear.

"I wish you'd let us help."

Of course she does.

Our family's version of love: guilt sifted fine, passed down like flour.

Before I can answer, Ava's face appears—lighting, lip gloss, and an energy level fit to scorch the phone screen.

"Is that my nephew?" she squeals, claiming space like it's a birthright.

Luca beams at her. I shoulder the phone while grabbing his coat.

"Hi, Ava."

Her name tastes like an old door I shut hard enough to rattle the frame. I love my sister. But being close to Ava has always meant being close to the people—and choices—I'm not ready to face.

"It's been forever," she chirps.

"Almost six years."

"Exactly!" she sings, missing the point by a universe. "So . . . you're coming home this year, right?"

"Haven't decided," I say, steering Luca toward the door.

Ava barrels ahead. "You HAVE to. The Christmas market's back. The cider, the gingerbread competition —remember—"

I do remember. Too well. The place where everything went sideways. The night I mistook a kiss for a promise and woke to a blank page pretending to be one.

That morning sits like a scar under everything. A truth I learned to work around, not heal.

Mom pounces. "Your father wants to meet his grandson properly."

Properly = In person, with judgment.

"He's met him," I say.

"Screens don't count."

Sure they do—when distance is the only thing keeping me upright.

"Mom, can we do this later?"

"We just want a real Christmas with you," she says. "Everyone's coming home."

Everyone.

Right.

Translation: *Him.*

Ava takes the stage again, bright as a flare. "Actually, we have news."

Mom tries to stop her. "Ava—"

"What? She'll find out."

I freeze on the landing. "Find out what?"

"I'm engaged!"

The word pierces, sharp as Frost Harbor's December air. Something inside me folds—old grief, old joy, old versions of me I thought I'd buried.

"That's . . . wonderful," I manage. "Congratulations."

"The engagement party's before Christmas Eve. You have to come. You're my sister—you're supposed to be my maid of honor."

I grip the railing. "Ava, we haven't even—"

"Exactly!" she cuts in. "Fresh start. Perfect timing."

Mom adds, "It would mean so much."

There it is—the tripwire.

"I'll think about it." Hollow words spoken by the older version of the girl who ran.

They launch into plans, colors, expectations—auditory clutter.

Luca trots toward me, lashes jeweled with snowflakes.

I end the call before anything cracks open.

"Mom, can we build a fort?" Luca asks.

"After we get home."

"It's not home yet," he says. "We gotta go home for Christmas."

I swallow hard. He has no idea what he's asking—for whom *home* is a door I welded shut on purpose.

I kneel to zip his jacket. "You really want to see Nana and Papa?"

He gives a solemn nod. "Nana has cookies."

Of course she does.

He doesn't need their sugar-dipped affection, but he deserves the origin story.

We walk to the car. I buckle him in, drop into my seat, and let the conversation linger.

When the engine wakes and the dashboard blinks 11:42 a.m., my excuses are fraying faster than my patience.

Red light. Airline app. The screen glows like it's judging me.

Break starts next week. Clinic's quiet. Classwork paused. No more obstacles.

"What's the worst that could happen?" I mutter—as if the universe hasn't answered that question before.

Book.

Losing the hush.

Losing the version of me that equated stillness with safety.

Losing the buffer that keeps Luca's father theoretical instead of real—keeps the past safely boxed in a version he'll never have to meet.

Truth: *I don't want to go back.*

Dare: *I book the flight anyway.*

Confession: *Some part of me is still hoping for a ghost.*

2

MISFITS NEED HOMES TOO

MIA

The snow here is an archivist—it settles more than it falls, preserving the things you never meant to bury.

I haven't glimpsed the house yet, but it edges toward me: the porch with its weary slant, the wreath tilting like it's eavesdropping, the mismatched lights my father insists on because he says, *Perfection is for people who don't understand wonder.*

"It's a gingerbread house," Luca breathes from the back seat, fogging the glass. "Mom, look—gumdrop lights!"

"Your grandpa would call that high praise." My voice does its best not to splinter.

Three hours never counted as distance. It still doesn't. The real measure is what your heart can endure when stepping toward.

"It's only two weeks," I tell myself. "Two weeks is survivable."

Fourteen days of smiling. Fourteen days of dodging questions. Fourteen days of protecting Luca by guarding the one truth that could undo us.

I park. Luca rockets out before the engine settles—boots scattering snow, limbs spinning like he's trying to catch every piece of sky at once. He hasn't been here since he was tiny, yet he tears across the yard like the place remembers him: past the old oak, up the porch steps, stopping before the wire-frame snowman with candy-cane buttons.

"Does he light up?"

"When your grandpa remembers to plug him in. Drama runs in the family."

A memory rises—Jake, a glue gun, both of us crouched behind the school carnival in the midnight frost. He'd dragged the battered snowman from a drift, lifting him like a wounded soldier.

"He's hideous," I'd laughed.

"He's perfect," he'd said, already plotting the resurrection.

We had stayed up rewiring him, coaxing light back into his hollow chest. Misfits deserved homes too, we'd said.

I believed Jake was born to mend broken things.

I didn't understand he was practicing to leave them behind.

The air outside carries smoke and pine—his scent, or an old echo dressed as the present. It drifts across the porch; a reminder I never asked for.

"There's my baby!" Mom bursts through the doorway, effusive as ever. She races down the steps and scoops Luca up, laughing into his hair. He folds into her without hesitation.

"Nana smells like cookies," he mumbles.

"She always has." My smile wavers, honest in its brittleness.

I pop the trunk, hauling our suitcases toward the steps. Mom catches my forearms, holding me in place the way she used to at train stations—those rare pauses where sentiment outran caution.

"Hi, Mom."

"Hi, sweetheart."

Her hug is warm in that cardigan-scented way only she has, soft with the faint floral hum of the wool.

Dad waits in the doorway, a mug between his palms. "Look at you."

He doesn't move, giving me space to choose. I step into his arms. His hug is brief, solid—the kind that lives in the silence between words.

"Good to see you, Mia."

"You too." The reply gets lost somewhere in his coat.

He studies my face, tallying years. "You look tired."

"It's my brand."

A muted laugh slips out of him, edged with concern.

Inside, Luca narrates the décor as if he's hosting a holiday special.

"Mom! There are twinkle lights on the stairs. It's not safe, but it's pretty."

"Both things can be true."

Mom brushes a hand across my cheek—an old gesture, part blessing, part apology. "We put your favorites in the kitchen. And your father insisted we start decorating early. He's sentimental in his own stubborn way."

Dad gives a loose roll of his shoulder. "Tradition keeps a home anchored."

Or pinned, I think. But the thought stays caged.

The house is exactly the way I last saw it—photos frozen in their frames: blueberry-knee summers, frosting-smeared

Decembers, the popcorn-garland year when our thumbs took the damage.

Time didn't shift a thing except the people inside it.

"This is . . . something," I murmur.

"It can be more than nice." Hope tiptoes through her voice. "We're just happy you came home."

A buttery, nutmeg-rich heat rolls out from the kitchen. A timer chimes, and Mom flutters toward it, brushing Luca's hair as she passes.

"Come on, Chief Engineer. Sprinkles await."

Luca pauses, checking my face. Independence is his kingdom, but even kingdoms need boundaries.

I nudge my chin toward the kitchen. "Go. Bring me back one."

"Two," he bargains.

"You drive a hard deal. Two."

He darts off. Dad lifts the suitcases from my hands.

"You don't have to—"

A weathered smile. "Let me pretend I'm useful."

"You are." The truth slips out bare.

We cross the threshold, my nerves fizzing like over-carbonated soda.

Dad sets the bags by the stairs. "Your room's the same. We freshened it, but didn't move things. Figured you'd want familiarity."

A tiny pause opens between us.

"Thanks."

He steps back, hands pocketed, gaze drifting toward the living room as if anticipating a storm front.

And again, I see it—my parents navigating their home like renters when I return. Careful. Polite. Quiet-footed.

"Hungry?"

"Always."

"Good!" Mom calls. "I overcooked with intention."

The hallway glows with memory. The glove table. The mirror where Ava practiced her smile that wasn't really a smile.

At the kitchen doorway, I freeze. Luca stands on a stool, raining red sprinkles over a cookie while Mom steadies the world beneath his small hands. Tears shine openly on her cheeks now.

An ache unfurls beneath my ribs—a room remembering what I was before I learned to leave.

We hover in a fragile constellation—the four of us spread across three rooms. Mom aligns cookies. Dad washes a clean mug because his hands need purpose. Luca hums a tuneless melody full of life.

And me? I stand still enough to let the moment hold.

Ordinary. Disarmingly so.

Then the shift—small, unmistakable.

Laughter floats in from the living room. Ava's quick spark twined with a deeper, embered sound I haven't heard in years.

The center of me locks hard.

"Who's here?" The words fall steadily. My pulse doesn't.

Mom keeps her tone light. "Just family, sweetheart."

The scent hits before the sight—pine, smoke, that faint aftershave my body recognizes before my brain catches up. The house narrows. Footsteps. A voice.

"Higher—yeah, hang it higher."

Recognition cleaves through me.

Jake Carter.

My breath stops—not a gasp, not a choke, just a sudden, brutal stillness.

He's beside my sister, guiding her hands as she hooks a pinecone ornament—*my* pinecone, once. His fingers brush her waist in that careful, polite way people use when they're trying to look like a couple instead of feeling like one.

A load-bearing part of me gives with a clean, brutal snap.

Not just because he's here, in my parents' living room, but because he's here with her—my twin—and neither of them knows he's already stitched into my life in a way that has Luca's eyes.

Ava glows. Jake looks up.

"Mia." My name leaves him like a confession.

They're still frozen there—hands lifted, bodies leaning—but the moment halts before it becomes anything more.

It isn't the almost-touch that undoes me. It's the truth in their silence.

Love remembered wears gentler colors than betrayal, but it wounds deeper.

"Bear!" Luca's shout slams the world back together. I turn, my smile barely holding.

Ava pivots, her façade crackling. Lit for a heartbeat, then brittle.

Jake doesn't move. Doesn't blink. His gaze snags on Luca, then on me—confused, searching, like he's feeling something he doesn't have language for yet.

And I feel it—the truth shivering through the room.

A fault line waking.

"They're here for the engagement party," Ava chirps, stepping closer.

The word lands like a misfired spark—small, but enough to burn through the air around us.

She lifts her hand; the diamond scatters stars across the room. "Told you you'd like him."

My twin. My mirror. Same hazel eyes, same long sweep of brown hair—only she glitters. Still.

I used to shine like that. Before Luca. Before stretch

marks and too-late nights and learning how to rebuild myself around a tiny heartbeat that wasn't mine.

I carry all of it now—and proudly. Luca is the best thing I've ever done.

Jake doesn't look away from me. His jaw trembles once.

"I'm so happy for you," I say, the lie shaped softly.

Ava slides beneath Jake's arm, her head settling on his shoulder like she's found her forever place.

Every brush of his hand.

Every easy lean.

Every piece of what once felt like mine—

No. What was never mine.

She loves him.

She loves Luca's father. And she doesn't even know she's loving the one person who could undo everything I've built.

"Mom, who's that?" Luca tugs at my sleeve.

One sentence could redraw his entire life.

One truth could cost me both of them in a single breath—Jake and Luca—if this blows up wrong.

What I want to say: *That's your father, sweetheart.*

What I say: "That's Aunt Ava's fiancé."

He squints. "What's that mean?"

"It means he's going to be part of the family."

Ava crouches. "It means he's going to be my husband."

Jake's voice breaks softly. "Is he . . . ?"

No one knows who Luca's father is.

And I plan to keep it that way—especially him.

If he knows, I don't just risk my heart—I risk Luca's whole world shattering before he even learns the rules.

Not fear.

Mercy.

Truth can shatter a family faster than any lie.

"Mom?" Luca hovers.

"Nana said she saved you two cookies, remember? Go make sure they're still there."

He studies our faces, reading more than he should, then runs.

I move to follow, but a hand closes around my wrist.

A touch I once knew by heart.

Ava sees the movement—one flicker—then looks away.

Questions crowd Jake's eyes. None escape.

We stand in a ring of adults and pretty lies. And I refuse to be the first to crack.

So I smile. Swallow the splintering. "I'm so happy for you, Jake."

Then I turn before my legs betray me.

My hand skims the wall—the chipped paint, the lived-in texture of a life I once wore without thinking. By the time I reach my old room, my pulse hammers, wild and arrhythmic.

Laughter rises through the floorboards, slipping into every crack I didn't know I'd left open.

Truth: *Jake is engaged to my twin.*

Dare: *I walked into this house anyway.*

Confession: *I brought his son with me.*

3

DOOR 12

MIA

You'd think I'd sleep better without Luca's feet in my kidneys. No blanket theft. No whispered dinosaur theories at 3 a.m.

But the room disagrees.

It's always disagreed.

Same window staring into the woods. Same door that refuses to latch. Same closet full of things no latch ever held back.

I still lock it anyway. A habit cosplaying as protection.

Frost Harbor wasn't supposed to scrape me raw. I told myself nothing here could cut anymore.

But then—

Jake. Ava. The ring.

A neat little constellation designed to undo me.

They kissed like people who knew others were watching —beautiful on the surface, but hollow in the room's acoustics.

One night. Perfect, reckless, unrepeatable.

Then, the vanishing act.

Now he's moving through my parents' kitchen as if he's trying to act like he belongs there, familiar motions that don't quite fit.

He didn't choose me.

Didn't even try.

But he left me with Luca—or maybe I chose Luca when everything else collapsed beneath his silence. Chose him, chose distance, chose a life where Jake Carter stayed hypothetical instead of a man who could look at my son and recognize the consequence he never had the courage to face.

I shove the blanket off and stand. The floor nips at my feet. The air smells of cedar and unresolved history.

Then I see them—my pajamas.

Red flannel boxers. Jake's face repeated, bait threaded into every square inch of fabric.

He gave them to me one Christmas, smug as sin.

"Poetic justice," he'd declared. *"My face on your ass instead of the other way around."*

I laughed until it hurt. Now it just folds inward.

Not grief—just old wiring tightening under my ribs. Six years, and some threads still know exactly where to pull.

My gaze hooks on the closet. The same brass latch from senior year—my DIY attempt at privacy. I haven't touched it since before adulthood started charging rent.

The key waits in the drawer, hiding under hair ties and fossilized nail polish. My hand hesitates, then digs.

A brittle click.

I drag our luggage out from in front of the closet—the suitcase scraping softly, the weekender bag sagging in complaint—and clear the way. The door groans as I pull it open, a sound older than the house and twice as dramatic.

Dust blooms as I lift the weekender bag. The leather has

aged into itself—scuffed and steady. It hits the bed with a soft grunt from the clasps, judgment noted.

Inside—peonies blazing on mustard fabric. Cheerful. Ridiculous. Ava once mocked it. I pretended not to care.

I toss out clothes, chargers, notebooks—excuses disguised as belongings.

My patch stares back: *Feelings are data.*

My shield. My loophole.

This bag shouldn't soothe me. Yet it does.

I reach for Luca's things and catch a flash of white behind a dead string of fairy lights—a box.

My box.

White cardboard. Thick green Sharpie: **MIA'S**, underlined twice—territory I claimed before I knew how.

It shouldn't weigh anything, but my arm braces as if expecting blowback.

Vanilla drifts up as the dust settles. Mom's perfume.

Of course she's been in here. She calls it tidying. I call it rearranging the bones.

I trace my name and lift the lid.

Inside: a handmade Advent calendar. Felt warped with time, crooked seams, my ten-year-old stitching wandering like a heartbeat learning its pattern. *Twenty-four doors.* One askew.

Door 12.

My nail slips under the flap. The felt resists, then yields.

A pinecone waits inside—small, gold-painted, dusted with silver. My initials on one side. His—*J.C.*—partially blurred by glue.

Glitter jumps to my thumb, bright as a secret turning itself in.

It's ours. The original. The one that shouldn't have survived. The one I thought Ava was hanging.

I sink to the floor, the ornament cupped like a wish or a warning.

Light hits it—glints, wobbles—and suddenly the room tilts. Snow cutting across the yard . . .

Jake beside me on the grass, hoodie sleeves shoved up, glitter paint clutched like contraband.

"Here." A toss. "This one's yours."

I eyed the uneven little thing. "Because it's lopsided?"

He nudged me, grin kicking wider. "Exactly. You're consistent."

"Wow. Romance isn't dead."

"Cute," he fired back.

He painted as if equilibrium depended on precision— tongue caught between teeth, brows furrowed, fully focused in that way he only ever was with me.

"Operation: Personal Ornament," he declared. "Code name: Don't tell Ava."

"She ditched for the Christmas market."

"She claims glitter triggers migraines. Convenient." His grin sharpened. "Besides—you're the fun one."

"That bar's underground."

He ignored that, lifting the finished ornament. "Initials. Mandatory."

"Why?"

He didn't look up when he answered. "Because it's ours."

He painted my letters first—M.S.—slow, like the moment deserved ceremony.

His own—J.C.—followed on a breath he pretended wasn't shaky.

"Official," he murmured.

"Officially what?"

A shrug. "Something."

And then—closer—he brushed paint from my cheek with his thumb.

No warning.

No permission.

A touch that meant nothing if you weren't paying attention.

Everything if you were.

The room returns—cold floor under me, the box beside my knee, glitter clinging like static searching for a home.

I should put it back. It doesn't belong to this version of life.

Jake belongs to Ava now. Full stop. Period. Doctrine. A truth I repeat like it might someday feel true.

And Luca belongs to me. That's the one line I won't let him cross. But my hand ignores all of it.

The pinecone slips into my weekender bag, behind Freud and my stitched mantra.

Hidden. Not gone.

"It's just one ornament," I whisper.

A draft of a life that never made the final cut.

Something shifts beneath my ribs—not quite pain, not quite nostalgia—more like an old hinge remembering it can move.

Luca's laugh fires up again—wild, bright enough to crack the ceiling open.

This—*him*—is real. Everything else is glitter on a memory.

I rise, brush gold flecks from my palms, and set the calendar back in its box.

Footsteps pass beyond the door.

The closet latch hangs crooked, leaving a thin seam of darkness watching me.

Truth: *It's just one ornament.*

Dare: *I keep it anyway.*

Confession: *I'm not done with us, no matter how loudly I say I am.*

Even though I know better. God, I know better.

4

REFLECTIONS IN SNOW

JAKE

The road dissolves into white haze, each exhale a sharp ghost in the air. Four miles behind me and the hush still crowds my heels.

Frost Harbor sits under a hard crust of winter that forces everything to hold its breath. My body falls into old rhythm —heel, toe—muscle memory built long before war turned it into instinct.

The lake to my left lies flat and silver, a frozen pane. I used to think winter made this place magical. Now it looks brittle enough to crack under a breath.

I tell myself the run is for my lungs. Truth is, I woke before dawn and couldn't take another minute in that rental— the lemon cleaner, the holiday candles, the curated quiet. Even Ava's steady breathing pressed against me like a reminder I couldn't name.

Silence used to calm me.

Now it feels like something closing in.

I push harder.

A truck glides past, tires writing lines in the slush. The driver lifts a gloved hand. My fingers twitch before I shut the impulse down.

I veer toward the ridge where the trees thicken and the Snowdens' roof breaks the horizon. I tell myself I'm not searching for her. Only taking the long way home.

Their crooked red mailbox appears first. Then movement behind the window—a small body darting. A laugh, clear and high.

Luca.

I stop. The street, the trees, even my lungs lock around the moment.

I knew Mia had a child. Small-town whispers travel on their own time. I never asked questions. Never asked her. Never asked Ava. Maybe I thought distance kept the past simple.

Knowing is abstract.

Seeing him—seeing the way he moves—strikes deeper.

Hazel eyes—*hers*. And the tilt of a nose I remember from mirrors when I was seventeen.

My gut does a sharp, off-center lurch.

My gut does a sharp, off-center lurch.

Don't start doing the math, Carter. If you start, you don't get to pretend you didn't leave more than a girl in that bed.

You have Ava. You have a plan. Getting close has a blast radius. Distance is the only thing I've ever done right.

My breath fogs in a white, needling cloud.

I force myself forward until their house disappears behind the trees. By the time I reach the porch, a cold weight has settled between my shoulders.

Ava's SUV sits under a dusting of snow—everything neat, staged, curated.

Inside, the rental smells like eucalyptus cleaner and new

drywall—clean edges over a house that hasn't learned us yet. Ava loves it. Big yard. Good schools. Plenty of storage.

Not my home.

My place has always been Northlight Cabin—open sky, open air, quiet that doesn't demand you earn it.

The house meets me with a stillness that feels expectant. I move through routine because it's the only thing that hasn't changed.

My gloves hit the counter.

A memory hits harder.

Northlight. Two days before Christmas.

Mia curled in the back of my truck, knees tucked under my old hoodie, cocoa steaming between her hands. Moonlight pooled on the cabin roof like it had been waiting for us.

"It's not about the stars," she whispered. "It's perspective. When something's far enough away, your problems shrink."

"Perspective," I teased. "Is that what you call dragging me out here in twenty-degree weather?"

She nudged me. "You're just upset I'm smarter than you."

"Not upset." I leaned closer. "Just trying to understand how staring at dots makes you profound."

She laughed, fogging the air. "You feel something when you look up there. You can't deny it."

"Oh, I feel something." Our shoulders brushed. "Not sure it's about the stars."

Her mug stilled midair, steam curling around that half-smile that always knocked something loose in me.

"And you like it."

Her voice softened. "Maybe. When everything feels like it's shifting, this makes it easier to breathe."

The joke died on my tongue. We both knew what she meant—the duffel already packed upstairs, the day after Christmas looming.

"Hey, Mouse?"

She looked at me, Christmas lights mirrored in her eyes. "Yeah?"

"When you're famous for decoding brains, don't forget this place."

Her eyes warmed. "Only if you buy me a telescope."

"A telescope? Planning to name a star after yourself?"

"No." A bump of her shoulder. "I want to see what you see when you look up there."

Something in my chest pulled tight. "Then I'll find you one. Strong enough to find home from anywhere."

"And you'll write?"

"I'll write," I promised. "Even if it's just to tell you what the stars look like from the other side of the world."

Her breath caught. "Then maybe I'll keep looking. So I don't miss you."

Cold held those words between us, bright and breakable.

I blink, and the memory dissolves.

The girl too.

The kitchen hums softly. My duffel sits open on the counter—the same one from overseas, still half-packed because I keep telling myself I'll unpack tomorrow.

When I grab my old jacket, something slips free—a folded scrap of paper.

Her handwriting, steady.

Star-Hunting Spots

- Harbor Lake Overlook
- Cedar Ridge Pull-Off
- Old Weather Station Hill
- Northlight Bluff — *the one we always said we'd get to . . . and never did.*

I stare at the last line.

We planned it every year—hiking up before dawn, freezing our asses off, watching the whole town wake in the valley below.

But deployments. Exams. Missed chances.

Life.

Something always pulled one of us away before we ever reached the ridge together.

The place we never touched.

The place every version of us seemed to orbit but never land on.

The place that suddenly feels less like a missed hill and more like unfinished gravity.

My phone vibrates—unknown Vermont number.

I answer out of habit. "Carter."

A familiar gravel slides through the line. "Sergeant. You change your number again, or you just screening me?"

I huff out something that isn't quite a laugh. "Harlan."

"That's better." A beat. "Winter drills are lining up. We kick off tomorrow at oh-seven. Thought you might want in. You've shown up every Christmas for six years—figured I should at least pretend to give you a choice."

Despite myself, something eases. "You need bodies?"

"I need *you.*" He says it as if it's logistics, not sentiment. "Recruits listen when you talk. You up for running a few sessions?"

The part of me that always salutes answers first. "Yeah. Sure."

"Good." Paper rustles on his end. "And Carter? If you want more than seasonal drills this year . . . we can talk. You've earned a steadier role."

There it is. The offer he's slipped across the metaphorical table more times than I've admitted.

Stable hours. Predictable pay. A life with walls that don't shift under my feet.

My throat goes tight in a way I ignore. "We'll see."

"You don't have to decide now." He doesn't push, but he doesn't buy it either. "Just don't ignore it out of habit."

Habit is exactly what I do. Every damn year.

"I'll be there for drills," I say instead.

"I figured." Another pause, gentler than he probably means it. "Drive safe."

I hang up before he can read more in my voice.

The low thrum of the house doesn't settle.

Upstairs, water runs.

Soon, the place will smell like lavender steam. Ava will come down smiling, arranging the day the way she arranges everything.

I pour coffee. Watch snow drift sideways. The Snowdens' chimney threads smoke into the sky.

"Morning!" Ava's voice floats down. "You already went running?"

"Couldn't sleep."

She appears in the doorway, wrapped in a towel, hair dripping—effortless, like always. "You've been quiet."

"Just tired."

She reads what I try to hide on my face but lets it go as she crosses the kitchen, her shampoo scent trailing behind her.

"You didn't say much last night." She holds up her hand. The diamond splinters light across the counter. "Still can't believe it's real."

I try to mirror her smile.

"And you picked this one yourself," she says. "You always notice more than you admit."

I chose the ring between deployments. She said yes before I understood the weight of the question. Before I understood she was in love with the version of me who sent texts from airports, not the one who wakes at 0300 waiting for the next blast.

"You deserve it," I tell her.

Her smile softens. "You really think so?"

"Yeah."

She leans into my chest briefly, then brushes snow off my shirt.

"Promise you'll try today. No soldier face."

I give her a crooked look. "Soldier face?"

"The one that looks like you're waiting for orders."

"Maybe I am."

She laughs, swatting my arm. "Dork."

Her phone buzzes. "Dylan," she says. "Planning the engagement party."

"Right. The dream team."

She winks. "Exactly."

Redirecting is Ava's quiet superpower. Maybe that's why I fell for her—how she smooths sharp edges without asking where they came from.

"Mom says Mia's helping with the Christmas market," she adds. "You should stop by."

A casual sentence. Not casual at all.

I keep my voice easy. "How's Mia?"

A shrug. "Same. Quiet. Locked up tight."

"And Luca?"

One brow lifts. "Luca? Why?"

"Just . . . why didn't Mia ever tell anyone?"

"You know her. She hoards her secrets."

She stirs her drink, straw squealing. "She almost kept the whole pregnancy to herself until she landed in the hospital."

My pulse spikes—fast, immediate. "Hospital? Why?"

"Hey—easy there, soldier." Ava softens, though her blink is quick, assessing. "Dehydration. Mom and Dad were her emergency contacts."

The word *emergency* hits like a ripcord yanked inside me.

"You never told me," I say, hearing the roughness scrape through.

Ava tilts her head. "You never opened that door."

No. I locked it. Bolted it. Told myself distance was mercy. That leaving one girl in a warm bed with a blank note was better than dragging her through the wreckage of my life.

I swallow against the dryness gathering in my throat. "Still. I thought you would've mentioned it."

"I didn't think you needed the fine print," she says gently. "We all moved on. Mia left for Rutland after Luca was born. Came back for a bit. Then she just . . . left."

My jaw works. "Just like that?"

"That's Mia. Always moving before the questions hit."

I study my hands. There's a tremor there—slight, but not ignorable.

That's the version everyone knows.

Not the girl who pressed cedar into my palm and whispered that the stars made the world honest.

Not the girl who stayed in my head through every deployment until silence replaced her.

"No one knows who the dad is," Ava adds. "She never told anyone."

"Doesn't that bother you?"

"Should it?" she asks. "Luca's incredible. Sweet. And he adores her. That's enough."

But it isn't enough for something old in me—something that flares hot and wrong and protective.

"Hey, where did you just go?" she asks softly.

I exhale slowly, trying to shake the tremor in my chest.

"Are you surprised she has a son? Or surprised you didn't know more?"

"I'm surprised at everything right now."

Her face eases, though something thoughtful lingers behind her eyes. "Don't let the past unhouse what we're building."

But the past doesn't unhouse things.

It knocks. Patient. Persistent.

Waiting for you to answer.

"You okay about all this?" Ava asks. "About us?"

"I'm okay." The lie crunches like grit.

Men like me aren't built for soft houses and registries and forever. We're built to leave, follow orders, pretend the blast radius doesn't hit the people we love.

She leans in, caramel breath warm. "Good. Because I love you."

I nod into the kiss out of habit. "I love you too."

My hand brushes the folded scrap of paper—*Mia's handwriting, a shape my heart remembers before my eyes do.*

Truth: *I'm not built for the life I keep promising Ava.*

Dare: *I say yes to the drills anyway. Pretend orders feel safer than feelings.*

Confession: *I'm still carrying Mia in my pocket, and part of me never stopped trying to find my way back to Northlight.*

5

THE SNOWMAN

JAKE

By the time my truck noses into the Snowdens' drive, I've already repeated the lie twice: I'm here to help with market prep. Ava said her mom needed extra hands. End of story.

Sure. And you jog at dawn for the scenery.

Truth is, I wanted to see them. Wanting has never been safe—that's how I ended up on planes and in places I shouldn't have survived, in beds I shouldn't have touched, leaving Mia with an empty pillow and me with a pocket full of ghosts.

The yard is loud with laughter and questionable architecture. A snowman slumps as if winter's been a personal attack. Mia stands beside him, posture familiar—steady attention, lashes freckled with snow. Luca pinballs around her, full chaos incarnate.

I kill the engine, pull on my beanie, and step out. "Frosty's lesser-known cousin? Frosty the Structurally Unsound?"

Mia turns. A crease forms at her mouth. "Jake."

Luca slams into my legs, one glove missing. I scoop him up easily, his grin its own tiny sun.

"You keeping your mom out of trouble?"

"She hates glitter," he reports gravely. "And snow in her boots."

I chuckle. "Two of life's greatest joys."

"Frosty's doing his best," Mia says, dry as snowfall. "Not everyone peaked in high school snow sculpting."

I crouch beside the snowman and tap his belly. A chunk falls off like wet drywall. "Diagnosis: grim. One more breeze and he's modern art."

"He needs presence," Luca declares.

"He needs scaffolding," I counter. "But sure. Presence."

"You can fix it?"

"What's the going rate these days?"

"Payment is half a juice box and a broken candy cane," Mia says.

"A savage market," I mutter.

We work side by side—packing snow, straightening the lean. Cold gnaws at my knuckles, but the rhythm between us warms fast—the old banter slipping back into place, a choreography my body remembers before my brain catches up.

And just like that, I'm sixteen again, reckless enough to believe wanting her wasn't a danger.

"Is that supposed to be a snowman?" I called once.

"No," she answered without looking up. "He's a penguin."

"He looks like he got hit by a plow."

"He's sensitive."

"He's horrifying."

She glanced up, narrowing her eyes. "You're jealous he has more personality than you."

I raised a brow. "That a challenge?"

"Only if you're brave enough to build something better."

I crouched beside her, fingers burning. "Fine. Let's give him legs. He's waddling into an identity crisis."

She laughed—quick, unguarded.

"I knew you'd cave."

"I'm saving him from public shame."

"Uh-huh. Keep telling yourself that."

"Next year, I'm making a better one," I said, squinting at her lopsided penguin.

"Oh, it's a contest now?"

"It's always a contest."

She nudged my shoulder. I nudged back. Maybe I leaned in. Maybe she didn't lean away.

Then, my overbuilt headpiece collapsed, burying her in a white avalanche.

She shrieked, "Jake!"

"That was a structural issue!"

"I hate you!"

"Not possible," I said, breathless with laughter. "You like me way too much."

"Do not."

"Do too."

She lunged and tackled me into the drift, and cold found every seam. Her arm across my chest. Her hair damp on her cheek. The world stilled around us.

A heartbeat where falling didn't hurt.

Luca jams an Oreo into Frosty's chest and steps back, triumphant. Mia ties a ribbon around the snowman's neck.

"*Still* leaning," I announce.

"*Still* criticizing," she fires back.

I huff a laugh. "You remember the penguin?"

Her hands freeze. Snow clings to her lashes when she finally turns toward me.

"The avalanche?" I add.

"Hard to forget."

"Built him like a Jenga tower."

"And you buried me alive."

"You deserved it."

"Probably," she admits, a small smile tugging.

I forget to breathe.

Snow explodes against my head. I spin, and Luca stands victorious, mitten raised.

"Sorry, Jake! I was aiming for Mom!"

Mia's laugh breaks free, sending me a look that says, *You deserved that.*

"Every year," Luca says proudly, "Mom and I have a snowman contest."

"Oh yeah?" I wipe snow from my collar. "Who's the reigning champ?"

Mia lifts a brow.

I squint. "Figures. You've always been a cheater."

"Strategist," she corrects.

"Cheater."

She sticks her tongue out.

The moment stretches, almost easy again—until Ava's voice rings from the window.

"Hot chocolate!"

Luca bolts, and Mia follows. I stay a beat, letting the world level.

Inside, the air is thick with vanilla and static from the radio. Ava owns the kitchen with her stride—sure steps, cream sweater, red scarf.

Mia moves differently—low-moving. She hums one low

note before reaching for a mug. It shouldn't hit me the way it does.

Ava glances back. "What'd Frosty do to deserve all that attention?"

"Just making sure he's OSHA certified," I say.

"He's avant-garde," Mia deadpans.

"Postmortem."

Ava laughs, unaware of the cold front between Mia and me.

Mia brings me a mug. I don't need to look to know her thumb will anchor the rim—her way of steadying things she doesn't trust to hold.

Our fingers brush in the handoff. A pause, faint but real.

"You never stopped adding cinnamon," I murmur.

She inhales, barely. "Old habits."

"Not all of them are bad."

Silence thickens.

I sip and flinch.

"It's hot," she observes.

"Still making it lethal, as always."

She bites her lip, fighting a smile.

Ava calls from the counter, "At least you didn't start a fire this time!" She's grinning at her phone, missing the frost under her own joke.

Mia turns away first, grabbing a dish towel. "You're dripping," she says, offering it.

Our hands meet on the cotton—intentional this time. A quick current runs through the fabric.

"Yes, ma'am."

Her blink—the slow-quick one—hits center mass.

Not now. Don't start reading weather in the wind.

She moves on, stacking mugs. Luca hums over his cocoa. The room crackles. I feel half a step behind everything.

Ava checks her phone. "Mom wants to know if Dylan's coming to the market." A private smile flickers.

It slides past me. Mia notices, though. Her shoulders narrow a fraction before she smooths them out. Then she slips toward the living room—an exit she's perfected.

I tell myself to let her go. I don't.

She stands by the fireplace, claiming the only quiet patch of floor like she always has—a small island carved out of noise. She hasn't turned, but she knows I'm here—chin lifted, breath evening, armor settling into place.

Then I see it.

Red and green fabric. Uneven stitches. The Advent calendar.

Ours.

Heat from the fire brushes my knuckles before I move another inch.

For a second, I actually think about leaving—about backing away before memory opens its teeth—but my feet don't move. They never do with her.

The flap for Day 13 is ajar. Mia's fingers brush it. Something slips out, catching the light. She snatches it before it falls.

I know it instantly.

Two stick figures.

A dog with a red collar.

Orion.

A quiet, sharp ache folds inside me. "The dock that winter," I say. "I said I wished the constellation were a dog."

"You said it made the stars less lonely."

"Yeah. And you said even stars take time."

A smile ghosts across her mouth—something between nostalgia and regret.

"Comforting," she says.

"Necessary."

She studies the drawing until her hand steadies. I step closer, slow enough to let her pull away. She doesn't.

"You kept that?" My voice roughens. "All this time?"

She swallows. "I thought I'd gotten rid of it."

It lands like a seam tearing open.

"Why keep it?"

Her thumb skims the paper's edge. "Some things just . . . stick."

She folds it carefully and tucks it into her pocket.

The ache goes clean through me. She kept the calendar, but never wrote back. Never opened Door 24. Never found the letters I crammed behind that flap when I had been stupidly sure love and ink could outlast distance and deployments.

The fire cracks. Ava laughs from the kitchen. Life moves on.

The calendar waits on the mantle—imperfect, familiar. Day 13 still ajar.

Twelve doors left.

Twelve days.

Truth: *She kept the pieces of us I thought she'd throw away.*

Dare: *I keep showing up at this house like I'm not the one who disappeared first.*

Confession: *There are words behind Door 24 that could blow this fragile ceasefire apart.*

6

COUNTING WITHOUT ME

MIA

The house wakes first—stretching itself into morning.

Mom hums over her cookie trays, coaxing them toward rising with nothing but patience and habit.

I'm shrugging into my coat when the door knocks—two quick, one slow. Harper's code. She sweeps in on a wave of winter air, scarf coming undone, coffee cupped in her hands with the care of someone transporting a volatile substance.

"Delivery from the gods," she announces. "Caffeine and questionable judgment."

"You specialize in the second one." The smile forms before I can stop it.

"And yet you keep inviting me in." She grins. "Tragic cycle."

"Only because caffeine outranks self-preservation."

"Mutual enablement," she says, handing me a cup smudged with her lipstick.

Steam coils between us—roasted beans and that citrus

perfume she refuses to abandon. Her gaze skims my face, quick and assessing.

"Tree Day," she reminds me.

"You didn't think I'd skip."

"I wasn't sure you'd want to. Considering . . . "

"Yeah." I exhale.

"The whole engagement-announcement ambush." She winces. "Not my proudest moment."

"You were caught in the middle."

"I was standing next to him, Mia. Not the same thing." Her thumb circles her cup. "Silence does its own damage."

Her words find the soft spot I pretend isn't there. She doesn't know she's brushing against mine too—the silence wrapped around Luca, the truth beating under every choice I make.

If I talk, I risk everything. If I stay quiet, I'm the only one who pays for it.

"You were trying to protect someone."

"Maybe. Or I simply couldn't watch either of you give way." She sips, grimaces. "Still volcanic."

"Haaaaarper!"

He launches at her. She drops into a crouch without hesitation, arms wide. He hits her in a burst of laughter and wool.

"Whoa!" she laughs. "When did you get this strong? Pulling sleds or causing mischief?"

"Mischief," he declares proudly.

She brushes flour from his hair. "You smell like Nana's kitchen."

"That's 'cause she made cookies!"

"Explains everything." She kisses his cheek. "Any superhero skills in kindergarten yet?"

"I'm learning math! And washing my hands."

Harper clutches her chest. "A man of discipline. I'm obsolete."

The sight tugs at something deep—my friend holding my son like it's instinct. My lives touching.

Harper always checked in. Showed up. And still there were nights—fever nights, lonely ones—when I almost called.

Almost.

She catches my expression and gently brings me back. "Hey. Stay with me, okay? You don't always have to keep it together."

Holding it together is the only thing keeping my world from splitting open. One crack, and Luca's life unravels.

A thin laugh escapes. "I'm working on that."

Her olive eyes sweep over me—thoughtful, sisterly. "And you're doing better than you think."

Her energy rebounds. "Now—your mom. Where is she? We've got a noble fir to liberate."

"In the kitchen, negotiating with cinnamon rolls."

"Fearless woman." She heads off for the thermoses, opening cabinets like this house still remembers her hands.

Dad hovers near the hall, promising to "finish a few things" and meet us later—his favorite exit line.

We're about to leave when something glitters on the mantel.

The Advent calendar.

Door 14 cracked open, felt lifted like a half-blink.

I step closer.

Inside rests a flattened, thin sprig of pressed cedar. A cold pinch tightens at the base of my throat. A door opening without me carries like a warning. Secrets don't survive on drafts. Not mine. Not Luca's.

Jake had tucked a fresh sprig behind my ear on our first

Tree Day—two teenagers pretending we could name trees by heart. I'd mixed up fir and cedar; he'd shown me how to tell them apart by scent. I had pressed that sprig into a book without meaning to.

Yet here it is.

I run a finger along the brittle edge. It trembles—or maybe I do.

How did it end up in the calendar?

Who's been opening them? Mom barely sleeps; Dad wouldn't notice. Ava hasn't been here since yesterday. Which leaves—

Luca.

The thought softens me. Curious hands. Drawn to anything that glitters.

Still, unease slips through me. Truths opened when I wasn't keeping an eye.

"Ready?" Harper calls.

I let the flap fall and slip the sprig into my pocket before joining her.

Outside, snow drags sideways in the wind.

Harper drives. The radio hisses—more static than song.

"I'm mad at you," she says suddenly.

I glance over. "Specifics help."

"For pretending it didn't wreck you. Hearing about Ava and Jake—taking that call—acting like it was weather."

The wipers thump a slow rhythm.

"People get engaged," I say. "It happens."

"Not them. Not after . . . everything."

"What do you want? A speech? A meltdown?"

Her knuckles are pale around the wheel. "I want you to stop pretending you're made of steel. You don't have to armor up every minute."

"Harp. Drop it."

"Mia Jane." Her voice softens but still digs in. "I know you. And I was there that night. I saw it."

Silence drifts through the car, cold as the storm outside.

"You make friendship an Olympic sport," she mutters.

A reluctant smile tugs at me. "You keep competing."

"Hell yes, I do."

Luca sings "Jingle Bells" in the back seat, slightly off-beat, perfectly himself.

"Tone-deaf," Harper says. "Definitely inherited."

I roll my eyes. No point arguing.

A truck rumbles past—CARTER TREE FARM stamped across its tailgate. My pulse trims itself to a tight, painful beat. Even the name feels dangerous.

Truth: *Hearing about him and Ava did wreck me, no matter how calmly I acted.*

Dare: *I'm going to his family's tree farm anyway.*

Confession: *A small, treacherous part of me wants the past to stop staying buried.*

7

CARTER TREE FARM

MIA

The Carter Tree Farm looks almost exactly the same—rows of firs climbing toward the ridge, hand-painted signs remain pointing toward Cocoa & Cookies, the Photo Booth, and Community Tree Day.

Luca presses his mittened hands to the window. "It's like a forest that got sparkly on purpose."

Harper sips her coffee. "Organized sparkly. And if Cherie Carter's running the show, there's a clipboard planning our oxygen intake."

I huff a laugh. "You say that like it's a problem."

"Only if you enjoy being volunteered into crafts with power tools." She scans the lot. "Alright. We hang ornaments, drink cocoa, and escape before nostalgia drags you into emotional quicksand."

"Copy that."

When I open the door, pine and sawdust and Cherie's cinnamon cocoa drift on the breeze. Sleigh bells jingle. Kids squeal. Frost Harbor beating just the way it always has.

Then I see his truck.

Parked by the barn. Tires dusted with slush. Same dent in the passenger door. Same cracked bumper sticker—*Keep Frost Harbor Weird.*

My pulse stutters. My body reacts before my mind catches up.

The sight tugs me backward.

Seventeen. Christmas break. Cinnamon cocoa sweating through paper cups. His truck parked in this exact spot—barn lights flickering behind us, the smell of hay and diesel steady in the cold.

Jake drummed his fingers on the wheel, eyes doing that thing—I'm about to screw this up or save it.

"Let's play the game," he said.

"It's not even a real game."

"Neither's Santa," he shrugged. "Doesn't stop me from wanting my stocking full."

I rolled my eyes, smiling. "You're comparing confessions to candy canes?"

"Exactly." His grin curved like a dare. "One truth. One confession. One stupid dare."

"It's not even Christmas Eve."

"Still counts."

He tapped the wheel. "Truth first. Your turn."

I traced a circle on my cup, pretending my hands weren't shaking. "Truth? Fine. Sometimes I think if I leave this town, I won't come back."

He went rigid. "You say that like it's a bad thing."

"Maybe it is."

"My turn." His voice dipped. "Confession? I hate thinking about you leaving."

My breath snagged. He noticed. He always noticed.

"Dare," I blurted, needing to breathe.

His voice dropped. "Kiss me."

I laughed, nudging him. "Funny."

"Not a joke," he murmured, and everything inside me tilted.

Before I could answer—

"Jake! Need a hand!" his dad called from the garage.

Jake cursed under his breath, pushed the door open, and cold air rushed in.

He looked back once.

Then, he slipped away.

The memory blows out like breath on glass. Snow falls again. Same place, different decade.

And there he is.

Sleeves rolled, hammer on his belt, laughing with a customer. Darren stands next to him holding a star topper, shoulders bumping. Their old friction has sanded down.

Air punches out of my lungs, sharp and humiliating, because they look . . . healed.

Last time I saw them together, they couldn't get through a sentence without splinters.

Harper nudges my elbow. "You okay?"

I lie. "He looks . . . different."

"Peace'll do that," she says. "Or lack of sleep."

Before I can answer, a familiar voice cuts through the snow.

"Well, deck me in tinsel and call me sentimental—Mia Snowden?"

Cherie Carter bursts from the barn in a whirl of red scarf and clipboard. "Honey, what are you doing here?"

"Community service?" I offer.

"Oh, hush." She folds me into a cinnamon-and-pine hug. "Haven't seen you since before Jake shipped out. You were barely out of college, ready to conquer the world and leave us old folks behind."

Harper loops an arm around her. "Some of us held down the fort while she went adventuring."

Cherie laughs, eyes crinkling. "True. You were the Home-Guard. She was the escape artist." She shakes my coat with affection. "Town's been quieter without you—and that's not a compliment."

Heat pricks my cheeks; Cherie Carter could still disarm me like I was seventeen.

She studies me with that motherly, unsettling accuracy. "You look wonderful. Older, sure, but in a good way. Lord, I used to think . . . " Her eyes sparkle.

"Used to think what?" I ask.

Her smile tilts conspiratorial. "That you and my Jake were just taking the scenic route to the inevitable." She pats my cheek. "Shows what mothers know, hm?"

A sharp cold hits my lungs. If she only knew how close she was—how close she still is.

"Guess so," I manage.

Luca barrels over, mitten flapping. "Mom! I found the cocoa tent!"

Cherie lights up. "And who's this handsome helper?"

"This is Luca," I say carefully. "My son."

"Well, aren't you a sight." Cherie crouches, scarf brushing the snow. "I'm Cherie Carter. I make the best cocoa in Frost Harbor—don't tell the bakery girls."

"How?" Luca asks shyly.

"Easy. You stir in a secret and never tell." She taps his nose. "Can you keep a secret, sugar?"

He nods, solemn. "I'm really good at that."

A twist cuts deep through my ribs.

He has no idea the size of the secret he's keeping for me.

Cherie smiles and smooths his hat with such casual tenderness it nearly floors me. "You've got good hands—Carter hands, we call them."

My chest tightens so fast it borders on pain. If she ever links that line to his face—to Jake's—everything detonates.

Please don't see it.

Please don't see him.

"My Jake used to—" she stops herself, smiling instead. "You'd make a fine tree scout."

A tender spot flares—every place I've tried to keep numb lighting up at once. The way Cherie looks at him, claiming him without even knowing she is.

Harper steps in. "Tree Twelve, right, Cherie?"

Cherie straightens, business snapping back. "Alphabetical this year. Snowden, Carter, Hale."

Harper squints. "That . . . is not alphabetical."

Cherie shooes her off, cheeks rosy. "Oh hush, it's alphabetical in spirit."

She bustles away, shouting about ornament hooks. Luca chases after her as though she hung the stars.

Harper throws me a look: *Brace yourself.*

When I pivot, Jake is standing fifteen feet away with a box of lights in his hands.

Our eyes meet across the falling snow.

Heat. Shock. And beneath it—*fear.*

Truth: *If he really looks at Luca, the lie I've been living won't survive the second.*

Dare: *I brought our son here anyway. Told myself it was just Tree Day.*

Confession: *I'm not only afraid he'll recognize Luca. I'm afraid of what happens if he recognizes us.*

8

THE ROW WHERE IT HAPPENED

MIA

"Alphabetical order," I echo, pretending my pulse isn't tripping over itself. "Sure. Let's pretend fate's got a filing system."

Jake's mouth curves. "Carter, Carter, Carter, Snowden. My mom's alphabet is . . . interpretive."

Harper snorts behind me. "Cherie alphabetizes by mood. Or caffeine level."

Jake's laugh rolls out warm—I hate how my body responds before my brain can brace.

Wanting something you can't have isn't romance; it's reflex. My heart should know better.

He nods toward an open section of trees. "You'll want that row. Good branches. Could win Best Ornament Placement."

Harper plants a hand on her hip. "Still upset I won that year?"

"Upset?" Jake scoffs. "You cheated."

"I used symmetry," she fires back. "*Art*, Jake. Look it up."

"Right. Tell that to the lopsided star you nearly decapitated the top row with."

They slip effortlessly into their old rhythm. I try not to sway with it.

The more they settle into familiarity, the more a piece of me wants to follow—and that's exactly what I came here to avoid.

Cherie's voice bellows from the main tent. "Harper! The wreath station needs bodies before the garland revolts!"

Harper groans. "If she hands me glitter, I swear." She squeezes my arm, then peels off toward the chaos.

And suddenly it's just Jake and me. And the quiet we never learned to manage.

Quiet used to feel like possibility. Now it's where the truths I've avoided crouch and wait.

We start working—him with the lights, me with ornaments—Bing Crosby humming faintly from somewhere on the farm.

He breaks first. "Didn't expect to see you back."

"Didn't expect it either." I dig through a handful of hooks. "Apparently, maid of honor duties come with frostbite."

He looks away the way people do when they learn something they were afraid to ask about.

"She asked you already?"

"You didn't know?"

His jaw flexes once, a tiny tell. "No. Didn't think wedding business would start this soon."

The space between us pulls tight as thread.

"She probably just wants to feel ahead of schedule," I say lightly.

He exhales, hands slowing on the wire. "You said yes fast?"

A sharp little snort escapes me—too loud—and heat rises

in my cheeks. "I don't think she gave me a choice. You know her."

He nearly smiles. "Yeah. Bulldozer."

Then, softer: "I missed that, you know."

I keep my hands buried in the ornament crate, because looking at him right now feels like the ground might tilt.

Steady. Stay steady.

Steady is safer. Steady keeps the past from finding its footing.

"Mmhmm," I manage.

Jake huffs a laugh. "Your . . . what did I used to call it? The snorf?" A grin tugs at his mouth. "The Mia Snorf™. Limited edition."

I groan, but the sound cracks into a real laugh—unexpected and bigger than I meant it to be.

God, this is how it happens. Joy sneaks in first, then attachment follows like it owns the place.

We float through a brief pocket of almost-peace until I reach too high for an ornament.

Snow shifts. Boots crunch.

Jake's hand lands on my waist, steadying me. Not possessive. Just him.

"Careful," he murmurs, breathing warm against my neck.

My heartbeat jolts, too quick to hide.

Want and warning spark at the same time.

And then the memory rises—unwanted, vivid.

Fifteen. Same farm. Same row.

I stretched on tiptoe, reaching for the top branch.

"Stop reaching like that," Jake teased behind me. "You're going to face-plant into a fir, and I'm not explaining that to your mom."

"I can do it," I snapped.

"Sure. Or you could let your extremely capable spotter assist."

His hands slid to my waist, lifting me just enough that the world tipped, then steadied.

"See?" he murmured, chin brushing my shoulder. "Taller already."

"I'm not short."

"You're fun-sized," he said, like it was a compliment he shouldn't say out loud.

The ornament clicked onto the branch. He didn't set me down right away.

His fingers had curled—just barely—as if letting go was the one thing he wasn't ready for.

"Got you," he whispered. "Always."

Twenty-seven now, and it still hits the same. And that's the problem . . . nothing about him feels like it aged out of me.

Jake straightens, stepping back. The thread between us snaps clean. "Better finish your row, Mouse."

The nickname slices right through every wall I built around him.

Cherie's voice rises again, calling for help with the garland line.

Jake lifts his chin toward the tent, half smile, half retreat. "Duty calls."

And then he's gone, but my skin doesn't register the absence.

If I keep reacting like this, the truth will show through me before I can cage it.

Ridiculous, how something so small—pressure through fabric, the whisper of his breath—can unmake years of distance.

I swallow hard. *Focus, Mia. Lock it down.*

My fingers sift through the ornaments, searching for something to ground me. Instead, I catch the cedar sprig I shouldn't have brought.

Before I can second-guess it, I tuck it between two branches near the trunk. Not hidden. Not displayed. Just . . . there.

Another piece of that calendar life sneaking into this one.

I step back, brushing my palms against my coat as if I can shake the memory loose.

Across the clearing, Luca's laugh rings out buoyantly.

I latch onto the sound. That's my tether. The reason I'm here. The thing that keeps my walls right where I built them.

Home is him now. Not Jake. Not Frost Harbor. Not the memories with teeth.

By the time Jake turns toward the garland line, I've nearly convinced myself to believe the lie I keep rehearsing:

I'm fine.

It meant nothing.

But fear whispers its truth anyway: Things that meant nothing don't come back this hard.

Truth: *My body still answers to him, no matter how many lies my mouth rehearses.*

Dare: *I keep showing up in his orbit anyway—tree farms, kitchens, old traditions.*

Confession: *I'm not just afraid he'll see himself in Luca. I'm afraid he'll see the part of me that never stopped wanting him.*

9

LUCKY

MIA

The house is still wearing last night—cocoa rings by the sink, stray pine needles, Luca's scarf draped over the radiator like it wandered in from a storm and fell asleep. Mom is humming somewhere in the distance. Harper is on the couch in a dramatic starfish pose, lost to sleep and a blanket that clearly won the battle.

I should be unconscious. Instead, my pulse keeps hammering like yesterday hasn't ended.

I wander to the living room. The lamp paints the room in winter gold. The Advent calendar sits on the coffee table, *suspiciously tidy*. Day 15's flap is lifted, tilted just enough to look guilty.

"Luca," I whisper, because blaming small hands is easier than considering anything else.

I open the door. A solid weight drops into my palm.

Lucky. Cold. Hard. *Impossible.*

Everything pitches sideways

A plastic soldier. Bent leg. Chipped paint. The one I

carried for years before I ever understood why letting go felt impossible.

How?

I didn't put this here. Mom wouldn't single out this one from a pile of old toys, and Dad . . . no. And Luca? Please. He won't even keep a LEGO guy if it loses a hand. A soldier with a bent leg wouldn't make the cut.

So how? The memory hits fast, unasked for.

Seventeen. Jake's room.

Snow whispered against the cracked window.

He didn't look at me when he said, "I want to enlist."

Four words, and suddenly nothing in me was where I'd left it.

"Okay," I said, trying to sound casual while my insides curled. "Do your parents know?"

"Not yet."

"Shocking." I nudged him. "You're still standing."

His mouth twitched like a smile might show up, then thought better of it. "It's the only thing that's ever felt like mine. Everyone here already wrote my story."

I didn't know how to fix anyone's life. I barely knew how to fix a collapsing snowman. But I knew the ache of wanting something so badly it scared you.

So I dug into my backpack and pulled out a fifth-grade superstition I'd never spoken aloud: A plastic soldier with a bent leg and a name I never admitted to.

"For when you tell them," I said. "For when you go."

He took it carefully. "I can't—"

"You can." My voice only trembled at the end. "And you will."

He closed his hand around it, a flick of vulnerability

breaking through. Then he pulled me in, arms tight, his steady heartbeat under my cheek.

"You're the only one I was scared to tell," he murmured.

"Why?"

"Because you're the only one I don't want to leave."

We stayed like that—closer than friends, shy of anything real—as snow gathered on the sill. Lucky sat between us like a promise neither of us knew how to keep.

The living room returns—radiator ticking, Harper snoring, morning testing its light.

Door 12. Door 13. Door 14. Now 15. Each one feels less like coincidence, more like someone marking time.

If he remembers too much—If the wrong memory rises at the wrong moment—I lose both of them. Him. And Luca.

"Hey." Harper's voice is gravelly with sleep.

She pushes up on one elbow, hair a tangle of rebellion. Then she sees my face—and the soldier—and *comes fully online*. "Is that who I think it is?"

I nod. The tension in her face eases, fierce and protective at once.

"For the record," she says, sitting up, "if you want me to launch that tiny man into the sun, I will. I have questionable aim but boundless enthusiasm."

A laugh slips out. "You'd miss."

"Rude but fair." She swings her legs over the couch. "You okay?"

"No," I admit. Then, because honesty feels contagious around her, "Maybe."

She nods like that's exactly right. "Okay. Working theory? Luca loves unauthorized flap activity. But if this is *that* soldier, my bet is on Small-Town Logistics. Jake dropped it last Christmas, your mom rescued it, and now it's part of the décor. Snowden women do weaponize tradition."

"That . . . does track." Though a small, stubborn part of me whispers, *Or it found its way back.*

"You want to talk?"

I cup Lucky in my palm. "Not yet."

"Then he stays with you." Her voice is stripped of its usual sharp edges. "Until talking feels less impossible."

Luca runs in, curls floating from static, sliding dramatically to the coffee table. "Can I open the little door? Nana says the numbers are patient."

"Numbers are extremely patient." Harper points her finger at him. "But breakfast before flaps. It's in the bylaws."

"Okay." He peers at my hand. "Whatcha got?"

"Just a worn-out toy." I slide Lucky into my pocket fast, too fast.

Not because he'd care.

But because some pieces of the past are still too jagged for him to touch.

He accepts this without question and races off.

Harper groans as she stretches. "I'm making eggs and a plan."

"What plan?"

"One that keeps you from building a nostalgia bunker. Light errands. Minimal people. And maybe karaoke at Riley's tonight. Holiday Karaoke / Trivia / Poor Decisions Night. Loud enough to drown out your brain."

My *no* melts into a *maybe.* Riley's is where everything once split open. And where noise is allowed.

"Fine," I give in.

"Love the enthusiasm."

She grabs a spatula from out of nowhere. "I could tell your mom the calendar had a tragic crafting accident."

The idea shouldn't make my pulse jump. But it does.

Because objects remember. And memories always find a way to surface.

"Don't," I whisper. "Not this one."

Harper salutes with her spatula. "Then we'll eat and do the least destructive thing next."

By the time she's murmuring with the kettle and Luca is lobbying for maximum chocolate chips, my phone buzzes where it lies face down.

JAKE

For what it's worth . . . I'm glad you were there yesterday.

I swallow hard. My thumbs hover, useless. If I start talking to him, it's only a matter of time before the truth slips out dressed as a joke or a late-night confession.

Before I choose, his bubble appears.

I shouldn't say this, but . . .

It felt different seeing you again.

I've missed you.

The words spark something too close to the edge, heat licking at all the places I keep boarded up.

Wanting him is dangerous.

Letting him close is worse.

Every piece of the past he remembers is a step closer to the truth I can't afford him reaching.

"Eggs in three! And somebody better be singing!" Harper shouts, clattering a pan as if knowing she just saved me from myself.

I turn the phone face down like it's a wound.

Truth: *Hearing from him still shatters through me faster than I want to admit.*

Dare: *I don't answer. I let the silence stand between us like it's a wall instead of a choice.*

Confession: *If I let one word slip, I don't trust myself to stop before I tell him everything.*

10

RILEY'S BAR

JAKE

Riley's greets me like it always has—nostalgia sunk into the wood.

The place hums with low conversation and old ghosts. Neon buzzes overhead, too loud, washing the room in unfinished business I never quite outran.

My body angles toward our old booth before I've even cleared the doorway. Muscle memory beating common sense, like always.

The radiator ticks—two soft knocks. The rhythm I used to tap against my knee whenever she sat across from me in that red dress she loved.

Not festive.

Not soft.

Not friendly.

A red that dared you to look and warned you what it would cost.

Her laugh still sparks in my head. If I shut my eyes, I can almost taste cinnamon on her lips.

First heartbreaks don't fade. They root deep and stubbornly. Case in point: I texted her like an idiot last night and the only thing that answered me was silence.

I keep telling myself that's fair. Doesn't stop me from checking my phone as if it owes me an apology.

We slide onto stools at the bar. I told myself I wouldn't come back here. Swore it.

Then Houston called in a Veteran Mandatory Morale Hour, and the truth is, I don't have the stamina to dodge both my past and my best friend on the same night.

I reach for my beer, and pause when something glints by the tip jar.

A lone brass sixteenth-note charm. Edges worn from someone's thumb.

Sixteen notes. One song. Door 16.

Someone remembers.

My gut twists—reflex, stupid. It's probably nothing. A stranger's keychain. But my brain doesn't care; it vaults straight to the same question on repeat.

What if she left it?

What if she remembers?

"Hey." Houston's hand cuts across my line of sight. "You're wearing the thousand-yard stare again. Real brooding Hallmark hero stuff. Blink if you're about to say the word fate."

I huff out a breath. "Fate and I aren't on speaking terms."

"Cool. Then let's call it second chances." He leans in, claiming the space like he owns it. Like he didn't just drag me into the one bar in town that feels like a live wire.

Before I can answer, he flags the waitress. She drops two beers and a karaoke flyer: Sing. Drink. Repeat.

Houston raises his glass. "To second chances."

I lift mine, but don't add anything. The words snag somewhere behind my ribs, lodged in the place that never stopped picturing one specific what-if.

The bar grows louder. Lights dim a notch. The jukebox wheezes through a heartbreak song I don't need help remembering.

Houston scans the room like he's reading a new country. "Okay, so . . . this place is tragic. Sticky floor, questionable lighting, vibe of a crypt with a liquor license."

"Maybe it's sentimental," I tell him.

"Or haunted." He tilts his head, considering. "Which fits your brand if memory serves."

That's Houston—three tours, two ex-wives who still text him, and a duffel bag full of more distraction techniques than clothes. He moved to Frost Harbor a month ago on what he calls a Short-Term Sanity Lease.

Translation: *I won't stay.*

I recognize the type. I used to be the type.

"Met my neighbor today," he goes on, stretching his legs like the bar is a couch. "Redhead. Freckles. Drives a tank disguised as a Subaru. Waved like she was auditioning for a peppermint commercial."

"Sounds aggressive."

"Sounds incredible." His grin is sharp. "Harper. Ring a bell?"

Something coils low in my ribs. "Yeah. Mia Snowden's best friend."

His brows climb. "As in . . . ?"

"Yes, Ava's sister, Messner."

Houston watches me for a long beat—eyes sharper than he pretends. He knows of Mia. Only what I've let slip over late-night talks and shared screwups. That we grew up together. That Ava is her sister.

That's it. But knowing Houston, he's filled in more blanks than I handed him.

"You only hit me with my last name when you're wound tight," he finally says. "Feels like I'm back in formation waiting for a sergeant to smoke us. What's got your panties in a wad?"

I roll my eyes. "First off, you and panties don't belong in the same sentence."

He barks out a laugh. "Please. Half this town wishes I belonged in theirs."

I shake my head, fighting a smile. "Secondly, nothing's bothering me."

We both hear the lie, but Houston lets it sit. That's his real gift—room without pity.

The speakers shriek as the MC taps the mic like he's starting an evacuation. Feedback knifes across the bar.

Houston winces. "Jesus. I thought this was a beer run, not a community event."

"Welcome to Frost Harbor," I say.

He's gearing up for another comeback when the door opens and winter rushes in, dragging laughter behind it.

And just like that—the noise drops out.

Because she walks in.

Snow dusts her coat. Her cheeks are pink, curls loose around her face. She looks . . . God. Older where grief brushed her, sharper in the edges it left. The same everywhere that still undoes me.

Harper barrels in first—bright confidence and chaos, practically towing Mia behind her. Mia moves as if she's trying not to disturb the air—careful, cautious, tugging at her sleeve the way she always did when she felt too exposed. Her eyes sweep the bar, a slow pass over Riley's, catching on all the memories I can almost see forming.

Houston breathes, "Well, damn. Miss Freckles Redhead brought reinforcements."

A hitch catches low in my throat. "Yeah."

"Okay," he murmurs. "Now I understand."

"Understand what?" My voice dips, braced already.

He gestures toward her, eyes narrowing in approval. "Why you used to say you'd marry someone like her."

I choke so hard my beer nearly hits the floor. "Jesus —Houston."

"What?" He lifts his hands. "She's beautiful."

Something hot and unreasonable flares through my chest.

I have no right to it.

Doesn't matter. It lands anyway.

He watches her again, more impressed than anything. "That smile? Those curls? Carter . . . "

"Shut up," I growl.

He grins, satisfied. "Helmet's on backwards again."

He's not wrong. But he doesn't know the rest. The kid who calls her mom now. The life I only heard about from a distance because I told myself distance was safer—for her, for me, for whoever that kid's father is.

Before he can push further, the MC screeches into the mic, and Harper starts waving her hand, volunteering Mia for karaoke like she's on a mission.

"Ladies and gentlemen," he crows, "we're starting strong tonight! Give it up for Mia Snowden!"

Mia halts mid-step. Her expression sharpens from easy to cornered in a blink. "Harper, no—"

The crowd roars over her.

She heads toward the stage with the resigned grace of someone being marched to their fate, laughter tucked under her breath like a secret.

"She looks railroaded," Houston mutters.

"That's Harper's whole brand."

Harper cups her hands around her mouth. "Make us sob, Snow Queen!"

Mia jolts—the same startled jump she used to give when a teacher called on her unexpectedly. Color climbs her neck, spreading across her skin in a flush she can't hide. Snow melts in her curls, catching the light like winter shaking glitter loose.

The piano starts—gentle, waiting.

Mia steps up to the mic.

A breath.

A beat.

Then—with her eyes drifting shut—she lets the first note slip.

Something in me shifts hard enough to rattle bones.

Mia at fifteen snaps into focus. Backstage. Wrapped in a robe she swore made her look like a blueberry. Chin tucked, fingers clamped tight around the fabric.

"Jake, I can't do it," she whispered. "Everyone's staring."

I stepped closer, tilted her chin up. "Mouse . . . you don't sing for them. You sing for you. And for me. Because I like hearing it."

Her eyes were huge, unsure. "You do?"

I shrugged casually; everything else wasn't. "Yeah. Makes the world sound better."

Her smile broke over me—bright, impossibly wide—and branded something I'd never managed to sand down.

Now, years later, she carries that same low, secret burn when she sings. She only lets the world see it when she's too lost in the music to remember she's exposing herself.

Houston exhales, "Well, damn."

I barely hear him. I'm somewhere between the girl on that stage and the woman standing here now, between the notes and the years we never spoke.

When she leans into the mic on the chorus, something in her unfurls—unguarded and fierce in a way that hits square in my chest. She's singing straight into the place I've kept sealed tight.

The last note hovers—fragile, breathtaking—before it slips free.

Applause erupts. Chairs scrape. Someone whistles.

Her eyes snap open, startled, then soften as color blooms up her neck again. She laughs, tucking a curl behind her ear, looking overwhelmed and luminous and so damn herself I forget how to stand.

My heart stumbles. Forgets its job.

From the front row, Harper yells, "Told you! She can still wreck a man!"

Mia hides behind her hands, a flustered grin peeking through the cracks.

Houston nods toward Harper. "Bold for someone I met six hours ago."

Harper clocks him instantly. "Well, hey there, neighbor."

He raises his beer. "Please return my snow shovel sometime this decade."

"No promises," she fires back.

They're off in their own orbit—his dry, hers blazing—and I know already they're headed straight for some kind of slow-motion disaster.

But I barely track it.

Because Mia steps off the stage carefully, eyes on the warped floorboard near the edge. She's looser now, but the second she zeroes in on me, the room narrows. All the noise compresses into a distant hum.

I'm on my feet before I realize I've moved.

When she reaches the edge of the crowd, I offer my hand. Nothing showy. Just . . . there.

She looks at it, then at me. A question settles over her face, over both of us.

Harper swoops in like a one-woman weather system. "Oh no, ma'am. You don't get to ignore that look. Man's asking you to dance. And Riley's has a strict no-refusal policy."

Mia sighs—this theatrical, put-upon sound—but when her hand slides into mine, the protest disappears.

My inhale snags. No sound, just impact.

Her palm is smaller than I remember. Or maybe I've just been gone too long. Either way, the contact jolts through every place I thought I'd boarded up. I curl my fingers around hers carefully. She's too real in my hands again.

The jukebox sputters awake. A coin drops. Electric noise flares—and then, of course, that song spills through the speakers.

Jessie Ware's "Say You Love Me."

Harper squeals, grabbing Houston's arm like she's been waiting for this exact cue. "Guess it's a theme!"

"Guess so," I say, though the word feels thin compared to what's happening inside my chest.

This is the closest I've been to Mia Snowden in years. Too close for what I deserve.

Every rational part of me knows this is dangerous—too much history, too much unsaid—

But I don't let go.

She steps in—adjusting—calculating each inch of distance she can tolerate. Her hand hovers a second before it settles against my chest, right over the frantic thud I can't calm down.

We move. A slow, steady sway that feels like muscle memory dragged out of storage.

And then sixteen hits me full force—my mom's borrowed paper crown slipping over my eyes; Mia drowned in my mom's dress; both of us pretending the song was a joke when it never was.

"You remember this?" she asks, eyes tipped up toward mine, those hazel flecks catching the string lights.

"Yeah."

I guide her into a spin—once, twice, a third time just to hear her laugh. It bubbles out, unguarded, the way it used to back before we knew what hurting each other would feel like.

And all I can think is:

What would it feel like if this was the life I got?

If she were the one I was marrying.

If this—her in my arms—was my every day.

If her little boy called me Dad.

The thought slams into me—betrayal and relief braided tight—and that alone should make me sick.

I'm engaged to her twin sister.

If Ava saw the way I'm holding Mia right now, she'd know exactly how uneven the math has always been.

I'm an idiot for even letting the idea breathe.

But with Mia this close, it's like Frost Harbor keeps nudging us toward each other.

The Advent calendar signs.

The fig ornament she tucked onto the tree when she thought no one noticed.

The sixteenth-note charm by the tip jar.

Pieces of us surfacing as if the universe is done being subtle.

The room tilts quieter. People still move around us—laughing, clinking glasses, brushing past—but they're background noise now. The only sharp thing in focus is Mia. Her hand in mine. The careful way her fingers flex against my shirt as if she's testing whether this is real.

The radiator knocks in its same two-beat pattern. Her shoulders twitch—barely—but I feel it under my palm. She hears it too. Remembering has a sound tonight.

The silence stretches between us, gaining weight. It's the same kind that used to live in the wall between our rooms— thick with things we never admitted out loud.

I angle us just enough to guide her around a couple weaving off the dance floor. Her breath catches at the shift— quick, sharp—and she looks away like she can will her reaction back into line.

Her gaze skims the bar. The lights. The MC. Anywhere but my face.

But the space isn't big enough for cooperation. Every time she tries to pull back, the crowd presses us closer—her shoulder grazing my chest, her knee brushing mine when our steps cross.

My hand settles at her waist, thumb brushing the fabric of her dress. Familiarity and restraint knock heads under my skin. I shouldn't hold her like this. Not now. Not ever again.

But she fits exactly where she used to.

"Mia . . . " Her name slips out quieter than I meant—low, more breath than word. It folds the air in half.

She stills.

Slowly, she looks up. It's deliberate resistance, that angle of her chin, like she already knows that meeting my eyes is a risk she shouldn't take.

But she does it anyway.

And when her gaze locks with mine, everything else drops out. The bar. The years. The people. It's just her, and the version of me I was when loving her felt simple.

I see the moment she feels it too—the gravity of it. The remembering. It flashes across her expression before she can hide it.

Her fingers twitch against my chest. Just once. Small movement, big impact. She pulls her hand back a fraction, like she touched something too hot.

She swallows. "Jake . . . " The word catches in her throat, something raw and unguarded leaking through.

The song swells, slow and pleading. It nudges us closer without asking permission. My thumb grazes the side of her hand—barely anything—and her breath stutters. She looks away, but she doesn't step back.

She stays inside the line we both know is there. Inside the line I've had no right to cross for years.

I feel every inch of her restraint. Every inch of mine.

The rest of the bar crashes back in waves—Harper laughing, someone ordering shots—but none of it really lands. It's all moving around the edge of whatever we're standing in.

Her gaze flicks down. For half a second, she looks at my mouth. It's quick, almost nothing.

But I notice. God, do I notice.

Wanting punches through my chest. It's so familiar it makes me angry. At myself. At timing. At all the choices that got us here.

She must feel some echo of it, because her fingers curl against my shirt, pulling her in before she shifts her weight again, like she's trying to erase it.

The space tightens again. So do we.

I take one slow breath, careful, because if I move too fast, this moment will rip apart.

Something in her eyes *opens*. There's so much there—hurt and history and something that looks too much like the way she used to look at me—that I can't stop my hand from rising.

Slow.

Measured.

Almost touching.

My fingers hover just shy of her jaw, close enough to feel the heat of her skin. One more inch and I'll cross a line I've been pretending doesn't exist.

She draws in a breath that says she feels it coming.

She doesn't step away.

For a second, all I can see is the night I finally held her the way I'd wanted to for years. The night I almost asked her to wait for me and didn't, because duty called and she deserved more than a life hinged on whether I came home.

My throat tightens around all the things I never said. All the things I still haven't.

"Mia . . . "

I'm so close to saying I'm sorry. For not making sure she got my letters. For leaving. For letting her believe she didn't matter.

She did.

She does.

Her lips part. My hand tilts closer—

And Harper's laugh crashes through the moment as she and Houston stumble past, still arguing about his attempt at a dip. Houston's elbow clips my shoulder. Mia flinches back enough to jolt the spell.

She blinks as if waking up. The air between us goes from private to public in an instant.

"Well," she says, clearing her throat. "That was . . . not terrible."

"High praise," I manage.

"You still dance like you know what you're doing."

"And you still pretend you don't."

We stand there; the song winding down around us, close enough for memory to bruise. The room feels too small for the things I almost said.

"Jake . . . tonight was . . . " She trails off, meeting my stare head-on. For a second, there's nothing between us but the truth we've been avoiding.

Across the bar, Houston calls, "Carter! I told you tonight's your U-turn!"

He's joking, but the words land too heavily.

Maybe he's right.

There's the life I promised Ava . . . and then there's the one that goes feral inside me whenever Mia lets even a little of herself show.

And those futures don't line up. No matter how hard I pretend they could.

Truth: *I never stopped wanting her, no matter how many other futures I tried to build.*

Dare: *I hold her, dance with her, imagine a life that isn't mine to claim.*

Harper waves Mia over from the bar. "Snow Queen! Get over here before I sign us up for a duet!"

Mia huffs out a breath that might be a laugh. She steps back, our hands sliding apart. The loss of contact is stupidly loud in my body.

She turns to go.

Then—right at the edge of the dance floor—she pauses. Looks back at me.

Just for a second. Then, one heartbeat more than is safe.

It's not long. It's not dramatic.

But it's enough.

Because in that extra moment, in that held look, I see every version of us we never let happen.

Confession: *And I know—if I keep looking at Mia Snowden like this, being engaged won't be enough to stop me from falling all the way back.*

11

INTERLUDE

HARPER

If Frost Harbor had a national anthem, it'd be the crack of Margaret Snowden's clipboard hitting a table.

I'm camped at the Snowdens' kitchen island at 7:12 a.m., with a Sharpie between my teeth, the glue gun warming, as if it has opinions, and Margaret on speaker, insisting she's "absolutely not pressuring me" about the market schedule.

"Harper, sweetheart, we're short a cocoa runner, and—oh! —Gingerbread Showdown check-in moved to eleven. Can you make sure Mia knows? And tell Luca we've got a very important lanyard with his name on it."

"Copy," I say, fluent in Snowden-ese. "One cocoa mule. One five-year-old with unchecked authority."

Mia slips into the kitchen like she's trying to make herself smaller than the steam from the coffeepot. Hair scraped up. Yesterday's sweater. Her hand brushes her pocket—quick, automatic, protective. I clock it. I don't ask.

"Morning," I chirp, deliberately bright. "Pick your sign: 'STRUCTURAL ONLY' or 'GUMDROP ECONOMY'."

Her expression flickers . . . wanting to respond but weighed down. "You slept?"

"Like a saint on NyQuil." Lie. "You?"

She doesn't answer. The mug rattles when she sets it down. I angle myself between her and the speaker, ready to intercept Margaret's next tactical request.

"Margaret—quick update," I cut in. "We're coming to the market, but Mia's on a timer. Grad-school brain fry."

"Of course," she says in a tone that means: *Over my gingerbread body.*

"Just an hour, sweetie. It'll be light."

It will not be light. Frost Harbor doesn't do light; it does traditions with teeth.

The radiator clicks. The house goes silent, like it knows better than to interrupt.

Mia's hand moves toward her pocket again.

I let the stillness speak in her place.

"Go ahead," she mutters. "Whatever speech you've prepared."

"No speech." I tilt my head, taking her in. "Just gauging where you're at. Seven on the 'I'm fine' scale?"

A dry huff. "More like six."

"Six works." I ease my stance. "We match the day to that. Market for an hour. Gingerbread check-in. If it gets spiky, we disappear. I'll fake a plumbing emergency—wet paper towel and everything."

A thin release of breath. Not a laugh, just relief trying to get its footing.

"You're absurd."

"And devoted." I nod at her pocket. "Not prying, but you gonna tell me why you're guarding that like state secrets?"

"It's nothing."

Which is the exact kind of lie you tell when the truth has knives.

I let it lie between us. Open door, not open pressure.

"So," I ask gravely, "how're you holding up after last night?"

"It threw me . . . "

"You danced with Jake."

"It . . . happened."

"And then it kept happening," I tease, gently.

Color crawls into her cheeks. "You and Houston didn't look like wallflowers either."

I snort. "*That* man had the audacity to step on my foot, not once, Mia, but three times!"

I swipe a bit of frosting and dab her nose before she can dodge.

She startles, but the tension in her shoulders slips half an inch. "Harper!"

"That's for misdirection."

And because I needed to break whatever spiral she was sliding toward.

"You still didn't stop dancing with him," she says, trying for control.

"Because he's my new neighbor. HOA-level friendly. Barely."

This time, the air around her shifts. Not quite a smile— more so her lungs unlocking.

"Last night shook you," I say, softer now.

"Yeah." She swallows. "It did."

The silence turns tight, so I step into it for her.

"You don't have to reach for clarity today. We move slowly."

"That better not involve more frosting."

"Debatable."

Luca bursts into the kitchen—sunrise in human form, grinning bright enough to shame daylight.

For one beat, he tilts his head exactly like Jake used to when he was puzzling over something too big for words.

It hits me low and fast. I shut that thought down fast. Not my dots, not my puzzle.

"Nana says there's a badge!"

"Indeed," I say solemnly. "Chief Candy Supervisor. Perks include gumdrop embez—taste-testing."

"One per row," Mia adds, voice loosening.

"Per row?" he gasps.

"Use it wisely," I tell him.

He salutes and charges out.

Mia watches him disappear, her fingers brushing her pocket again—this time with a flash of guilt.

I drop my voice. "Hey."

She looks up. "Hey."

"You can tap out."

"I don't want to." Her shoulders fold inward. "It's just . . . him. His parents. Seeing him with Ava."

Her palms press to her eyes. "It's like staring at the version of my life I didn't choose. And feeling the loss of something I shouldn't want."

There it is. The *truth* of what she's been trying to walk around.

And definitely *not* my truth to spill. But, if the truth ever hits daylight, I know exactly whose side I'm on . . . and it's not subtle.

"I get it," I say.

"Do you?"

"Know you've been building a fortress out of doing the right thing and hoping no one notices the cracks? Yeah." I angle closer so she doesn't have to meet my eyes if she can't.

"Know you don't have to hold the entire damn thing up alone? Also yeah."

A fragile smile crosses her lips. "Your pep talks used to swear more."

"High school was a lawless era." I cap my Sharpie. "Okay. Market, then check-in. Ava's doing engagement-party prep with Dylan. Jake's on drills all week."

A millimeter of tension leaves her shoulders.

"I thought the engagement party would be the hard part," she says.

"You thought you could ghost your way through Frost Harbor," I answer, not unkind. "But people still see you. Still care. That's loud when you're not expecting it."

Her gaze dips. "I hate that I want to go. To the market. All of it. After years of swearing I wouldn't."

"Mia." I brush my elbow lightly against hers. "Wanting isn't weakness. It's your heart going, 'Hey, remember me?' while your brain tries to play dead."

A startled sound escapes her, somewhere between a laugh and a breath. "When did you get wise?"

"Right after I turned unbearably nosy."

I slide a sign across the counter: **STRUCTURAL ONLY — NO GUMDROP BRIBES.**

She rolls her eyes, color returning to her cheeks.

We move easily—her scarf, my signs, Luca streaking past like a tiny meteor. The house thrums with Frost Harbor energy, that earnest kind of chaos that tries its best to look organized.

At the door, she hesitates. Her hand hovers near her pocket.

Whatever she's carrying is heavier in meaning than mass. She's not ready to share it. And I'm not going to ask before she's ready.

Cold air greets us—pine, frost, and morning light. Down the hill, Frost Harbor is already overachieving: lights everywhere, distant carols drifting off-key.

"Ground rules," I say as we head down the steps. "If it gets too loud, we break. If you need to vanish, I create a distraction. And if someone corners you with cookies and life lessons—"

"You'll bite," she finishes.

"Exactly."

"You'll be arrested by noon," she murmurs, looping an arm around Luca.

"Worth it. You're my person. Extraction included."

She looks at me—eyes clearer, the storm in them settling a notch.

Luca sprints ahead, fearless.

Mia follows carefully.

And me?

Truth: *She's hanging on by threadbare grace and caffeine.*

Dare: *I'm going to stand between her and whatever the past throws next, even if I have to bite a Santa.*

Confession: *I see more than she thinks I do, and I'll keep her secret until she's ready for it not to be one.*

12

BEFORE THE WAR

JAKE

Frost Harbor isn't awake yet, but the world pretends. Thin blue light slips over the treetops, breath hanging in the air like a thought caught mid-rise. The *Carter Tree Farm* sign wears a skin of frost sharp enough to bite through gloves.

Dad's already in the driveway, wrestling a fir toward the flatbed, boots grinding against the frost as if the tree insulted an ancestor.

"You're late," he calls without looking up.

Carter-speak for *Good time, proud of you, don't push it.*

"It's 7:11," I say, grabbing the other end.

"Trees don't keep track of clocks." He hefts the branches higher. "Mrs. Zanetti wants this delivered before her energy fields collapse."

Wouldn't want that. "Chakras slipping again?"

A snort—his version of a smile.

We settle the trunk onto the flatbed. Frozen bark cracks at the impact, releasing pine and cold earth—scents that drag me home whether I want them to or not.

Dad folds his arms. "Straps. Need the good ones. Your mother reorganized."

Which explains the half-labeled avalanche on the porch.

"Coffee?" I ask.

His grunt translates to *Yes, but don't expect gratitude.*

Inside, warmth gathers in layers—coffee, sugar, pine sap. For a suspended moment, I'm seventeen again, racing Mia to Door 17 on the Advent calendar we pretended wasn't a competition.

I shut the memory down before it wakes all the way.

Mom sits at the kitchen table in one of Dad's flannels, hair pinned up by two pens and sheer determination. She's unpacking a holiday tote when a rogue jingle bell skitters across the wood.

"Oh good," she says. "You can keep your father from rupturing something."

"That's the plan." I take the coffees. "Morning."

She hums as she shakes out the tote. Something small and brown tumbles onto the table and spins to a stop.

Her breath catches. "Well now. I didn't expect to see this again."

I step closer.

A gingerbread boot, half of one, iced clean across the break.

The sight of it tilts something in me, a quick, breath-stealing wobble.

Door 17. The year we split it—half in my house, half in hers. A superstition we never named, as if keeping both pieces meant we kept each other too.

Mom smiles faintly. "You and that Advent calendar. Door 17 never stood a chance."

Mia's shoulder leaned against mine, her grin conspiratorial as she broke the cookie. *Yours,* she'd whispered, like the word carried a promise neither of us named."

The boot fits in the palm of a child. A wayward thought flickers—*Luca would love this*—and I smother it before it sticks.

Mom's voice drifts in. "Does it bring back memories?" Her eyes light in a way that says she sees right through me.

"You knew?" I ask.

"Honey, I'm a mother. I see *everything.*" She points a piece of tinsel at me like a truth wand. "You two practically tackled each other trying to get that cookie."

I exhale. "And here I thought we were subtle."

I slip the gingerbread boot into my pocket. Ava would lose her mind if she saw it, and she should. This is history I shouldn't be carrying.

Mom stands, brushing glitter from her hands. "Straps are in the blue bin, bottom shelf. And take the breakfast sandwich. Fuel, not a suggestion."

"Yes, ma'am."

The bin coughs up a tangle of straps. I find a usable one and snag the sandwich.

On my way out, she calls my name, a thread of affection in her voice. "Having you home . . . seeing you here for Christmas again . . . I'm just grateful."

Warmth and ache collide in my chest, that familiar pull between wanting to stay and knowing I never fully do.

I know what she means—the brutal stretch after Christmas, the drills, the long days that forced me to say too many hard goodbyes. She hated military life for me, but she still stood behind every choice I made. Besides Mia, she always was the next.

Cold meets me outside, blunt as truth.

Dad eyes me. "Find 'em?"

"And breakfast." I lift the sandwich.

He grunts approval. "Your mother's making spice cookies again. House smells like December's guts."

We fall into work—strap tossed, strap caught, ratchet tightened. Our silence is practiced and comfortable. My mind is not.

Last night intrudes in flashes—her hand in mine, her laugh, the look she tried not to give me.

Dad breaks the quiet. "Not much coming from you this morning."

"Thinking about drills."

He lets the lie sit. "Houston said your division's got a rough week coming. Long rotations."

"Nothing we can't handle."

A few years ago, he would've snapped that the tree farm was safer and closer. Now he just nods.

"You're good at it," he says quietly. "Military life. You've grown into yourself."

His words find their mark—approval mixed with regret I didn't expect.

Part of me wonders if there's a version where I grow into myself here too, and what I've cost to get this far. Another part wonders if I could ever be enough for someone else. If I'd screw it up. If I'd turn into him or fail trying.

"I didn't think we'd get here," I admit. "After I left, it felt like I had drawn a line."

"I know." His voice softens. "But every Christmas you came home, I started seeing the change. You needed to find your direction."

I swallow hard. "Thanks."

"The Showdown should be big today," he says. "Your mother's vibrating over it."

"When is she not?"

"You used to be the same way." He tightens the strap. "Christmas hit you hard. The anticipation. You liked it more than the sugar."

He's right. Some part of me still likes it, especially now that the something I liked is walking around Frost Harbor with memories that match mine.

Dad claps the truck. "Go on. Don't keep Mrs. Zanetti waiting for her spiritual awakening."

"Yes, sir."

I climb into the cab. The seat groans in the same place it always has. My coffee steams. The world is too bright for how early it is.

Ava's photo comes to mind—cream sweater, perfect smile, a future I keep trying to step into.

But as the truck rolls down the lane, each bump taps the little boot against my thigh, steady and insistent.

Truth: I shouldn't still be carrying pieces of a life I walked away from.

Dare: I pocket the boot anyway.

A breath. A beat.

Confession: Every knock from the past sounds too much like her name.

13

GINGERBREAD WAR

MIA

Frost Harbor rises from the winter haze like a memory I thought I'd buried. White lights sweep across the square, catching paper snowflakes that spin through the air. Booths overflow with gingerbread chaos—gumdrops scattering, icing stacked in tubs, peppermint shimmering across stone. A choir hums beneath an awning.

It should feel magical. Instead, it pulls at seams I spent years stitching shut.

Luca's mitten squeaks in my grip as he bounces. "Mom! They have chocolate roofs!"

His excitement hits a tenderness I don't let myself examine. "I see them, bud."

Harper nudges me with her elbow, scarf eating half her face. "Jesus. Frost Harbor weaponized nostalgia."

I laugh, because the alternative is letting my chest crack open. The Advent calendar flap this morning was Door 17— little gingerbread boot, heel snapped clean through. I'd stared at it too long.

Jake used to tease me about that cookie. Said I, "baked emotional foreshadowing."

We split that boot one year. A silent pact we never said aloud: Both halves meant we'd find our way back.

I tuck my hands in my pockets, fingers grazing the boot half I stole before Luca could see it.

"Smells the same," Harper murmurs. "December and . . . unprocessed history."

"History is seasonal," I whisper back.

Before we make it three feet into the chaos—

"Mia, honey, over here!"

Mom is wearing flour like armor. Dad's beside her, leveling gingerbread walls with the concentration of a man defusing explosives. Luca beams. He loves them instantly, the way kids do when they finally meet the people they've only heard stories about.

Mom kneels. "Chief Candy Supervisor, reporting for duty?"

Luca straightens. "Yes, ma'am!"

Dad solemnly awards him a sparkly lanyard. "Quality Control Division."

The sight blindsides me. Because Luca fits between them like he's always belonged.

Mom's hand squeezes mine—brief, warm, almost like she's forgiving me for leaving years ago. Or forgiving herself for letting me.

Harper leans in. "This is either cute or psychological warfare. Scale?"

"Seven," I breathe.

"Copy that."

Mom straightens. "We're short on gumdrops, and the Carters brought extras. Be a dear and check with them before the contest starts. Darren and Cherie are around here somewhere."

Harper sighs. "And so it begins."

We cross the lane, boots squeaking. My pulse climbs.

The crowd shifts right as we take a turn.

He's carrying a toolbox and a bakery box, frost dusting his dark uniform. A streetlamp back lights him, catching the line of his jaw, the metal at his collar, the breath he exhales like he's trying to steady himself.

Memory hits hard—Jake at seventeen, leaning against a railing, looking at me like he knew a truth neither of us could say yet.

His eyes lock onto mine with that same unnervingly precise attention.

Something inside me pulls tight, painfully, like a seam giving way.

"Oh no," Harper whispers.

"Uncle Jake!" Luca launches toward him, mittens flailing.

Jake drops the bakery box, kneeling in one smooth motion. He catches Luca like he's done it forever. Like his arms knew the shape of him before his mind did.

The sight punches the air out of my lungs.

Jake looks up at me—slowly, reluctantly—and it's all there:

Recognition.

Longing.

Regret.

A truth he's been swallowing for years.

Then—

"Jake!"

Ava sweeps in as if she's been cued by the universe. Scarlet coat, perfect hair, smile bright enough to belong in a bakery window.

Dylan follows half a step behind, clipboard tucked under

his arm. He nods at me—gentle, observant—but his eyes catch every detail.

Ava slides her hand down Jake's sleeve. "There's my hero. Toolbox and treats. Literal perfection."

Jake shifts Luca to his hip. "Backup supplies."

His eyes flick toward me again. He can't help it. It's instinct.

And something sharp flares under my ribs.

"Are you gonna help me build the best gingerbread house?" Luca asks, clutching Jake's collar.

Jake softens in a way I've never seen him soften for anyone but me. "Wouldn't be a gingerbread build without you."

Ava's laugh snaps like brittle candy. "Adorable."

Mrs. Carter barrels through the crowd, cookies in hand. "There's my favorite boy!"

She hugs me one-armed, presses a kiss to Luca's forehead, chatters about icing techniques.

Jake sets Luca down gently. "Go show her your badge, buddy."

Luca bolts off.

Jake doesn't look away from me.

Not right away.

"Apron time," Mom says, appearing with my old green one—frayed edges, my name stitched in little gold loops. A wound disguised as fabric.

I fumble with the straps.

Someone steps behind me.

A shift in the air.

A quiet, familiar breath.

Then—

"I've got it."

Jake's fingers graze mine, careful and ember-warm.

Confident in a way only someone who once knew every inch of me could be.

My pulse free-falls.

He ties the straps carefully, ike he remembers how I always hated when they twisted.

"You still double-knot," he murmurs.

"You . . . remember that?" My voice is soft. Too soft.

His mouth ghosts into a half-smile. "I remember too much."

The apron settles against my spine—the knot firm, neat, exactly the way he used to do it.

He steps back.

I'm still unraveling.

"Walls aren't gonna level themselves!" Dad calls.

Chaos erupts again, scattering the moment but not breaking it.

Jake ends up beside me. Of course he does. Gravity always had opinions about us.

At the worktable, it's madness:

Mom herding candy canes.

Harper running structural commentary.

Ava arranging gumdrops like she's auditioning for a holiday catalog.

Luca on a crate, supervising everything.

Jake braces gingerbread walls. I hold icing bags. Our hands brush—a feather-light collision—and I feel it everywhere.

"You always did the ridges best," he says, unguarded.

"I taught you the ridges."

"That's why you perfected them."

Harper mutters, "Weaponized domesticity. Terrifying."

Ava doesn't laugh. "We're doing symmetry."

She watches Jake watch me.

"Yes, ma'am," Harper salutes.

Luca sneaks a peppermint where it absolutely does not belong, and I sweep a frosting flourish over it. He beams, our small secret.

Across the lane, Cherie lifts her camera. "Snowdens! Over here!"

We shuffle together—Mom, Dad, Ava, Luca, me, Jake. Someone counts down.

Three . . . two . . .

I swear I feel a hand settle at my waist. Maybe imagined. Maybe not. My pulse misfires either way.

Flash.

Another.

Jake steps back quickly. Ava watches him like she's waiting for an answer he hasn't given.

"Perfect," Mom says. "Now—"

"Mia, Jake! Just the two of you," Cherie calls. "It's been years."

Ava laughs too quickly. "Cherie, they're covered in icing."

"That's what makes it cute."

I turn, ready to dodge, but I don't move. And Jake steps beside me like he's always belonged there.

He doesn't touch me. He doesn't have to. The heat of him finds me, anyway.

We lift our eyes together. And we look.

A heartbeat suspends.

Then everything shatters back into motion.

Mom claps. "Back to work. We're short on shingles."

"Gumdrop-tiled," Dad corrects.

"I'll get them," Ava offers.

"Mia and Jake," Mom decides, with the casual cruelty of a woman who loves romance novels.

Jake meets my eyes. "Come on, Mouse," he says, gently.

Truth: *Standing this close feels wrong in all the familiar, impossible ways.*

Dare: *I keep slipping into places that put us side by side.*

Confession: *If I let this keep happening, the risk isn't just my heart—it's everything I've rebuilt.*

14

THE OUTBUILDING

MIA

The outbuilding door thuds shut behind us, soft enough not to echo, loud enough to rearrange something in my chest. The noise of the square fades into a distant hum—laughter muffled, music swallowed, winter pressed against the walls like it's waiting for us to remember we don't get to hide in here.

The air is warm and faintly sweet, like old frosting and forgotten December afternoons. A place preserved in sugar.

Jake stops just one step inside. He exhales—long, shaky, unplanned.

Not the controlled, steady breath I'm used to.

Something looser. Something that sounds like a man who's been holding together a structure too heavy for too long.

"I forgot how loud this town gets," he says quietly. But the softness in his voice isn't about the noise.

"I think chaos is Frost Harbor's love language," I say,

trying for lightness. My hands brush dust from a shelf because looking at him head-on feels too much.

His laugh is small and startled. Like he didn't expect to find ease with me still existed.

He steps closer—not crowding, not intentionally, just . . . pulled. The air shifts. Warmer, tighter. My pulse jumps.

I open the bin of gumdrop shingles, lid creaking. "Inventory," I mutter.

Jake hums behind me, the sound settles along my spine. "This place hasn't changed."

"It feels like a room waiting for its next December," I say.

He moves around me thoughtfully. Like he's walking inside a memory, and each object touches something buried.

"That corner," he says, pointing behind me, "is where we stashed extra frosting. You mislabeled everything."

"I didn't mislabel," I say. "You hid them just to watch me panic."

A real laugh slips out of him. "And there—" He nods to the dented workbench. "That's where I tried to hammer gingerbread together."

"You broke three nails."

"One," he insists.

"Two and a half," I counter.

He smiles. Quiet. Wistful. The kind of smile that comes from remembering a life you thought you'd lost.

His gaze drifts upward to the highest shelf. "You climbed that every year even though you hated it."

"You always caught me."

His eyes flick to mine. They soften. Break open a little. "Of course I did."

The silence that follows isn't empty. It's close. Pressured. A held breath stretched thin.

I sift through the bin, pretending I'm counting gumdrops. Jake steps in behind me.

Close enough to feel rather than hear the breath he draws.

Close enough for the edge of his jacket to graze my back when he shifts his weight.

Close enough so the air grows heavier with every second he doesn't step away.

"Mia," he murmurs.

I turn.

His hand lifts—hesitating for a heartbeat—before brushing the side of my jaw. His thumb sweeps gently, knocking loose a dusting of powdered sugar.

It's not a casual touch. It's a memory resurfacing with skin-level clarity.

"You've got sugar here," he says softly.

My breath trembles. "You're . . . still giving directions," I whisper.

His expression cracks—quietly, like a man breaking in a way he hopes no one sees.

But I do.

His fingertips trail down to my wrist, curling lightly, carefully around it. Not gripping. Not claiming.

Just . . . holding.

As if he's asking a question without speaking:

Are we still us in here?

Is this still something?

Will you pull away?

I don't.

The air tilts. The floor shifts. Something unsustainable presses between us.

"Mia," he says again, but this time it's a confession wrapped inside my name.

I lean in without meaning to—just enough that our foreheads almost touch. His breath brushes my lips. His hand tightens a fraction around my wrist like he's afraid I'll vanish.

"If you look at me like that . . . " His voice breaks. Actually breaks. " . . . I'm going to forget I'm engaged to your sister."

The words are sharp, hot, and tangled as Ava crashes into my mind—bright coat, flawless plans, the absolute trust she has in both of us.

I pull back a sliver, enough to breathe.

Jake doesn't follow. He closes his eyes, like the pull toward me is something he has to physically fight.

The loudspeaker snaps on overhead: "TEN MINUTES REMAINING! Teams, ten minutes!"

We flinch apart.

Jake scrubs a hand down his face—hard, punishing, the way someone does when they regret showing too much.

When he drops his hand, his eyes are too wide.

That's the real crack.

The one that whispers, *Collision is coming and you both know it.*

The medal on his collar glints in the dim light—sharp, proud, earned. A marker of everything he became while I raised a small, bright, Jake-shaped version of him alone.

"Jake . . . " I whisper, reaching before sense catches up. My fingers graze the medal. Cool. Solid. Grounding.

His breath catches. He looks down at my hand like it's dangerous.

"You did it," I say quietly. "You became exactly who I always hoped you'd be."

Something raw flashes across his face—gratitude, hurt, longing, apology.

He covers my hand with his, gently, like he's afraid of shattering it.

Then he lowers our hands together.

"Better get out there before your mom declares a frosting emergency."

We step outside. The cold hits. The noise rushes in. Kids shriek, bells ring, someone yells about a collapsing candy-cane chimney.

But Ava is the first thing I see.

Laughing with Dylan. Easy. Uncomplicated.

Then she spots us.

Her smile stutters. Just a fraction. A tiny crack.

Dylan follows her line of sight. His gaze lands on Jake. On me. On the too-small space between us. His fingers tighten around his clipboard before he smooths them out.

Jake doesn't notice.

Of course he doesn't.

He's too busy pulling the door shut behind him, brushing dust from his sleeve like innocence.

But I feel the shift. The fracture.

Truth: *We didn't just almost cross a line. We dragged it somewhere none of us can unsee.*

Dare: *I pretend we can keep everyone safe.*

Confession: *The look on Ava's face—and the brief silence from Dylan—tells me otherwise.*

15

WHAT WE DON'T SAY

MIA

The market noise follows me home—laughter tugging at my coat, powdered sugar still threaded through my hair. But it's the shed that hums under everything. Luca sleeps in the backseat, lanyard crooked across his chest, content in a way I can't seem to imitate.

I tuck him into bed, peel off my frosting-stiff sweater, and find the boot still in my pocket. I sit at the edge of my bed, thumb following the split line again and again, chasing the sharp little bite it gives back.

The truth I've been holding buckles open, rising in my throat like it's desperate to breathe first.

The night I left Frost Harbor, I promised I would give my son the best life I could. That meant sacrifice. Silence. Swallowing every word I ever wanted to say to Jake.

Everyone knows Luca's father was a one-night stand, and that's not a lie. I just never said it was with my best friend.

The boy who could pull a laugh out of me so hard it left my ribs tender for hours.

The boy who knew every dream I was too scared to voice.

The boy I loved before I knew what love was.

I press the boot to my chest until the sugar smears warm against my skin.

"You did it, Jake," I whisper.

Truth: *Luca's father isn't a stranger. He's the boy I loved before I even had the language for what I was feeling.*

Dare: *I let the world believe he was a mistake instead of a miracle.*

Confession: *Even after everything, I'm still proud of Jake Carter—and part of me wishes he knew why.*

16

THE POLAROID

JARGE

December 18. Door 18.

Five days into winter drills.

Eight days until Christmas.

Three days until the engagement party I keep pretending I'm prepared for.

Snow has been falling since before sunrise—thin, relentless, indifferent to the glare of the field lights. It layers over the bleachers, the flags, the recruits' shoulders until everything feels muted.

"Reset." My voice cuts through the wind.

The line hesitates, shifts, still nowhere near the precision I need from them. They think I'm pushing discipline.

Truth is, I'm trying to find a rhythm I can trust—feet, breath, command. Something that doesn't bend when I do.

Step. Breath. Command.

Anything but Mia's laugh in Riley's bar, or the warmth of her body in that outbuilding. Anything but the kid looking at me like he's known me his whole life.

Boots grind against the frozen ground. Everyone exhales fog. Cold knives through my uniform, and at least the sting keeps the world clear.

Pain usually means focus. Focus usually means quiet. Today, the quiet slides off.

Don't think about Mia standing in the snow, staring at you like time never moved. Don't think about the way she leaned in before she realized she shouldn't. Don't think about Luca's hand in yours—small, certain, instinctive.

And don't think about the truth sitting behind that.

Because if you let that truth breathe, you'll have to admit you didn't just walk away from a girl—you walked away from a life you never believed you had a right to want.

The whistle shrieks. "Positions."

A couple of recruits flinch. I ease the edge in my tone and move through the line, adjusting shoulders, grip, stance.

Correct. Repeat. Reset.

The only things I've ever known how to do cleanly.

"Carter!" Houston's voice bounces over the wind as he steps in, adjusting a recruit's stance without asking. "Your Bravo group is drifting left. Again."

"I see it."

Houston shadows my pace—calm, infuriatingly perceptive.

"Wrist higher." He nudges a recruit's elbow up, then lowers his voice. "You good?"

"I'm fine."

Automatic. He steps right over it.

"Because you've got the eyebrows again."

I cut him a look. "What eyebrows?"

"Pre-deployment," he says. "The ones that say you're thinking too loud."

The wind steals the retort I want to make.

He smirks like he knew it, anyway.

We move down the row, adjusting form in sync the way we've been doing for years. He calls cadence; I correct the angle. He spots movement; I redirect posture. The recruits snap sharper under the dual pressure.

For the first time today, the rhythm locks into place.

"Better," Houston says. "Almost impressive."

"Don't get sentimental on me."

"Please. I save that for my neighbor."

I don't look at him, but he's waiting for me to.

There it is—*Harper*.

"She's not your neighbor," I state. "You said you were only staying in town for a month."

He lifts a shoulder, pretending not to care. I know the truth—he's settling in, lying about it, and Harper's the reason.

"Yeah, well. Plans change."

"Because of your neighbor."

"She's loud. Hard to ignore."

"Sure," I answer, watching him correct another recruit. "*Just* a neighbor."

He doesn't rise to the bait, which is how I know I'm right.

I don't press. He'll get his own December reckoning soon enough.

He hands me his coffee like a peace offering. I take a sip because he'll hound me if I don't.

"You've been quieter," he says. "Which is concerning."

"Training cycle."

"You're a shit liar."

Before I can answer, another whistle sounds from the far end of the field.

"Carter!" Harlan calls. "Office."

Houston winces. "Oof. Dad voice."

I pass him back the coffee. "You've got the line."

He gives me a lazy salute. "Roger that, Sergeant Running-From-Things."

"Not running."

"That's the other eyebrow look."

I leave him with the recruits because, irritating as he is, he keeps them sharp. And he keeps me from spinning too far into my head. Houston's the only person who can ground me without trying.

The admin office hits too warm—radiator rattling, heat billowing up from the floorboards. Harlan stands behind his desk, arms crossed, watching me; measuring something.

"You've been steady this cycle." He doesn't layer it with praise—just observes. "Focused. The recruits respond. You're good with them."

"Thank you."

"But," he adds, leaning a hip against the desk, "I'm not asking about the drills. I'm asking about *you*."

My shoulders tighten like a reflex I can't shake. "I'm fine."

"You're not. You're here, but not *all* the way. Most people would miss it. I don't."

I look past him, at the peeling paint on the window frame.

He softens. "Son, there's a difference between functioning and standing on solid ground. I've known you long enough to see which one you're doing."

I don't move.

"You carrying something?" he asks. "Something family-related?"

He doesn't press harder, just leaves the space open.

I stay silent.

"Jake . . . you don't have to tell me what's going on. But you need to figure out what you want before it's chosen for you."

His words sink in, prying loose something I've been holding shut for years.

"I'm offering you something stable," he continues. "Civilian contract. Logistics lead. Housing. Benefits. Room to build a life with structure. You'd be damn good at it. And you deserve a life that doesn't require constant armor."

There it is—the safe path. The good-man-settles-down path. The stop-running path.

On paper, I *should* want this.

Ava deserves a man who wakes up rooted in his life.

A man whose heart isn't stuck in two timelines.

Someone *not* me.

While he sketches out the life I'm supposed to want, my head wanders somewhere else.

A square full of gingerbread and lights.

Luca laughing at a snowman that barely stands.

Mia's hands trembling while I tied an apron around her.

Her voice when she whispered, *You did it.*

Her pride. Her fear.

Mine.

"You've spent years setting yourself on fire for everyone else."

I shift at his voice bringing me back, but he keeps going.

"The question is whether that's still who you are." His voice settles into something quieter. "Or whether you've outgrown running."

He's too close to the truth.

"Think about it," he says. "Not the version of your life that sounds good on paper. The one that lets you breathe."

I swallow. "Copy."

He watches me closely, as if deciding whether he should push again, then gives a slow nod. "You're a good man,

Carter," he says. "But even good men get to choose their lives."

Good men choose; cowards drift. And I've been drifting so long I almost convinced myself it was movement.

I step into the cold like breaking the surface after too long underwater. I climb into the truck. Shut the door.

Something awaits on the passenger seat.

A Polaroid.

Mom's handwriting curls on the back: Snowden–Carter, 12/21.

My stomach free-falls as I lift it from the seat.

It's me and Mia at the gingerbread table—her body angled toward mine, mine toward hers, gravity slipping back into a language we pretended we forgot. She's flushed from the heat; I'm smiling in a way I only ever did with her.

The photo blindsides me with a truth I've been outrunning since twenty-one.

Something slips from the visor and lands in my lap.

Another Polaroid. Older. Warped, edges bleached.

Sixteen. Tree farm behind us, half-decorated. Her curls were full of snow. My arm hooked around her waist like it belonged there. Her smile was small, private—only for me.

I hold the two photos together.

Different years. Different versions of us.

Same stance.

The same quiet gravity pulling us back into orbit.

All the distance—tours, silence, years with Ava, Luca—suddenly looks less like moving on and more like a cover story. One I told myself so I wouldn't have to admit I never stopped wanting the same girl.

Air punches out of my lungs in a single, uneven breath. The Polaroids bite through my jacket when I press them to my chest. I should be thinking about Harlan's offer. About the life Ava thinks we're building. About the woman who has no idea half my heart is still stuck beside a gingerbread table with her sister.

About the man *I* promised I'd be.

All I see is Mia in both pictures, and the empty space where a little boy with her eyes and my nose might fit.

Then the memory slams in. *The Advent calendar. Door 24. The letters.*

Three years of them—written under barracks lights-out, folded small enough to hide behind one felt square.

Every December 24th, I pictured her opening that door, finding them.

She never said a word.

Never wrote back.

I took her silence, stamped it as rejection, and marched straight into deployments. Straight into Ava. Straight into a life that looked stable but never fit.

But she kept the calendar. Kept the stupid Orion-dog drawing like it meant something, and I'm the idiot who turned my own heart into a scavenger hunt and then punished her for not following clues I never gave her.

Mouse, I should've kissed you that night. Dare me to believe you still think of me. You're my home. Always have been.

Pressure stings behind my eyes.

If I'm wrong, chasing this could blow up more than one life. If I'm right . . . we've been walking around the blast radius for years, pretending it's just weather.

My hand finds the keys before my conscience can talk me down. The engine growls to life, heat sputtering through the vents.

I'm not starting the truck to think.

I'm starting to think that whatever I do next, someone is

going to get hurt. The question is whether I keep hurting the one person who never deserved it.

Truth: *I never stopped wanting her, no matter how many lives I tried on.*

Dare: *I'm about to chase answers that could blow my life wide open.*

Confession: *For the first time, the thought of wreckage feels less scary than staying in this lie.*

17

THE ICEBOUND TERRACE

MIA

Snow streaks sideways across the roof of The Icebound Terrace, piling along the beams until they glow like frost-lit iron. Inside, Ava has orchestrated perfection—gold-rimmed glassware, precise garlands, a tree polished for magazine covers. Everything gleams.

But nothing compares to the floor.

Panels of glass stretch beneath us, revealing the rink below. Skaters carve clean lines into fresh ice, their movement sending pale ripples upward—brushing my shoes, my legs, my ribs.

It feels as if I'm standing over a heart still beating under glass. One that used to sync with mine.

Luca kneels beside me, palms pressed flat to the glass. "Mama! Look! They're right under me!"

His voice is pure awe. I kneel too—mostly so he won't see how tight my chest feels.

"I see," I whisper.

But my eyes drift to the rink. To that corner.

The one where Jake held my hands while I clung to him like the world might open under my feet.

"Relax your ankles, Mouse."

"They are relaxed."

"They're stiff enough to break concrete."

"Then catch me."

" . . . I always do."

I remember the scrape of our blades, the sting of cold on my cheeks, the way the stars blinked awake as the town lights dimmed. How Jake had looked at me, like winter carved out a moment meant only for us.

I can still feel it.

I hate that I can still feel it.

"Mama?" Luca asks gently. "Did you get 'gaged here?"

"No, baby."

"Will you someday?"

"Maybe." The word scrapes by.

He takes that as fact and sprints toward the dessert table.

Mom appears beside me, holding two cups of cider. Her eyes do that gentle sweep she's done our whole lives—scanning for cracks we pretend aren't there.

"You okay?" she asks.

"I'm fine." My voice betrays me.

She passes me a cup of cider. "Mm. You've always gone hush when something hurts."

"I'm not hurting."

She studies me—not prying, just present. "Honey . . . growing up next to someone your whole life doesn't mean you never lose pieces of yourself along the way."

My throat knots. "This isn't about Ava."

"I didn't say it was." She touches my arm. "I said you're hurting."

I stare down at the rink. I've spent years trying not to remember this place.

"Sometimes," she says, softer now, "we tuck old pain into corners because we think we shouldn't feel it anymore." Her hand glides over my shoulder. "That doesn't make it disappear."

The cider thaws my fingers; my chest stays frozen.

"Mom . . . what if I don't want old pain? Or old anything?"

Her smile deepens, all-knowing warmth. "Mia, healing isn't betrayal."

I blink. "What?"

She shrugs casually, as if she didn't just split something open. "Life nudges us to look at what we're carrying. Sometimes we need help seeing it."

I frown. "Why do I feel like you know something I don't?"

"Because mothers pay attention. Even when their daughters don't."

"Mom."

She leans in, thumb brushing my cheek. "Just this: Don't shut a door that's still knocking."

Before I can ask more, she scurries away, leaving me rattled—holding warm cider with thought echoing in my ribs.

Healing isn't betrayal.

Betrayal isn't just cheating on a person. It's rewriting history. It's admitting the story everyone believes about Ava and Jake was never the one I was living.

Snow whistles outside. The rink glows beneath my feet.

The far door opens.

Cold sweeps through the Terrace—and Jake steps inside. Snow dusts his hair; his shoulders fill out the coat; his breath curls in soft white ghosts. His gaze lands first on the glass floor, then the rink. Something in his posture loosens—just a fraction.

He comes straight toward me.

"Mia." Soft. Low. Careful.

My name catches low under my ribs.

"You made it," I manage, aiming for steady.

"Wouldn't miss it." His gaze drops to the glass again. "Didn't expect this."

"You did," slips out before I can stop it. "You always talked about the rink."

His mouth curves. "Yeah. I guess I did."

He steps beside me, close enough that his coat brushes my sleeve. His scent—cedar, winter air, a hint of soap—pulls at something unguarded inside me.

"Look," he says, pointing down. "Right there—that's where you fell and wiped me out with you."

I laugh. It feels like breathing after being underwater too long. "You tripped over nothing."

"False. You dragged me."

His smile lingers—real, unguarded, and unbearably familiar.

"And that corner?" he continues, pointing again, "that's where you finally let go of my hand. You were shaking."

"You pretended not to notice."

"I noticed everything," he says softly.

My breath stutters.

Then he leans in, his shoulder brushing mine. His fingers graze the railing near my hand—gentle and deliberate. Heat curls straight through me.

"I used to lie on that ice with you." His voice sinks lower. "Watch the stars come out. You said winter made everything feel truer."

"Jake . . . "

He inches closer—barely, but enough. His breath warms the shell of my ear. "I always thought . . . if I ever got married, it would be here," he murmurs. "Above the rink. Stars overhead. The world quiet. Just . . . "

He hesitates. His eyes find mine, raw and open.

" . . . us."

My heart lurches.

If I let myself want that, is it healing like Mom said . . . or betrayal in a prettier dress?

"I know. I was there the first night you said it. I just never thought you'd hand that dream to someone else and call it new."

His jaw clenches, but he doesn't step back.

He steps closer.

"Mia," he breathes, "I need to tell you something."

His hand grazes mine, the brush sending a shock straight up my spine.

He leans in; his breath skims my cheek. I can feel his heartbeat in the inches between us.

"Mia," my name again, his voice rough, "I—"

"There you two are!"

Ava's voice fractures the moment.

Jake jerks back, but not all the way—not fast enough. His hand hovers near mine, like his body hasn't gotten the memo yet.

Ava hooks her arms through his effortlessly. "Babe! You vanished."

Jake straightens, expression slammed shut. "I was —just—"

"Isn't this place stunning?" She beams. "Jake's the one who found it! I didn't even know he skated until he told me he used to come here all the time."

She nudges him. "He said it always felt romantic. That he could picture a wedding here."

My pulse drops straight through the floor.

Jake's eyes flash to me—panicked, aching.

"And look what he got me," Ava chirps, rummaging in her clutch.

She pops open the box.

A flash of silver. A star catching the light in that impossible way.

A fissure of ice runs through me.

I know this necklace.

I know exactly what it carries with it.

Jake once held that same star up to a black Frost Harbor sky and told me I was his north point—what he'd look for when everything else went dark.

It's not just that he reused a memory. It's that he handed my sister *the* future I used to picture for us and called it theirs.

Ava lifts it by the chain. "He said it reminded him of the first night we watched stars together. Isn't that so sweet?"

Jake's eyes slam shut for half a second—just long enough to give him away: He knows. He remembers. He regrets it.

I force the words out. "It's beautiful."

Ava smiles brightly. "Okay—mini meltdown time! Champagne glasses didn't arrive, and the favors are still at Whim & Whistle. I'm drowning."

"I'll go," I offer instantly.

Ava beams. "You're a lifesaver."

Jake steps forward. "I'm going with her."

I shake my head. "Jake, you don't have—"

"You're not going alone," he says, firm.

Ava waves a hand. "Perfect! Mia, favors. Jake, glasses.

Divide and conquer. Love you!" She kisses him—quick and clearly unbothered.

He doesn't kiss back.

Not really.

Minutes later, the cold outside hits like truth.

We stop beside his truck. Snow swirls between us, a moving wall we can't cross and can't step away from.

"Mia," he hesitates, "what happened in there—"

"Don't." It scrapes out of me.

His breath fogs in a harsh exhale. "I can't lie about what I feel."

"Jake—"

He steps closer.

Too close; his voice brushes my skin when he speaks. "I can't keep pretending we're nothing."

Pretending we're nothing used to feel like safety. Now it feels like suffocating.

Truth: *I don't want to be the woman who pretends her heart never picked him.*

Dare: *I keep agreeing to be alone with the man I'm supposed to have moved on from.*

Confession: *Every time he looks at me like that, it feels less like betrayal and more like coming up for air.*

18

WHITEOUT

MIA

The storm eats the world one mile at a time.

Snow sweeps sideways across the windshield, turning the road into a tunnel of white. The cab is overheated, and every breath I take steams against something fragile strung between us.

Jake hasn't spoken in seven minutes.

That's how I know he's thinking too loudly.

Finally, he shifts his grip on the wheel, knuckles ghost-pale.

"Alright," his voice low, "is this gonna be a silent drive? Because if so . . . that might actually kill me."

I keep my gaze on the swirling storm. "I'm thinking."

"About what?"

I lie instantly. "Nothing."

He snorts very, very Jake-like. "Mouse . . . you've never thought about 'nothing'. Not once in your entire life."

"Can you not—" I start.

"Call you *Mouse*?" His jaw works. He stares at the road too hard. "Yeah. I've been trying to stop."

"Trying?"

He laughs under his breath. "Failing miserably."

He exhales, fogging the glass. "Storm's picking up."

"Outside or inside?" I say before I can stop myself.

His head turns.

Slow. Startled.

A little wrecked.

"Mia . . . "

"Don't."

I grip the seatbelt. "Whatever you're about to say, *Carter,* don't."

His brows lift. A smirk tugs at his mouth, one of the dangerous ones.

"Carter?" he echoes. "You only called me that when I was in the doghouse with you."

I whip my head toward him. "You *are* in the doghouse."

"Oh?" he asks calmly. "And which particular sin got me there this time?"

I glare straight ahead, refusing to take the bait. "Pick one. Dealer's choice."

"Just one?" His smirk deepens. "We're underselling my talents."

I want to laugh.

I want to punch him.

Mostly, I want to crawl out of my own skin.

"Jake," I mutter, "don't start."

But now he's mute.

He taps his thumb once on the steering wheel—a nervous tell he probably doesn't realize he still has. The tension knots through the cab so fast it's dizzying.

"You always do that," he says quietly. "Feel something real and then slam the door on it."

I swallow hard. "Someone has to keep both of us on the road."

He huffs a humorless laugh. "And here I thought the snow was the thing that was going to kill me."

I don't answer.

The road narrows into white static. His shoulders tense as he leans forward to see through the blur. The motion sends a shiver of memory rolling through me—Jake, always leaning in. Always steadying. Always trying.

Except when he left.

He clears his throat.

"Look . . . if I'm already in the doghouse, I might as well be in the—"

He stops, searching for the word.

" . . . deep end."

A breath jerks out of me. "Jake."

He ignores the warning in my voice.

"I owe you an apology," he admits. "A *real* one. Not the bullshit, mission-ready version I've been handing out to everyone else."

My stomach flips. "Jake—"

His jaw flexes. He keeps his eyes on the road as if he needs something solid to aim at.

"I'm sorry," he continues quietly. "For a lot. For the way I left. For shutting down instead of talking to you. For making you carry the fallout for something I should've met you halfway on."

The air in the cab thins. Outside, the storm claws at the glass. Inside, it's just his voice and the one night I've tried not to relive.

"And I might as well admit the part that's been eating me alive."

"That night," he confesses, "the one before I left . . . I don't replay the bed." His fingers tighten on the wheel. "I replay *after*. When you were curled against me. When I had my hand on the back of your neck and every part of me was screaming to say something *real.*

"I should've kissed you goodbye and told you what you were to me . . . asked you for something. Anything. Instead, I shut down, walked out like a coward, and pretended it was safer for both of us if I never asked you to wait."

My chest hollows out. I stare out at the whiteout so he won't see what that does to me. *How does he not know he's offering the one thing I crave and the one thing I'm terrified of?*

"Jake," I whisper. "You didn't owe me—"

"Bullshit." He exhales a short, self-disgusted sound. "I owed you honesty. At the very least."

His mouth tightens, regret shadowing his features. "You gave me everything that night. And I handed you silence and a deployment."

For a heartbeat, the only sound is the storm and Luca's ghost-laugh at the edges of my mind—him, with Jake's nose and my eyes, waiting back in a life neither of us is brave enough to name.

"Some days," he adds, voice fraying, "I still think about what would've happened if I'd asked you to wait. If I'd been braver. If I hadn't gone looking for the *safe* version of a life with your sister instead of the true one with you."

My pulse is a trapped bird.

"Jake . . . you can't—"

"I know . . . Mia, believe me, I know."

For one terrifying moment, I think he's going to pull the truck over.

He doesn't.

He forces himself to keep driving—like that's the only thing keeping him from doing something irreversible.

"Mia . . . "

Tension ropes through his shoulders. "Tell me you don't feel *this*." He winces, almost as if he hates himself for asking but can't pull the words back.

This = The heat.

This = The ache.

This = The truth clawing its way out.

This = Luca's button nose, laugh, and stubborn tilt of the head.

This = Everything we almost were.

Everything we *still* could be—if I weren't terrified of him looking at Luca long enough to see himself.

I grip the seat so hard my fingers ache. "*Jake* . . . "

I shake my head. "We can't. God, we can't talk about this."

The storm howls around us, a living thing slamming against the truck.

He whispers, barely audible: "Then why does it feel like we're about to crash into something we should've hit years ago?"

I can't breathe.

"Just drive, Jake."

And we do.

Truth: *We're not just driving through a blizzard; we're*

steering straight at everything we've been dodging for six years.

Dare: *I stay in this truck with him anyway, knowing exactly what's spiraling between us.*

Confession: *I don't know if I'm more afraid of us crashing . . . or of us finally landing where we were always meant to be.*

19

WHIM & WHISTLE

MIA

The storm pelts our backs as we cross the sidewalk, snow needling my cheeks, wind clawing at my scarf. Jake gets the door open with his shoulder, a gust of icy air following us in like it's offended we escaped.

The bell chimes overhead—its decibel stitched into every December of my childhood.

Whim & Whistle smells exactly the same.

Vanilla. Cedar. Old wood polish.

As if the universe bottled Christmas and never updated the recipe.

It's dangerous. Because Jake Carter standing in this lighting looks exactly like the boy I once quietly detonated my heart over.

He braces the door with his boot and glances up through the windows. "Ten bucks says we're not making it back before dark."

"You still drive like an eighty-year-old librarian." I stomp snow off my boots. "We were never making it back before dark."

He huffs a laugh, shaking snow from his hair. "Bold from the girl who refused to go over thirty on the back roads."

"Those roads iced."

His mouth cants. "Pretty sure everything about us iced."

The comment slices clean, catching right on an old heartbreak. He looks away too quickly, pretending to study ornaments while I pretend I didn't feel the crack reopen.

The shop is a narrow maze of shelves and twinkling lights, glass baubles reflecting us back in warped little duplicates. Jake's reflection shifts between them—broader than the boy I knew, posture strung tight.

Marcy pops up from behind the counter, hair in a messy bun, a spool of ribbon looped around her wrist. "Snowdens! I was wondering when the party elves would show. Favors are in the back, if they haven't been buried alive."

"I'll grab them," I say.

Jake moves with me automatically—step-for-step, shadow-close.

I shoot him a look. "Divide and conquer, remember? I've got favors. You were assigned to the champagne crisis."

He shakes his head, voice dropping. "Storm's shifting. Glasses place is farther out." His gaze tracks the windows, the gray, the sideways snow. "We'll hit that after. No point in making two runs."

"Jake, Ava wanted—"

"Ava wanted things done." His jaw works. "I'm still doing them. I'm just not sending you back out alone with the sky looking like that."

Something small and traitorous in my chest leans toward him.

He probably doesn't even realize he's doing it, but he's already scanning the space: door, windows, aisles, back hall. On the surface, it's casual. Underneath, it's not casual at all.

"Still on patrol?" I murmur.

He blinks. "What?"

"You're sweeping exits. Counting heads. Clocking sight-lines." I tilt my head. "I recognize a recon pass when I see one."

A wry smile tugs at his mouth, reluctant but real. "Maybe I just like to know where the candy samples are."

"Uh-huh. They teach you tactical deflection in basic? Or is that an advanced seminar?"

"Field-tested," he says lightly. "Repeatedly."

He moves differently now. Back straight. Weight centered. Shoulders coiled like he's listening for a sound no one else hears.

The softness I knew is still there—tempered steel now, not erased.

We drift past a display of glass ornaments. Tiny worlds curve around us, our silhouettes leaning close in their reflections. For a moment, it looks like we're almost touching.

He catches the image too.

"Still look good in Christmas lighting," he says, voice low enough it barely qualifies as teasing.

"Speak for yourself." My answer comes out a little too fast. "You're the one with snow in your hair."

"Adds to the effect." His smile edges toward real. "Chicks dig frostbite."

"Wow. Someone's been out of the game a long time."

He goes quiet for a beat, the joke hanging heavier than it should.

"Yeah," he says finally. "You could say that."

Before I can untangle that, Marcy calls, "Gingerbread Caramel?" and rattles a glass jar near the register. "First one's free, second is emotional support."

Jake's shoulders ease a fraction. "See? This is why I came home." He plucks two candies from the jar and holds one out to me. "Come on, Mouse. For morale."

"You realize you just fed me candy like I'm five," I say, unwrapping it anyway.

He watches my fingers a fraction too closely. "Old habits."

The ginger-spice blooms first—warm and honeyed—then the caramel crunch follows, loud in the intimate hush. Jake bites into his, and the crack echoes through the quiet.

The overhead lights flicker once.

Twice.

The atmosphere shifts, and suddenly I'm hyperaware of exactly where Jake is. How close. How keyed-in.

"Tell me that's not ominous," I say, looking up at the ceiling.

He doesn't follow my gaze. He's watching the front window, where the sky has gone from gray to iron.

"The storm's moving faster than we are."

"Story of us," I mutter before I can stop myself.

His head snaps toward me.

My lungs forget their job.

The lights go out.

The shop drops into thick, instant darkness. The sudden silence is so complete I can hear the faint creak of the old building and the wind dragging its nails down the outside walls.

For one suspended heartbeat, the only sound near me is Jake's low, calm, "Well. That's festive."

My phone is already in my hand, thumb finding the flashlight by muscle memory. A pale cone slices through the dark and lands on him.

It hits his face in stark angles—jaw tight, eyes alert, shoulders braced. He clocked the outage before my thumb even moved.

He looks at me first.

Not the door.

Not the window.

Me.

"Okay?" he asks, voice steady but pared down.

"I'm fine." Too thin. We both hear it.

His gaze softens by degrees.

"Breaker's in the back," Marcy groans somewhere near the counter. "Left of the stockroom, behind the wrapping paper. I was gonna get my dad to—"

"Got it," Jake calls. Effortless authority. "Stay put. We'll flip it."

We.

"Jake, you don't have to—"

"Mia." He's already moving toward the back hall. He jerks his chin for me to follow. "I remember what happens when you're unsupervised around electricity."

Heat prickles up my neck. "That toaster was faulty."

He huffs something almost-laugh-like.

The hallway to the stockroom is even narrower than I remember, lined with overstuffed shelves and leaning towers of cardboard boxes. It smells like cedar, dust, and ribbon glue —the behind-the-scenes version of Christmas.

My phone's beam bounces off tinsel and bubble wrap. Jake walks just ahead of me, one hand slightly back as if ready to catch me if I trip. His shoulder grazes mine every few steps, steady as a metronome.

Unintentional, my ass.

"You okay?" I ask quietly, because the darkness squeezes words down to their barest form. "You tensed when the lights went out."

"Training," he shrugs. "Generator failures. Power cuts. You learn to move before you think."

"You always moved before you thought," I say. "That's not new."

He glances over his shoulder. The light catches his eyes, turning them molten.

"That how you remember it?"

"How else am I supposed to remember the boy who dove into a frozen creek to get my boot back?"

"That boot was your personality," he deadpans. "Couldn't lose it."

My laugh cracks. "You used to say it made me look like an off-duty elf."

"It did." His mouth curves. "In a good way."

He slows as we reach the end of the hall, letting me catch up. For a second, we're close enough for our breaths to mix in the cold-stale air.

"Still doing it," I murmur.

"Doing what?"

"Deflecting with jokes anytime things get close to real."

He leans in a fraction, enough that I see the notch in his lower lip, the faint scar along his jaw I don't remember. "Mouse, if I stopped deflecting in the dark with you this close, we'd both be in trouble."

My pulse ricochets off bone.

The breaker box is a gray metal panel tucked behind a tangle of extension cords and wrapping paper tubes. Jake shoulders the boxes aside as if they weigh nothing, exposing the panel.

"Hold the light?" he asks.

I lift my phone, aiming the beam where he needs it. He steps in, close enough I can feel the warmth of him through his coat. One arm braces on the wall near my head as he flips the cover open. The other works the switches with efficient, practiced motions.

He's caging me in without touching me. And touching me *everywhere.*

"Still smells like someone bottled Christmas back here," he mutters, brow furrowing as he scans the breakers.

"Probably expired by now."

"Not everything does." Quiet. Almost to himself.

His fingers move along the switches, sure and steady. There's a soft click, then another.

The lights surge back with a hum and a buzz, harsh fluorescent flooding the hallway.

Jake doesn't move.

The sudden brightness makes everything too sharp—his hand beside my head, the flex in his neck, the rise and fall of his chest inches from mine.

Slowly, he looks down at me.

"See? Still good under pressure."

"I wasn't the one doing anything."

His gaze drops to my mouth, then up again. Something unguarded cuts through his control.

"You're standing in the dark with me," he says, voice low, edges frayed. "Not running. That counts."

"I'm not running," I whisper. "There's nowhere to go."

"Mouse." His voice catches on the nickname. "You've been running since the day I—"

He stops; the words hit something live.

I stay still. If I move, I might break whatever this is.

His hand lifts from the wall. For a second, I think he's going to reset the space between us, turn it into a joke.

Instead, his knuckles graze my cheekbone, brushing away a streak of dust or glitter or nothing at all. His touch is absurdly gentle, like he's afraid I'll flinch.

"I'm sorry," he whispers.

The words land like a weight on my sternum.

"For what?" My voice barely forms.

His throat works. "We don't have time for that list."

I swallow around the knot. "Start small."

He exhales something that isn't quite a laugh. His thumb drags once, barely there, along the side of my face, leaving heat in its wake.

"I'm sorry I keep putting you in the dark," he says. "Then acting surprised when you trip."

Air rushes out of me in one startled breath.

He drops his hand like he's just realized what he's doing and steps back, giving us both a sliver of air. The hallway widens. Cools.

Outside, the wind howls against the building, rattling something loose on the roof.

"Storm's getting worse," he says, voice back to clipped safety. "We should grab the favors and head out."

"Right." I clear my throat, remembering how to move. "Right. Favors. Champagne. Wedding prep. Totally normal errands."

He watches me a moment longer, like there's something he wants to say and is stopping himself.

"Hey, Mia?" he says finally.

"Yeah?"

"In case the roads go sideways . . . " His jaw tightens. "I don't want the last thing you heard from me to be a joke."

"Then don't make one," I say, heartbeat in my mouth.

He opens his mouth. Closes it. Something like surrender flickers through his expression.

"I meant it," he says. "Back there. At the Terrace."

"Jake—"

"I know," he cuts in softly. "I know we can't . . . not right now. I get it." He scrubs a hand over his jaw. "Just . . . know I didn't say any of it to mess with you. Or make this harder. It just . . . wouldn't stay in anymore."

The honesty scrapes raw against old hurt.

"I know . . . "

His shoulders ease, like that was the thing he'd braced for —a rejection, not understanding.

"Okay," he murmurs. "Come on, before Marcy sends a search party."

We retrace our path down the hall. My phone light is off; we don't need it anymore, but the memory of holding it lingers like phantom weight.

Marcy is half-swallowed by a stack of cardboard when we emerge.

"Success?" she calls.

Jake lifts a hand. "You're not cursed. Just overloaded a circuit."

"Says you," she mutters, shoving a box onto the counter and digging through it. "Here we go. Thirty of the little bags with the monogrammed tags. And—oh!" She grabs another smaller box, grinning. "Ava bribed me to hide the extra favors up here so no one steals them early."

She lifts the lid.

Miniature snow-globes wink up at us. Inside each is a tiny rink with two figures—one in a dress, one in a suit, hands almost touching, heads tilted together.

I suck in a breath.

Jake stills beside me.

Marcy beams, oblivious. "'A Winter to Remember.' That's the phrase she picked."

Jake's fingers curl around the box edge, knuckles whitening. "Yeah," he says, voice thin. "Unforgettable."

I force a smile. "They're beautiful, Marcy. She's going to be thrilled."

And she should be. She's building a wedding on a story she thinks is hers, and I'm the coward letting her.

Marcy wrangles the boxes into two piles. "Alright. Favors in this one. Extras and tags in this one. You kids need help carrying them out?"

"We've got it," Jake says quickly. He scoops up both stacks like they weigh nothing, muscles flexing under his coat.

"You sure?" I ask. "I can carry something. I contain multitudes. And biceps."

His mouth twitches. "I'm aware. Grab the door for me, show-off."

I roll my eyes, but warmth flickers through my chest as I move ahead of him.

The moment I push the door open, the storm smacks me in the face, wind tearing at my hair, snow gusting in wild, sideways sheets.

I brace against it. The boxes shift behind me.

Jake's voice comes low beside my ear. "Careful."

His palm grazes the center of my back—steadying. Not a shove. Not quite a guide. Just . . . there.

My body remembers that touch like a prayer.

We step out into the white blur together.

For a heartbeat, it feels like the world is nothing but wind and cold and the heat of his hand through my coat.

He drops it as we reach the truck, the absence so sudden it feels like a misstep.

"I'll load. You get in, warm up."

I haul the door open with stiff fingers. He catches the boxes I pass over, then leans in to open the passenger door for me.

"This isn't a date," I blurt, because my brain short-circuits when he does *old-Jake* things.

Something like a smile ghosts across his mouth. "I'm carrying presents into a blizzard and opening your door," he says. "Pretty sure high-school us would call that a date."

He shuts the door and disappears into the storm to stow the boxes.

I sit there, breathing in the faint mix of him and cold air, listening to the wind batter the truck and the blood rush in my ears.

We're about to be sealed in together again.

Cab. Storm. Nowhere to go.

Lightning struck us in the dark hallway, and we walked away.

I don't know whether we'll walk away again.

Jake climbs in, snow dusting his hair, cheeks flushed, eyes bright with challenge and something heavier.

He turns the key, and the engine growls to life. Warm air sputters from the vents.

He looks over once, searching my face for cracks. "Ready?" he asks.

No.

"Yes," I manage.

Truth: *This isn't an errand run anymore; it's two people*

standing on the edge of a life neither of us is allowed to admit we want.

Dare: *I get back in that truck knowing exactly what almost surfaced in the dark.*

Confession: *If something breaks tonight, I won't be able to pretend it was just the storm's fault.*

20

THE TIPSY REINDEER

MIA

Snow doesn't fall—it charges. It comes at us sideways, teeth bared, scraping at every bit of exposed skin. The streetlamps blur into smeared halos, pale circles swallowed by white.

We tried the truck. The bridge vanished into a sheet of ice and static—tires yawing; the world slipping a few inches out from under us. Jake didn't curse. Didn't panic. Just eased off the gas and pulled over with the same terrible calm he's always had when things go wrong.

"We walk," he said. Two syllables, no argument, like the storm and I were both his responsibility.

Now the wind tries to shove us back to town. Back to safety. Back to everything we're pretending isn't happening.

I almost say, *Let's call Ava. Let's be smart. Let's be good.*

But the words wither on my tongue.

Jake is already scanning the whiteout like it's a briefing map. "The Tipsy Reindeer's two blocks," he adds. "Give or take whatever fresh hell this is."

"The place with the deranged reindeer on the roof?" I hunch against the wind, scarf whipping my cheek.

His mouth twitches. "Those things survived five blizzards and one direct lightning hit."

My laugh rips out of me, high and startled and way too honest. His eyes cut toward me—sharp, then soft, like he's memorizing the sound.

The gust that follows feels personal. Snow stings my face, needles my lashes. Jake steps closer without even seeming to think about it, his shoulder taking the brunt of the wind, broad and solid in my periphery.

"Stay close," he murmurs.

I skid on a slick spot—ice hiding under a layer of powder. My feet shoot sideways.

His hand finds mine before gravity can finish the job.

Not a brush. Not a question.

A full, sure grip that jerks me back onto myself.

We don't let go.

His glove is rough wool against my palm. I can feel the shape of his fingers through the layers anyway, like muscle memory woke up and went, *Oh. This again.*

"You okay?" he asks, gaze tracking the road, not me.

"Just windy," I manage.

"One word for it."

Snow gathers on his lashes, his hair, the shoulders of his coat. He looks like the storm tried to carve him out of itself and then gave up, leaving him half-man, half-winter.

The motel sign finally swims out of the white:

THE TIPSY REINDEER — VACANCY

Half the bulbs are dead; the rest flicker in nervous protest. Jake exhales, a short sound. "Still upright. Still here."

"You've stayed here before?" I yell over the wind, forcing my fingers not to tighten around his.

"Once. High school. Pipe burst at home. Dad blamed my science project."

"Unfair slander."

He huffs out a laugh. Another gust slams into us. I stumble straight into him this time, no pretense of balance. His hand lands at my waist, anchoring me long enough that my heart does something reckless and traitorous.

"Easy," he says near my ear, low enough the storm can't steal it. "I've got you."

For one suspended second, we don't move.

Then the wind shoves again, and he drops his hand like he remembered who he's supposed to belong to.

He reaches the door first, bracing his shoulder against it. Of course he does—soldier first, human second. He steps in ahead of me, scanning the lobby in a quick, efficient sweep: exits, windows, occupancy, threat. Only when his posture eases by a millimeter does he hold the door wide.

"Come on, Mouse."

The nickname hits harder than the wind. Not teasing. Not casual. Just . . . true. A straight line back through years and snow and the girl who used to think December started and ended with the boy next door.

I step inside. The lobby smells like pine cleaner and something attempting to be cocoa. My whole body is shaking.

"It's cold," I lie, shrugging his name off my shoulders.

"You're shaking," he says quietly.

"I said it's cold."

He doesn't call me on it. He just shrugs out of his jacket and loops it around me, the inside lined with his heat. "Here. Before you start pretending frostbite is a personality trait."

The weight of him settles over my shoulders. The collar brushes my jaw. It smells like outside air and his soap and some clean, stubborn thing that has survived every deployment.

"Jake—"

"Storm's not letting up." He checks the front window; the glass rattles like it's rethinking its life choices. "We're stuck here."

"Ava's going to worry," I say, because worrying about my sister is so much easier than admitting what's rattling in my chest.

"I'll call her." No hesitation. "I'll take the hit."

"But she'll think—"

"She'll think the roads are a nightmare in a blizzard," he says gently, "because they are. That's the whole story."

No, it isn't. His eyes say the rest—the part where he's in a motel with the wrong sister and a history that won't stay buried.

The manager appears from behind the desk, hair sticking up in static-y tufts. "Rough out there, huh? Power's spotty, but we've got a few rooms left. Twins or queen?"

"Queen," Jake says.

The word lands like a dropped plate.

My lungs forget how to function. The manager nods, already reaching for a key.

Jake goes rigid. "Wait. I mean—two, if you have—"

The manager winces. "Storm's knocked most of the place offline. Only have one left that's got reliable heat. Everything else is iffy."

Silence spills out, thick and immediate.

One choice. One bed. One storm that does not care about our moral high ground.

Jake swallows. I watch his throat work. "We'll . . . take it."

I don't say a word.

Not from fear.

Because there's a traitorous, buried part of me that has been bracing for this exact moment since the snow started. The part that thought, *Of course. Of course everything would funnel down to one door and no exits.*

He takes the key, fingers brushing mine in the handoff.

Small contact. Big aftershock.

The manager disappears into a back room. Muted TV laughter leaks through the wall, wildly inappropriate.

Jake stares at the key like it's a live grenade. "Mia," he says, voice rough, "I don't want you thinking this means something it shouldn't."

The thing is, he's right.

It already means something it shouldn't.

His eyes shut—brief, like a flinch. When they open again, they're unshielded for the first time all night. Every emotion he's been white-knuckling is right there: want and fear and some deep, grinding regret.

"Let's go," he says. "Before the power decides to quit altogether."

We climb the stairs without touching. Our hands don't brush. Our shoulders don't bump.

But every step feels like a thread snapping.

Not touching, but unraveling.

The room is . . . a lot.

Reindeer. Everywhere. On the curtains. On the lamp. On the pillows. On the ugly duvet, prancing across a field of snow like they're trying to stage a coup.

I stop three steps in. "Oh my God."

Jake's gaze does another quick sweep—corners,

windows, fire map, heater. Only then does he really see the décor.

"I don't remember it being this . . . committed," he says.

"Committed? Jake, the carpet has hooves."

He actually chokes on a laugh. It hits my ribs in a weird, painful place, because this is exactly how it used to be—me mocking bad decor, him trying not to laugh too loud.

There's one queen bed. Center of the room. Holiday-embroidered within an inch of its life.

Ridiculous. Dangerous.

He clears his throat. "We can . . . make it work. I'll grab extra pillows. Line of demarcation. Or I can take the floor."

"With the reindeer carpet?" I point at the faded herd stamped into the rug. One of them has an eye that looks like it's following me. "I'm not having your military record end with 'killed by festive upholstery'."

His mouth tilts. "Right. Wouldn't look great on the report."

The heater in the corner rattles like it swallowed a bolt and is considering choking. Jake moves closer, testing the grate with the back of his hand, then glancing at the thermo-stat, the window seal, the gap under the door.

He never stops. Even here. Even now.

The part of him that's always on the perimeter doesn't know how to stand down.

I tug off my gloves, fingers throbbing as feeling returns in sharp little jabs. "At least it's not freezing," I say, holding my hands out toward the heater.

"Give it a minute," he mutters. "That thing sounds like it's ready to unionize."

His attention shifts just as my sleeve brushes too close to the metal. Heat bites my skin.

"Shit—" I jerk back, grabbing my arm on instinct.

Jake crosses the distance between us in one stride. The air moves with him. "Let me see."

"It's nothing," I say quickly. "Just a tiny—"

"Mia." Just my name. No rank. No joke. The sound of someone who has patched up too many burns to let this slide.

Reluctantly, I lower my hand.

A red line is already blooming on the inside of my wrist. He cradles my arm, thumb skimming the edge of the burn—not pressing, just mapping the damage.

It's not clinical. It's not detached.

It's Jake.

"I'm fine," I repeat, because that's the script and I'm good at it.

"You always say that," he says quietly.

"You make it sound like a flaw."

"No." His thumb moves once more, light as a question. "I make it sound like I know you."

The words land like the burn didn't.

"Does it still hurt?" he asks.

Only where he isn't touching. "Not really."

His mouth curves—sad, knowing. "Would hate to see history repeat itself."

"Which part?" I ask. "The injury or the part where we do something stupid after?"

He lets out a broken half-laugh. "Define stupid."

"Crossing a line we shouldn't cross."

"Maybe the line was always bullshit," he says, eyes flicking to mine. "Maybe we just liked pretending it wasn't."

My heart does a slow, sick roll. "Jake—"

He drops my wrist gently and steps back a fraction, as if he heard something in my voice and knows if he stays that close we're both going to forget how to think.

"Hold on," he says abruptly.

Before I can ask, he's at the door, coat already half on.

"Jake?" My pulse kicks against the inside of my throat. "Where are you—"

"Two minutes," he says over his shoulder. "Don't touch the heater again."

The door shuts. The wind roars against it instantly, like it's furious he got away.

Thirty seconds.

Forty.

Fifty.

The storm screams. The reindeer curtain sways in the draft. The room feels too small, too loud, too full of the fact that my son is back in town, asleep—or hopefully asleep—and the only man who might ever look at his face and see himself is out in hurricane-level snow because I touched a heater like an idiot.

Luca's nose is Jake's. I can't unsee it once I start. The stubborn set to his chin. The way he tilts his head when he's concentrating. I swallow hard, the old terror lapping at the edges of all the new ache.

If Jake ever looks too long—

The door bursts open.

He comes back in on a gust of cold, dusted in fresh snow, arms full of a battered metal box. His cheeks are red from the wind; his breath fogs in the air as he kicks the door closed.

He doesn't look at the bed.

He goes straight to the little table by the window and drops the box with a heavy clank, then shrugs out of his coat and sets it beside it.

"What is that?" I ask.

He flicks the lid open.

Of course it's an emergency kit. An actual, full-on, no-joke emergency kit that looks like it has survived three wars and a parade.

Bandages. Burn gel. Gauze. Flashlight. Thermal blanket. Portable charger. Pain relievers. Energy bars. A multi-tool. Zip ties. A tiny sewing kit. A miniature bottle of whiskey that looks like it's seen some things. A folded T-shirt—his, worn soft at the collar. Two candy canes.

My throat tightens for no good reason.

Then I see it.

Tucked near the bottom, wedged between gauze and the flashlight, is a silver packet with a cartoon reindeer whose antlers are forever drawn slightly wrong.

My cocoa.

The limited-edition hot chocolate I gave him on the nineteenth. I'd grabbed three at the Whim & Whistle counter, then shoved one in his hand and said, *Door 19 is a good omen. You're not allowed to waste good cocoa.* He'd laughed and pretended not to look weirdly moved.

I figured he drank it on base or tossed it or forgot.

"Mia—" he starts.

I already have it in my hand. My fingers shake around the foil. "You kept this?"

His eyes close for a beat, like he knew this moment was coming and still wasn't ready. His hand scrubs the back of his neck.

"Yeah," he says slowly. "Door 19."

My heart trips. "Today."

"Today," he echoes.

The storm claws at the window. The heater clicks, then hums. Somewhere down the hall, a TV muffles laughter that doesn't belong to this room.

"Don't judge me," he adds, gaze dropping, shoulders doing a small, useless shrug.

I couldn't if I tried.

Because this—this stupid, expired packet—is proof of something I've spent six years trying to convince myself I made up. The Jake who jumped into a frozen creek after my boot. Who labeled a whole compartment in his truck "Mia's Disaster Supplies." Who said December felt less sharp when I was in it.

He reaches for the burn cream with a gentleness that makes my chest hurt.

"Come here," he says.

The words aren't a command. They're a habit. A place we always used to end up.

I go. I don't pretend otherwise.

He squeezes a ribbon of ointment onto his fingers and rubs his hands together to warm it, like he's done this a hundred times in a dozen tents and trucks, just never for me in a reindeer motel while I hold proof of everything we never said.

When his touch finds my skin, the sting fades under the careful glide of his thumb. He works in slow, precise strokes, eyes focused, jaw tight.

"You kept this," I whisper, staring at the packet in my free hand, crinkling the foil. "Jake . . . you kept it all these years?"

His jaw ticks. He doesn't look up. "I kept everything from that night."

The room tilts.

"Why?" The word scrapes on the way out. "It's expired. It's—nothing."

He exhales once through his nose, humorless. "It was never 'nothing'." His voice drops, rougher. "You told me you don't waste good cocoa. Your words, not mine."

"That's not—"

"I didn't keep it for the taste, Mia." His thumb smooths

the last of the ointment into my skin. "I kept it because you handed it to me on the last night I knew exactly where home was."

Heat stings behind my eyes. I look away, because if I meet his gaze, this whole stupid room is going to come apart.

"Jake . . . "

"Don't," he murmurs.

It's not a dismissal.

It's a shield. For both of us.

He wraps the gauze carefully, circling my wrist, keeping the layers neat even as his fingers shake. Every pass of the bandage feels like it's winding something tighter inside me instead of holding anything together.

When he ties it off, he lifts my arm—just a little. Instinct, probably. Old muscle memory of pressing a kiss to my skin.

He stops just short, eyes flicking to mine like he caught himself at the edge of a cliff.

The almost-kiss hovers there, bright as a cut.

He lowers my arm slowly, his palm lingering on the inside of my elbow, thumb tracing a small arc like he can't quite let go. "You'll bruise," he says quietly, "but you'll be okay."

He's wrong. About the second part, anyway.

He steps back just enough to rearrange the space between us into something that looks like distance if you don't examine it too closely.

He stares at the cocoa packet still clutched in my hand. Something shifts behind his eyes—decision, dread, both.

"Feels like you deserve the truth," he says.

The lights flicker once. Twice. The heater groans and rattles in protest. The storm leans against the walls as if it's listening.

"Jake," I whisper. "What truth?"

Truth: *We didn't just skid off a road—we slid straight into the one scenario I swore I'd never end up in with him again. Alone. Trapped. With no exits that don't cost anything.*

Dare: *I stand there with his jacket around my shoulders and his history in my hand and let him talk anyway.*

Confession: *Under every excuse, every promise to be good, I wanted something exactly like this storm to pin us long enough that the truth stopped having anywhere to hide.*

21

CINDER LINES

JAKE

There's a moment—right after a blast, right before the dust settles—where everything goes quiet.

Not peaceful. Just . . . suspended. Like the world's holding its breath to see what's still standing.

That's what it feels like now.

Mia stands in the middle in a reindeer massacre of a motel room, my jacket hanging off her shoulders, that stupid cocoa packet in her hand. The foil glints in the lamplight every time her fingers tremble.

I've carried that thing across continents. Through sandstorms and airports and bases that smelled like jet fuel and fear. I shoved it into bags and footlockers and glove compartments and told myself I'd know when it was time to throw it away.

Apparently, it's tonight.

"Feels like you deserve the truth," I hear myself say.

Her head lifts a fraction. She looks wrecked and wary and braced all at once. Like she thinks I'm about to hand her another deployment instead of the thing I should've given her years ago.

"Jake," she whispers. "What truth?"

The part of me that trained for worst-case scenarios is screaming to shut up. To keep it simple. Keep it safe. Keep it survivable.

The part of me that walked away from her once knows there's no such thing.

"Door 24," I say.

Her fingers tighten on the cocoa, crinkling the foil. Her eyes close for a second as the words hit an old bruise.

Of course she remembers.

"Every Christmas Eve," I go on, voice low. "Since we were what—twelve? You'd come over in those ridiculous elf boots, and we'd wait until your parents went to bed, and then you'd yank the Advent calendar off the wall like you were staging a heist."

Her mouth twitches, but there's no humor in it.

"We'd scribble something on scrap paper," I say. "Confession, wish, dare. Fold it up, shove it behind Door 24. Read them after midnight. Laugh. Pretend none of it mattered."

Her jaw works. "It was a long time ago."

"Not to me."

The heater clicks. The storm claws at the window. The reindeer curtains flutter like they're eavesdropping.

"The year I left for basic," I say, "you wrote, 'I'm scared everything's about to change', and pretended it was a joke."

Color drains from her face. "You remember that?"

"Yeah." My throat feels tight. "I slipped in, 'I'm scared it won't'. You never called me on it."

She looks away, as if the air between us is too sharp to breathe.

"After that," I continue, "you went to college. I shipped

out. We both acted like the tradition would just . . . retire itself." I swallow. "It didn't. Not for me."

Her stare snaps back to mine. Confusion first. Then something darker.

"Three years," I say. "Three Decembers, I made it home around Christmas. Sometimes just for a weekend. You were always . . . somewhere else. Back at school. On the road. Stuck with flights. Never home on the twenty-fourth."

She swallows. I can see the muscles in her throat jump.

"But the calendar was still there," I say. "Your mom still hung it up like it was wired into the drywall. Same spot. Same crooked nail." I huff a humorless laugh. "Same stupid, smug reindeer."

"Jake—" she starts.

"I didn't trust mailing anything that mattered," I push on. "Didn't want your parents or Ava finding it. So I did the only thing that ever worked." I nod at the cocoa in her hand. "I wrote you."

Her fingers go white around the packet.

"Barracks, trucks, corners of hangars," I say. "On breaks. In parking lots. On my phone when I could get service, on paper when I couldn't. I wrote everything I never said. And every Christmas Eve I was home, I folded those letters up and slid them behind Door 24."

The silence that follows is so complete I can hear the heater rattling and the wind whistling in the frame.

She lets out a short, disbelieving sound. "That's not funny."

"It wasn't meant to be funny."

"You're telling me you—" Her hand lifts, then drops. "You hid letters behind felt, like some kind of puzzle? And just . . . left them there?"

"Yeah," I say simply. "Because you were the one who

said the calendar made December hurt less. Because Door 24 was ours. Because I was young and gone for the first time and stupidly in love with you, and it felt like the only place I knew how to put the truth where it belonged."

Her face does something I don't have words for. Shock. Hurt. Anger. The kind of betrayal that comes with realizing there was a second story running under the one you thought you were living.

"Jake, just—stop." Her voice frays at the edges.

"Mia," I say softly, because if I'm going to blow us up, I might as well use her real name for me to do it, "did you ever open Door 24?"

She freezes.

The answer's written all over her before she says a word.

She doesn't.

"You didn't," I breathe. "You never opened it."

"You left," she blurts. "I couldn't—" She bites the rest off, shoulders curling in like she's trying to fold herself around a wound. "It doesn't matter."

"It matters to me," I say, more roughly than I mean to. "I thought you read them. I thought you saw everything and just . . . decided not to answer."

Something inside her flinches like I reached in with my bare hands.

"So I stuffed it down," I say quietly. "Signed another contract. Told myself you were better off. That I'd been an idiot for making feelings into Advent homework."

"Jake." Now her voice is small and hoarse. "Don't do this."

"What?" I step closer before I can stop myself. The carpet muffles the sound, but she feels it; her chin tips up that fraction she always does when she's bracing. "Tell the truth?"

Her eyes flash—wet, furious. "You still left."

"I had to," I say. No excuses, just the fact. "I didn't want to."

"You always have a reason." Her lip trembles; she presses her mouth flat like she hates it. "Duty. Orders. Ava. There's always something that isn't you choosing."

"Standing here right now is a choice," I say.

"Is it?" Her laugh breaks on the way out. "Or is it just another moment you'll decide was a mistake because it doesn't fit whatever plan you've got scribbled behind Door 25?"

I take the last step between us.

I'm close enough to see the tiny freckle under her right eye. The one I used to try not to count.

"My plan," I say quietly, "was to marry you."

Her breath stutters. "Don't."

"After that night at Riley's," I say anyway, because if I stop now I'll never start again, "when you fell asleep on my chest and drooled on my shirt and kicked off every blanket like a menace? I lay there thinking, *This is it. This is the person. This is home.*"

Tears gloss her eyes, rage and hurt braiding together.

"I wanted to ask you to wait," I admit. "I wanted to say, 'Mia Jane, I'm in love with you, and if you still feel anything when I get back, let's build something that's ours.'"

"Then why didn't you?" The words rip out of her, raw. "You let me walk away thinking you didn't want me."

"I never said that," I protest.

"You didn't have to," she fires back. "Your silence did it for you."

"I wasn't silent," I say, and it comes out harsher than I intend. "I was folded up behind a felt flap on your kitchen wall like an idiot."

She lets out a strangled sound—half laugh, half sob—and

swipes at her eyes, furious at the tears. "You can't fix years with some secret letter stunt. You still . . . disappeared, Jake. You still let me think—"

"That you were discardable," I finish when she can't. The word tastes wrong in my mouth. "You never were."

Her chest rises and falls too fast. There's a tiny tremor in her hands now, barely visible. She's trying so hard not to show it.

"I'm not trying to fix years," I say, softer. "I'm trying to stop lying. To you, to myself, to everyone. About what we are."

"What we *were*." The correction is automatic and brittle.

"What we *are*," I say again.

The lights cut out.

One second, reindeer everywhere. The next—nothing. The heater shudders to a stop. The storm roars louder in the sudden silence, fingers scraping at the walls.

"Mia?" I reach for her before my eyes even adjust.

"I'm here." Her voice is closer than I thought. Too close to be safe. Too close to step around.

Her hand brushes my chest and freezes. Mine closes gently around her wrist.

"You okay?" I murmur.

"Define okay."

My grip tightens, just enough to steady. Her pulse is a frantic thrum under my fingertips. It's dark enough that I could pretend I'm imagining it.

I'm not.

"You always hated the dark," I say, thumb skimming along the inside of her wrist. "You used to climb through my window when the power went out and swear my closet was haunted."

"It made noises," she mutters.

"It had a vent."

"You told me that later."

"I tell you everything later," I say. "That's half the problem."

Lightning flashes outside, a white-hot flare that slices through the curtains. For a heartbeat, the room is a photograph: her face tilted up, eyes huge, lips parted, my jacket drowning her frame, that cocoa packet still clutched in her other hand.

When the dark closes in again, it feels thicker. Closer. Like it's pressing us together on purpose.

"I'm not leaving you in it this time," I say quietly.

"Jake . . . " Her voice has a crack in it I've never heard before. "We can't—this . . . we can't do this."

My thumb moves over her pulse again, slowly. "Tell me you don't feel it," I say. "Tell me I'm wrong, and I'll shut up. I'll go to my side of the bed, and tomorrow, I'll stand next to your sister like I haven't been in love with you since before either of us knew what the word meant."

She doesn't answer.

The motel groans around us. Somewhere down the hall, a door bangs. The wind howls, throwing itself at the windows like it's trying to get in.

"Mia," I say, and her name fractures in my throat.

In my mind, Door 24 is still hanging in her parents' kitchen. I can see my own handwriting, cramped from hunching over the counter so no one would see. I can feel the way my chest hurt every time I slid another folded confession into that stupid little cardboard square and told myself she'd find it. That she'd know.

I'm sorry I made the truth into a scavenger hunt. I'm sorry I left you with the wrong version of the story and then stayed gone.

"I'm sorry," I say finally, the words scraping on their way out. "That I spent six years pretending you're not the first person I look for in every room."

Her fists twist in my shirt so fast it knocks a breath out of me.

"You don't get to say that," she chokes.

"Mia." I let go of her wrist and find her face in the dark, fingers careful along her jaw. "Look at me."

"I can't see you," she whispers.

"Yeah," I say quietly. "You can."

It takes a second, but she lifts her chin, angles toward me. I can make out the shine of her eyes now, the shape of her mouth.

"This thing between us . . . " I swallow. "It didn't die just because we pretended it did."

Her breath stutters against my thumb.

"I can't stand here one more second," I say, voice dropping, "and act like you don't undo me just by breathing."

Another flash of lightning. Another frozen image: her face tipped up, lashes wet, mouth trembling, braced like she expects another hit.

"One of us has been bleeding from this in silence for years," I say. "Maybe it's time we both admit it out loud."

Not permission. Not a request.

Just a fact I've been carrying like shrapnel.

The darkness settles again, but I don't feel blind. My hand is still on her jaw. Her fingers are still knotted in my shirt like she's the one keeping me upright.

I lean in until my forehead almost touches hers. The air between us is hot and thin.

"I shouldn't touch you," I murmur. "I've told myself that a thousand times."

Her chest rises against mine, and I feel every uneven breath.

"But wanting you?" I shake my head once, the movement brushing my forehead against hers. "That never stopped."

She inhales a sharp, involuntary sound that punches straight through me.

"If you tell me to step back," I whisper, "I will."

She closes her eyes. I feel the flutter of her lashes against my skin, a tiny, traitorous touch.

"Jake . . . " she says.

Not *no*.

Not *stop*.

Just my name, wrecked.

That's all it takes.

I cover her mouth with mine.

At first, it's just contact. Warm. Shocked. Her lips still, like her body is a half-second behind her heart.

Then she moves.

Her fingers drag me closer by my shirt, yanking me down to her; gravity finally getting its way. Her mouth opens under mine, hungry and furious, like every unsent reply to every unsaid thing we've ever buried.

Heat hits me so fast my knees go a little weak.

"Mia," I gasp into the next kiss, the word breaking on her lips.

She swallows it and gives me another.

Her back finds the wall with a soft thud. My hands hit the plaster on either side of her head and stay there, because if I put them anywhere else, I'm not sure I'll be able to stop.

She arches. Just a little. Just enough so our bodies line up in a way that makes my vision white out for a second.

Years of restraint, of distance, of pretending, all snap at once.

Everything we buried catches fire.

22

BLIZZARDS & BAD DECISIONS

MIA

The first thing I realize is that I'm the one who moves.

Not him.

Jake's mouth finds mine—warm, stunned, careful—and for half a second, I can still call this an accident. A misstep in the dark. A storm-induced lapse in judgment.

Then, my fingers tighten in his shirt, and I drag him closer.

There goes plausible deniability.

He makes a sound against my lips—half-groan, half-prayer—like he's been holding his breath for six years and just now exhaled. His arms are still braced on either side of my head, elbows locked.

The wall is cold at my back.

He is not.

Every rule I've ever written for myself curls up and burns.

I should pull away.

I should say Ava's name.

I should remember that my sister is waiting for his truck

to roll back into the driveway, trusting him to come home safe and solid and *hers*.

Instead, my body does what it has always done around Jake Carter.

It tells the truth before my mouth can lie.

I angle up on my toes, chasing the kiss. His restraint snaps a notch. His weight shifts closer, nowhere near too much and somehow still too much. One of his hands drops from the wall, fingers hovering near my waist like he's negotiating with his own impulse.

"Mia," he gets out, voice wrecked against my mouth.

I swallow the rest with another kiss, because if he finishes that sentence it turns into a choice, and I don't know how to choose anything but him in this exact, terrible second.

His mouth answers like we've done this a thousand times instead of almost never. I taste winter air and regret and the sharp tin edge of fear.

His free hand finally lands—high on my hip, fingers curving in, careful and possessive all at once. My back presses harder into the wall. The world narrows to four points: his mouth, his hand, the pounding in my chest, the faint tremor in his.

"You have no idea," he murmurs against my jaw, words dropping between kisses like he can't keep them in, "how long I've been trying to kill this."

"Don't," I breathe, tipping my head to give him more room, hating myself and wanting him all at once. "Jake, don't say it."

Because I know exactly how that sentence ends. And if he says *love* out loud, everything I've built since the night he left will split clean down the center.

He doesn't listen.

He never has, not when it mattered.

His forehead rests against my temple for one ragged breath. I feel him shake. "I tried, Mouse. I tried to let it die. I tried to be what everyone needed."

His thumb finds that small spot beneath my ribs—his spot, the one he pressed during thunderstorms when I couldn't sleep. Even now, in the dark, he finds it without fumbling, drawing a slow circle that's more confession than touch.

"I still see you in every December," he whispers. "I still look for you in every room. I still—"

I kiss him again, hard enough to steal the word before he can give it shape.

I am a coward and a traitor and something else I don't have a word for, because the truth is this: I don't want him to stop. Not for the storm. Not for the promise circling both our throats. Not for the future I supposedly handed my sister with a smile.

Ava's face flickers at the edge of my mind like a warning siren.

Luca's laugh ghosts right behind it—bright and unmistakable and carrying too much of the man currently kissing me against a reindeer wall in the dark.

I should push him away.

I don't.

Tears sting my eyes, hot and useless. Something splits behind my ribs, sharp and clean, the kind of break you don't walk off. For one dangerous second, I feel the words building in my throat—every I *missed you* and *why didn't you* and *you're Luca's father, you idiot* clawing toward daylight.

The hallway creaks.

Footsteps pass too close. A door slams down the hall.

Jake jerks back like someone yanked him on a line.

His chest heaves. Mine tries to match it and fails. My

hands stay knotted around his shirt until the space between us forces my fingers to uncurl, one by one, like I'm prying them off a ledge.

In the new dark, all I can see is his outline. Broad shoulders. Bent head. The absence between us humming.

When he speaks, his voice is raw. "This isn't fair to you."

A laugh pushes out of me, thin and broken. "Fair?" My back is still pressed to the wall. I feel like I'm holding the building up. "You think any of this has ever been fair?"

He drags a hand over his face. His silhouette cuts across the sliver of light from the bathroom door, all edges and tension. "I'm engaged to your sister," he says, each word ground out. "And I—" He stops, breath faltering. "I shouldn't have kissed you."

"You did," I say, because if I don't say something true right now, I'm going to shatter. "And I didn't stop you."

The admission hangs there, hot and shameful and weirdly relieving.

I can't see his eyes, but I can feel him searching my face like he always has—that too-intense focus that used to make me feel seen and now makes me feel flayed.

He steps back a fraction. Then another. Each inch is like losing altitude, like the ground is dropping away and we're still somehow falling.

"I need space," he says finally, voice tight, "before I do something neither of us can walk away from."

There's a part of me that wants to ask, *What do you think we just did?*

Another part wants to tell him there's already no version of this we walk away from.

His gaze snags on mine one last time. I feel it—like heat, like impact. A whole conversation in a single look: I want you. I shouldn't. I'm already failing at both.

Then he backs away, slow and reluctant, until his hand finds the bathroom doorknob. Cold fluorescent light spills over his shoulder, harsh compared to the dark we're standing in.

He doesn't lock the door.

He just disappears behind it, and the slice of light narrows, then clicks off.

The motel room exhales. The storm surges louder in the sudden quiet, wind snarling at the thin walls like it's furious it didn't get to witness the scene.

I stay standing for three breaths. Four.

On the fifth, my knees give up on me.

I slide down the wall until I hit the reindeer carpet, my legs folding, my pulse rattling against my ribs.

His jacket is still around my shoulders, heavy with his warmth and the ghost of his hands. My lips are swollen. My wrist throbs where he bandaged it. The cocoa packet digs into my palm, foil edges biting my skin as if to prove it's real.

My brain runs in circles.

He kissed me.

I kissed him back.

He said he looks for me in every room.

He is still walking into a room with my sister at the end of all this.

And underneath it all, coiled in a place I don't let myself touch, is the worst truth of all:

If he walked back out of that bathroom right now and crossed the space between us, if he reached for me again, if he said, *Say the word and we'll tell her together*—

I don't know if I'd stop him.

I don't know if I could.

The thought terrifies me more than the storm, more than the roads, more than every worst-case scenario I've hoarded since the day I peed on a stick and sat on a bathroom floor and decided to raise a small, bright, Jake-shaped secret alone.

Thunder rolls somewhere far off, muffled by snow. The heater coughs back to life. A string of Christmas lights outside our window flickers, casting faint colors across the ceiling—blue, red, green, like a soft, stupid heartbeat.

I press the heels of my hands into my eyes until sparks bloom.

Truth: *I wanted this storm. I wanted something bigger than me to pin us in one place long enough that the lies couldn't keep getting in the way.*

Dare: *I let him kiss me, knowing exactly who was waiting for him back in Frost Harbor—and who was waiting for me.*

Confession: *The scariest part isn't that we crossed a line. It's that, for one blinding, impossible moment, it didn't feel wrong at all.*

23

LIPSTICK & LIES

MIA

Day 20 is waiting for me.

The Advent calendar leans against Mom's kitchen wall, a little more frayed every time I look at it. Seventeen's flap still sags. Eighteen's hook is bare. Nineteen is a ghost—door empty, cocoa gone, the memory of Jake pressing it into my hand in a motel room still too loud.

Now twenty stares back at me like it knows what tonight is.

Engagement party.

Glass floor.

Rink.

Speech.

"Mom, can I open it?" Luca bounces in his tiny button-down, bowtie crooked. He smells like soap and sugar and every decision I'm not brave enough to explain.

"Door 20 is officially a group effort," Harper announces from the island, eyeliner wand dangling, hair twisted into a reckless knot. "We need all available magic."

Mom stands at the stove, cheeks flushed from the heat, wearing her nice sweater and that necklace she only brings out for big nights. Dad is at the table, pretending to read the paper while absolutely not reading it.

"Go ahead," Mom says. "Just don't rip the whole calendar off the wall, Lu."

"I'm not a monster," he mutters—and tugs the flap open.

Something small drops, bounces once, and rolls to my feet. I scoop it up.

A peppermint.

Red-and-white swirl. Clear wrapper. *Simple.*

Something tightens low in my chest.

"What is it?" Luca asks, peering. "Candy?"

"Yep," Harper says. "Ancient artifact. Believed to ward off public embarrassment."

I turn it between my fingers.

Seventeen. Backstage. My first solo. My hands shook. Jake's palm closed over mine as he slipped a peppermint into my hand.

"For courage," he had whispered. *"When you want to run, bite. Remember to breathe. And remember I'm out there, cheering you on."*

The memory hits a place I've never learned to guard.

"You okay?" Harper asks, her edge softening.

"Jake used to hand me one before each performance," I say. "He never forgot."

"I saw him do it," Mom says, a small smile tugging at her mouth. "He'd steal them from the jar in the choir room. Always insisted you needed them more."

Of course she noticed.

Luca's eyes widen. "Uncle Jake gave you candy? That's so cool."

"Very cool," I manage.

Beside me, Harper angles a look, sharper now. "And the universe just sent you a retro courage disk. Rude, but on-brand."

"Do you think he . . . ?" I trail off.

Placed this one. Like the cocoa. Like Lucky. Like the boot.

Harper lifts a shoulder. "Either it's cosmic meddling or a man with access to old candy and too many feelings. Both check out."

I close my fingers around the peppermint until the edges indent my skin. "I can't do this," I whisper.

"Yes," she says instantly. "You can. Question is: What version of you shows up tonight? Snow Queen of Silent Suffering? Or the woman who knows her own heart and can fake a toast for twenty minutes without imploding?"

"Low bar."

"We love attainable goals." She taps the calendar. "Pocket the sugar spell. We'll build the rest as we go."

Mom stirs her pot, but her voice drifts over her shoulder. "Peppermint always meant courage in this house," she says. "And a little forgiveness."

"Forgiveness for what?" Luca asks.

"Spilled cocoa. Broken ornaments. Being human," she answers. Then, she meets my eyes. "You'll know when you're ready."

I hate when she does that—wraps the truth in something tender and leaves me to unwrap it later.

Luca tugs at my dress. "Do I get some too?"

"Not this one." I lower my voice. "This one's for nerves."

"You're nervous?" he whispers, like I've admitted a state secret.

"Just a little." I crouch and straighten his bowtie. "But I'll be okay."

He beams. "'Cause you're brave. Harper says so."

Harper doesn't even try to look innocent. "It's documented."

Dad folds his paper with a soft thump. "We should head out soon if we want to beat the traffic."

"It's Frost Harbor," Harper says. "There are like twelve cars."

"Thirteen, if Darren brings the truck," Dad replies solemnly.

The normalcy of it—the banter, the cozy bustle, Luca's excitement—collides hard with the knot I've been carrying all day.

I slip the peppermint into the pocket of my dress.

If the universe insists on sending me courage, I'm not leaving it behind.

Truth: *Last night against that motel wall didn't feel like a mistake; it felt like coming home.*

Dare: *I zip up my coat, paint on a smile, and agree to toast his engagement like I'm not still shaking from his hands on my skin.*

Confession: *I'm more afraid of what my face will give away than anything I might say into that microphone.*

24

PEPPERMINT & PROMISES

MIA

The Icebound Terrace looks like someone curated a snow globe and then cranked the volume. Garlands sweep along the beams, catching gold light. White tablecloths glow under candle halos. The trees in each corner are styled within an inch of their lives, every ornament deliberate. The glass floor reveals the rink below—a sheet of shifting blues and pinks, like it's breathing.

Luca squints through the glass, fogging a tiny patch. "Mama . . . were you ever scared down there?"

"Scared?" I rest a hand on his small shoulder, feeling the way he leans into my touch without thinking. The trust in that lands heavier than it should. "Sometimes. Mostly, I was cold."

He lifts his mouth in that sure little way of his. "You'd be brave now."

"Maybe." It's the closest truth I can offer without unraveling.

He presses his palm to the floor, lining it up with mine. "I think yes," he whispers, like a secret meant only for me.

My chest gives a small, traitorous pull, something loosening where I've tried to weld shut. Heat gathers behind my eyes. I slide my hand back before the moment opens wider than I can manage.

"Mia, honey!"

Mrs. Carter weaves through the crowd, cheeks flushed, red scarf tied with aggressive cheer. Mr. Carter follows a step behind, a little stooped, wearing his good flannel and the expression of a man who'd rather be hauling trees outside than making polite conversation.

I smile, bracing already. "Hi, Cherie. Hi, Darren."

"Oh, look at this one." Cherie crouches in front of Luca. "All handsome and official. Let me guess—Chief Ring Security?"

Luca puffs up. "Chief Chocolate Inspector."

"Even better," she says, eyes bright. "I'll need you to check the dessert table later. For safety." She ruffles his hair. He leans into it, grinning.

Darren folds his hands over his belt buckle, studying Luca. "Big question, my man. What's Santa working on for you this year?"

"A sled with real steering! And a robot dog that doesn't run into walls."

Cherie laughs. "Oh, Santa's got his work cut out for that one."

Luca shrugs, unapologetic. "Santa's magic."

"Mmm, that he is," she agrees. Her eyes soften toward him before flicking to me; something small and searching there.

"You alright, honey?" she asks, lowering her voice. She pulls me into a hug that smells like pine and bakery sugar.

I hug her back, my throat catching. "I'm fine," I say, which is . . . generous.

Cherie nods, not quite convinced but unwilling to push. "Big night. Lots of feelings flying around."

God, she has no idea.

"Margaret!" she calls when she spots my mom. "Those centerpieces! Tell me everything."

She lets me go before I can crumble.

The moms converge in a flurry of praise and logistical tyranny. Dad and Darren exchange a single nod that—translated from Dad-speak—covers an entire debate: lights good, music fine, crisis level acceptable.

I breathe out slowly, trying to smooth the rattle in my chest.

"Think you can survive this?"

Harper appears at my elbow in a dark green jumpsuit that should require a permit. The neckline alone could start a small riot. Houston stands nearby, pretending to admire appetizers and absolutely eavesdropping.

"Define survive."

"Make it through your toast without combusting." She steals a bacon-wrapped date with surgical precision. "Bonus points if you avoid tackling the bride-to-be mid-party."

Across the room, Ava spins toward us in a swirl of red silk. Dylan is two steps behind with a clipboard and the weary patience of a man who's rerouted three circuits already.

"There she is!" Ava beams, air-kissing my cheek without smudging her lipstick. "You look perfect."

I glance down at my dress—simple, dark, forgiving, made for people whose hearts are held together with tape. "You look like you mugged a holiday catalog," I say. "It works."

She laughs, squeezing my hands, energy buzzing off her.

"Okay. Skating block at eight. Toasts at eight-thirty. DJ at nine. Dylan is handling anything that might explode or short-circuit—"

"Actively on it." He raises the clipboard like a shield. His tie is crooked, and he somehow makes it look intentional. His eyes soften when they land on her.

"You just have to be your charming, supportive sister self for five minutes with a microphone," Ava finishes.

Five minutes.

The peppermint in my pocket presses a sharp edge through the fabric.

"Easy," I say. My voice absolutely disagrees, thin and papery.

Ava doesn't catch it. She's already pivoting as Dylan leans in with another question about outlets and surge protectors. He looks good in blue—more at ease than Jake has ever looked in formal anything.

"Ava, the string lights over the terrace keep flickering," Dylan says. "I can reroute, but we'll lose the back speakers if the surge hits again."

"I trust you." Her hand falls to his forearm as if she's done it a hundred times.

He stills for a beat, absorbing it, then smiles. "Then I'll make it work."

Their eyes linger a fraction too long.

Harper murmurs, "Interesting."

"Harper," I warn.

"What? I ship competent people doing complicated wiring together."

"Of course you do."

Houston finally abandons the appetizers and slides up on Harper's other side, smelling faintly of cedar and beer.

"Is this what I get for finally meeting my new neighbor in

the wild?" he asks her, mouth curving. "You show up looking like that and make everyone else feel underdressed?"

Harper lifts a brow, pleased. "Compliments and snacks?"

He chuckles, eyes dipping once down her jumpsuit before manners drag them back up.

She bumps his shoulder, pretending not to preen.

Houston takes a sip. "Hey, have either of you seen Jake?" he asks, aiming for casual and missing. "He texted that he was here with a couple guys from the academy."

Harper tips her chin toward the far end of the Terrace. "There. Balcony side. Pretending he's not the main attraction."

I follow her gaze.

Jake stands near the glass, flanked by two of his guys. Dark suit, tie already loosened like his neck refused the full Windsor. His hair is doing that wrecked thing it does when he drags his hands through it—and the sight hits me low, a sharp, traitorous swoop in my stomach, remembering those same fingers gripping my waist last night.

Jake in a suit should be illegal.

He laughs at something one of his guys says—brief, real —but his eyes keep skimming the room like radar, tracking exits, threats, and—

As if sensing me, his head turns.

Our eyes collide.

Just a second. Elastic. Dangerous. The noise around us blurs, everyone else softening while his gaze hooks into mine and holds. My skin tightens, hyperaware of every place his hands touched last night, like my body is replaying the map.

My back still remembers the chilled door, the scrape of his stubble along my jaw, the way his name cracked out of me like a confession I'd been swallowing for years.

Tonight, he's announcing his engagement to my sister.

Heat crawls up my throat—shame and want knotting—and my fingers twitch toward the peppermint in my pocket like it's a life raft. I curl my hand around it, the cool wrapper biting into my palm.

Harper shifts deliberately, sliding between us like a professional blocker, sequined shoulder slicing through his line of sight. "Okay, focus. You have one speech to give, zero hearts allowed to implode, and exactly one emotional support gremlin at your side."

"That gremlin is not you."

She grins. "You're right. I'm a full emotional support cryptid."

"Comforting," I mutter, pulling in a breath that doesn't quite settle.

"Practice," she orders. "Give me your opening line."

My mouth dries. "Um. 'Thank you all for being here tonight to celebrate my sister and—'"

"Wrong," she cuts in. "Try again without sounding like you're defending a thesis."

"I am defending something," I hiss. "My sanity."

"Then remember the peppermint."

I touch my pocket. *Breathe. I can do this.*

Pretend my chest isn't held together by gauze and stubbornness.

A sharp clink rings from the bar as someone taps a glass.

The bartender lifts his hand, smiling easily. Mid-thirties, warm brown skin, dark hair tied at his nape. His nametag reads *BEN*. He's wearing a sweater with a drunk reindeer on it and somehow making it charming instead of tragic.

"Alright, Frost Harbor," he calls. "Two-drink minimum on emotional honesty tonight, but the skating portion is complimentary."

Laughter ripples through the room, tension loosening.

"Skate rental's down the stairs," Ben continues. "If you're a danger to yourselves on ice, we've got railings, hot cocoa, and liability waivers."

Harper claps. "I like him."

Houston tips his beer. "Man knows his audience."

Ben's eyes skim the crowd before landing on me—long enough to spark interest. Heat flares along my collarbone, a flicker of awareness I am not equipped to manage.

Somewhere to my left, Jake drifts closer with his guys, just inside my peripheral vision. I don't have to see him to feel the way the air sharpens.

Jake stiffens. His shoulders climb a notch.

"Keep looking, why don't you," he mutters under his breath, low enough only someone too close would catch it.

I shoot him a side-eye anyway.

Bold, considering he's supposed to be celebrating an engagement to my *sister*, not glowering over who glances at me.

Ava loops her arm through his, oblivious. "Come on, babe. First couple on the ice gets bragging rights."

"You hate skating," he reminds her, amused.

"But I love spectacle." She tugs on his arm. "And I love you. Come fall down romantically with me."

Dylan's face folds briefly—something unguarded flickering through before he masks it. "I'll keep the med kit ready," he calls.

Jake startles at the words, then smooths it with a grin. "Guess I'm outnumbered."

As they pass, Luca darts forward, all legs and excitement. "Uncle Jake! Can I skate too?"

Jake stops immediately. "Yeah, buddy." He crouches to Luca's level, suit creasing, attention fully on him. "If your mom says it's okay."

Luca swings toward me, eyes huge. "Please?"

Ice rink. Jake. Luca. All the fragile pieces I've been balancing like glass ornaments.

He's five, I remind myself. *He deserves joy untouched by my fear.*

"Helmet," I say. "Gloves. And stay with a grown-up. No solo stunts."

He salutes. "Yes, ma'am."

"I'll take him for a slow lap," Jake offers. Like he's not offering to step straight into the center of everything that terrifies me. "We'll stay by the rail."

My throat narrows around everything I want to say.

You're his father.

You have no idea what you're holding.

He's yours in ways you don't see.

"Thanks," is all I manage.

Jake ruffles Luca's hair in that absent, instinctive way dads do—fingers easy, thumb lingering for a second. Then he straightens. "Meet me by the rental counter. We'll get you the coolest skates they've got."

Luca rockets away, sneakers skidding on the polished floor, Cherie and Mom trailing behind, already fussing about socks and laces and circulation.

I watch them—the grandparents, Jake, my son—all of them converging at the top of the stairs in a knot of affection and oblivion.

Harper leans in. "That," she exhales, "is a lot."

"Understatement," I mutter.

Truth: *Letting Jake take Luca's hand feels less like a favor*

and more like handing him a piece of a life he doesn't know is his.

Dare: *I pretend it's just skating and say yes anyway, even as my heart tries to claw its way out of my ribs.*

Confession: *Watching them walk toward the stairs, I can't tell if I'm more terrified he'll recognize his son—or that he won't.*

25

SKATES & SECRETS

MIA

Ten minutes later, Luca is on the ice with skates slightly too cool for a five-year-old, a helmet a size too big, and cheeks pink from cold and joy. He holds both of Jake's hands, stiff-legged, wobbling with every glide and laughing each time he doesn't fall.

Jake Carter, steady on the ice.

A little boy with his nose and my eyes.

Both grinning like the world is simple.

Cherie and Darren watch from the rail, pride carved deep into their faces. My parents stand a few feet down, Mom's hand over her mouth, Dad doing a terrible job hiding misty eyes behind a cough and a sudden fascination with the Zamboni schedule.

Houston murmurs at my side, "Hell of a picture."

Harper exhales hard. "You have no idea."

They're admiring a picture they don't realize is mislabeled: *Father.*

The thought spears through me, sharp enough that I curl my fingers around the railing to keep myself upright.

Ava totters onto the ice next, announcing herself with a shriek that ricochets off the glass. "This is so slippery!"

"That's the point," Dylan calls from the gate, half-smiling. He has a skate guard in one hand and a wrench in the other, because of course he does.

Jake guides Luca back toward the opening with careful pushes. "Trade-off, buddy," he says. "I'm taking your Aunt Ava for a lap. You hang with your nana, alright?"

"Okay!" Luca blurts. "You were so good at it! You didn't fall once!"

Jake's mouth pulls to one side, eyes crinkling. "High praise." Then he reaches for Ava's hand.

He doesn't look at me.

He doesn't have to.

The awareness sparks anyway—a live wire stretched between the ice and where I'm standing. It snaps through my nerves, my pulse stuttering in time with the rhythm of their skates.

Truth: *From up here, they look like the future I pictured once, back when I still believed we might get one. A man steady on his feet, a woman laughing beside him, a kid sandwiched in the middle. The Carter Christmas card.*

Dare: *I stay behind the glass and let everyone admire the pretty family picture without correcting the caption. Let them think this is simple. That I'm just the sister, just the friend, just the girl on the safe side of the boards.*

Confession: *If the truth finally cracks the ice we're all skating on, I don't know who I'm going to lose—Jake, my sister, or the version of me who thought she could keep them all. And standing here, fingers numb around the rail while my son laughs up at the man who doesn't know he's his, I'm not sure which loss terrifies me more.*

26

THE TRUTH BETWEEN THE TOASTS

MIA

"Hey," Ben calls as I come back to the bar. "You look like you need a pre-speech drink or a Mars-bound escape pod."

"Whichever's faster," I say.

"Hot toddy?" he offers. "Nerves' special. Won't ruin your enunciation."

Ben's hands move quick and practiced over the bottles, the soft clink strangely calming. My own hands are still buzzing from the mic I haven't touched yet.

"You're Mia, right? Sister of the bride?"

"Yeah." I wrap my hand around the glass he slides over, letting the heat soak into my skin. "Walking human toast."

"You'll crush it," he says with easy confidence. "Professional secret: Don't try to be funny if you're about to cry. And if you do cry, own it. People trust tears more than jokes."

Despite myself, my mouth lifts. "Are you secretly a therapist?"

"Only for people who tip well." He nudges the mug closer. "You skate?"

"Not well," I say.

A lie. I used to skate like it was the only place my body knew exactly what to do.

He glances toward the rink below. "I'm off shift after the toasts. If you want someone to cling to the railings with, I'm your guy. I only fall on important occasions."

It's a simple offer. Friendly. Easy.

No history. No hidden letters in felt. No six-year-old fault line waiting under every blade of ice.

"Maybe." I manage a smile.

He taps the bar. "I'll check back after your speech. Break a leg. Not literally."

Down on the ice, Ava wobbles theatrically, gripping Jake's arm. He laughs as he steadies her, slow and patient in the way he always was with anyone who didn't grow up on slippery surfaces.

It should be sweet.

It feels like a punch.

He glances up again. Our eyes catch, and the noise around me blurs until it's just him and me and a sheet of ice sitting between two catastrophically bad decisions.

My lungs misfire. Heat rushes up my throat, sharp and unsteady.

"Mia." Harper appears at my side, her hand brushing my elbow. "Time."

"What?"

She nods toward the stage area—really just a slightly raised patch of glass with a mic and a single speaker. People are already drifting toward it, drinks in hand, expectant, like they're all in on something I'm not ready to say out loud.

My stomach drops. "Now?" I croak.

"Now."

I take the peppermint out, turning it between my fingers, the wrapper crackling like a tiny thunderclap.

You're allowed to breathe. His voice. That night. The way my chest had listened.

I unwrap it, pop it into my mouth, and bite down.

Sharp sweetness floods my tongue—cool and bright, a jolt straight through my ribs.

My shoulders loosen a fraction. Air actually makes it into my lungs.

I'm not okay. But I'm upright.

And right now, that counts.

The mic smells faintly of sanitizer and nerves. I wrap my fingers around it anyway.

"Hi," I say—too close. Feedback squeals. I wince, pull it back. "Sorry. Still figuring out how to exist at normal volume."

Polite laughter ripples. My heartbeat is a drum.

"I'm Mia," I continue. "Ava's sister. Jake's . . . long-suffering best friend." I glance toward the ice. "I've known these two almost my whole life. One of them has been bossing me around since she was born. The other once jumped into a frozen creek to rescue my shoe, so make of that dynamic what you will."

Laughter again—real.

Ava presses a hand to her heart, smiling. Jake stands beside her, one arm over the rail, watching me like the rest of the room isn't here.

Peppermint cools the back of my throat.

"When Ava told me she was engaged, I asked her if she was ready. Not for marriage. For . . . choosing. For the part where you decide, every day, that this is your person. Even when it's hard. Especially when it's hard."

A soft murmur moves through the crowd. Something cinches behind my ribs.

"Ava has always known how to choose what she wants," I continue. "She chooses color. And joy. And the restaurant with the longest line because the food has to be better. She chooses big. She chooses loud. She chooses love with her whole, stubborn, glitter-covered heart."

My voice wavers. I swallow against the tightness.

"And Jake . . . " I search for words that are true and not cruel. "Jake has always shown up. For his family. For this town. For strangers in places most of us will never see. He's the guy who fixes things quietly at 3 a.m., who keeps jumper cables in his truck *just in case*, and who can apparently be talked into wearing a suit without spontaneous combustion."

A smile tugs at his mouth. His eyes stay locked on mine.

Heat prickles along my neck.

"That's what I see when I look at them," I say. "Someone who chooses with her whole heart. Someone who shows up with his whole self. And two people deciding they want to walk into whatever comes next together."

My vision swims momentarily. I blink hard.

"I wish you patience," I say. "And courage. And the kind of love that lets you be your gentlest and your bravest selves at the same time."

Peppermint burns a little now—bright and bitter.

"And—" My voice dips without my permission. "I wish you honesty. The kind that doesn't wait until doors are closing to tell the truth."

Jake's shoulders tense—barely. Ava squeezes his hand, mistaking the reaction for emotion instead of impact.

I lift my glass. "To Ava and Jake. To choosing. To showing up. To whatever wild, beautiful thing you build together."

Glasses rise. "To Ava and Jake," the crowd echoes.

They sip. I sip. Peppermint and champagne fizz together on my tongue, sharp and wrong.

Someone touches my elbow as I step back.

Dylan.

"You did great," he says quietly, "for what it's worth." His eyes are gentler than I expect—like he knows too much and not enough.

"Thanks," I murmur.

He glances toward the ice, where Ava is insisting someone take a picture of her and Jake against the rail. "She needed that," he says. "Hearing you say you believe in her."

I don't correct him—that belief and approval aren't the same thing.

He heads toward the DJ, sliding back into problem-solving mode.

Harper swoops in, looping an arm around me. "You didn't burst into flames. Ten out of ten, would toast again."

"I talked about honesty," I rasp. "At my ex-almost's engagement party."

She squeezes my shoulder. "If the shoe fits . . . "

"Don't say shoe."

"Right. Boot trauma. My bad."

Ben appears at the edge of the crowd. "Speech survived," he says. "Which means you officially qualify for post-toast skating."

"I never agreed to—"

"You did," Harper lies smoothly. "I heard it. Witnessed. Filed."

"Harper—"

Ben jerks his head toward the stairs. "Come on. I promised recreational clinging to the rails."

He's being kind. And I need distance—from the terrace,

from the mic, from the motel room still printed on my skin where Jake touched me.

"Okay," I say before I can overthink. "One lap. If I fall, I'm haunting this place forever."

"Deal."

We head toward the skates. Harper veers off toward Houston, clearly plotting mischief. Mom is near the dessert table, laughing with Mrs. Carter, thankfully not watching me closely.

At the rental counter, Ben finds my size with practiced ease. "Ever skate out there?" he asks.

"Once or twice," I say. "In another lifetime."

He grins. "Let's resurrect it."

We step onto the ice. Cold seeps through the thin soles; the sharp scent of fresh ice and faint metal hits me. The rink hums under my blades.

I take one careful step. Then another.

My knees wobble, muscle memory groggy but waking. Ben skates backward in front of me, offering both hands like a safety net.

"Got you," he says. "Bend your knees. Trust the glide."

I huff a laugh. "I know how physics works."

"Okay, show-off. Prove it."

I release a breath I didn't realize I was hoarding and push off.

The first glide is clumsy but real. The second comes easier. The third—my body remembers. Weight forward, center, back. Ankles angling instinctively. Arms balancing without thought.

Wind brushes my cheeks, bright and exhilarating. Something locked under my ribs loosens. We make it halfway around before I forget to be scared.

"Hey," Ben says, impressed. "You lied. You can skate."

I smile despite myself. "Had a good teacher."

"Let me guess," he says. "Tall, cocky, terrible at hiding feelings?"

A startled laugh breaks out of me.

He winks. "It's always that guy."

My gaze betrays me, finding Jake.

He and Ava are near the center now, moving carefully. She clings to his arm, laughing loud enough for the entire Terrace. His hand steadies her at the waist.

But his eyes—

They're on me.

Noticing Ben's hands around mine. The way I'm leaning into someone else.

His jaw tightens. His grip on Ava shifts too firm; she startles, then laughs it off.

"Jake!" she yelps. "Don't you drop me."

"Wouldn't dare," he says, but his voice doesn't land the way it should.

Houston glides past with alarming confidence, Harper on his arm, half-threatening, half-clinging. "Heads up!" he calls. "Newbies in motion. Watch your ankles."

"Speak for yourself," Harper fires back. "I was born for dramatic near-death experiences."

She clocks me and Ben instantly. Her brows rise. Then she follows my gaze to Jake and Ava. Her mouth presses thin.

We keep skating. Ben keeps a respectful distance, only tightening his hold when my balance tips. "You're a natural," he says.

The ice blurs under us. The scrape of blades, kids laughing near the rail, distant clinks of glass—all of it blends into a soft, layered hum.

And then we reach the far corner.

The exact spot where my eighteen-year-old self once lay

sprawled on the ice, breathless with laughter, Jake flat beside me, stars winking through frost.

"You okay?" he asked then, his breath fogging the air.

"Everything's cold," I said. "Except my chest."

"Good cold or bad cold?"

"Good." I turned toward him. "I think."

His smile was unguarded, rare, too much. "Yeah," he said quietly. "Me too."

We lay there until our fingers froze, talking about nothing and everything—college, tours, the terrifying size of the future.

I watched his breath rise in little clouds and realized, Oh. It's you.

That night was the one that changed everything.

My blade catches in a groove now, jerking me back.

I stumble. Ben's hands close around my wrists. "Whoa. I've got you."

My heart slams. In the reflection of the glass wall, another set of hands flashes through memory—another winter, another version of me.

Jake's still watching. Ava says something; he nods absently.

But his attention never leaves the place where Ben is holding me up. Jealousy cuts across his face—fast, bright, unmasked.

My stomach flips. It shouldn't feel like comfort.

But it does.

Because if he's jealous, I'm not the only one skating with ghosts.

"Want to keep going?" Ben asks. "Or break?"

"I—" My voice thins. "Maybe a break."

He nods and guides us toward the rail. "You did great. For the record."

"Debatable," I murmur.

At the wall, I grip the cold metal, grounding myself. My legs tremble—not from skating, but from everything dropping back into place at once.

Ben squeezes my shoulder. "If you come back later, I'll teach you how to spin."

"Let's not get ahead of ourselves."

He laughs and pushes off, gliding toward a cluster of tourists.

Harper appears at my side, slightly breathless, cheeks flushed. "So. Bartender looks delightful."

"Harper," I groan.

"What? I appreciate a man with balance. And a non-terrible sweater."

"You were watching?"

"Please. I'm watching everything." Her eyes flick toward the center. "Including the human storm front in a suit."

I follow her gaze. Jake has given up pretending not to watch me.

Ava follows his line of sight. Her brows pinch—briefly—before she laughs and tugs him toward the far side of the rink, away from where I stand.

Dylan stands at the rail with a headset, pretending he's only focused on the DJ. But when Ava clutches Jake during a stumble, Dylan's jaw tics before he reins it in.

Everything on this ice is a reflection of something else.

Old patterns.

New fractures.

People circling lives they haven't admitted they want.

Harper bumps my shoulder gently. "You okay?"

"I don't know." My breath fogs the air. "It feels like . . . stepping back into a sentence I never finished."

She nods, softer than usual. "Then maybe it's time to decide how it ends."

Below us, the rink glows. Above, the terrace lights flicker once and hold steady.

I tuck my cold fingers into my coat pocket. The peppermint wrapper crinkles.

Truth: *The ice just handed me the exact moment I fell in love with Jake Carter, and it still feels like one of the truest things I've ever known.*

Dare: *I let someone else hold me up while he watched, because it feels safer to wobble with a stranger than admit I still want to lean on him.*

Confession: *No matter whose hands were on my wrists, every glide still curved back toward him.*

27

THE NIGHT BEFORE

MIA

December 23rd.

Snowden Family Fun Night: The annual tradition where everyone pretends we're not one misplaced ornament from implosion.

Laughter spills out of the house—soft, lively—but it hits me like static, something I can hear but not feel. I sit on the porch steps, boots sinking into slush as my breath ghosts into the cold. Out here, the air bites honestly. No cinnamon. No manufactured cheer.

Through the windows, shadows drift across the glow—Ava twirling in a sparkly dress, my mom rearranging snacks she already perfected, Harper sneaking cookies like she's running black ops.

And Jake.

I don't have to see him to know he's there.

It's a new, unnerving skill: *Sensing him.*

Two nights ago on the ice, the way he watched Luca . . .

The way his smile faltered.

The brief pull in his eyes—keen, too aware.

Jake is close to the truth.

Maybe already holding it.

And I'm one wrong breath from everything cracking open.

The porch light snaps on.

"You planning on freezing to death out here," Harper asks. "Or is this your dramatic monologue arc?"

I let out a low exhale. "Option C: Avoiding the emotional minefield inside."

She hands me a mug of cocoa—extra marshmallows, lukewarm, exactly right. "Your mom just initiated Frostbite Roulette."

"Oh God."

"Oh yes." She grins. "Jenga with emotional prompts. A Snowden classic. Dylan is already regretting his life choices."

"Accurate."

She studies me. "You okay?"

No.

"I'm fine."

"You're lying," she says lightly, though her voice softens around the edges. "Want me to kidnap you? Fake a medical emergency? I can claim you swallowed an ornament."

A quiet laugh slips out. "Tempting."

But my eyes drift back to the window—to the glow, the movement, the picture-perfect calm.

Harper follows my gaze. Her voice lowers. "He's in there."

Something tightens low in my chest. "Yeah."

"And he's doing that thing."

I drag my attention back to her. "What thing?"

"The thing where he tries not to stare but absolutely fails."

Snow dusts my hairline as I close my eyes. "Harper . . . "

She bumps my shoulder. "Hey. You don't have to explain anything. I'm here for moral support and whatever chaos you require."

My throat pinches. If I told her—if I said it out loud—the truth would finally exist outside my body. And then everything shifts. The night. The holiday. Us.

I'm not ready.

Not yet.

Maybe tomorrow.

Maybe never.

Inside, someone squeals over a toppled Jenga tower.

"Come on," Harper murmurs. "Before your mom assumes elves dragged you away."

I take one last pull of cold—honest cold—then follow her inside.

Truth: *Jake knows something. Maybe everything.*

Dare: *I walk into that house anyway.*

Confession: *Tomorrow is Christmas Eve. Door 24. And I'm running out of places to hide.*

28

BE BRAVE, MOUSE

MIA

The living room is too lit. Every string of lights is cranked to high, blinking like they're trying to hypnotize us into cheer. Candles sugar the air with cinnamon and vanilla. A "Chill Christmas Vibes" playlist hums under it all, but even the soft carols feel brittle—like if anyone stops smiling, the notes might crack apart.

I stick to the edge of it all, half in shadow, cocoa cooling between my palms. Laughter bounces off the walls and returns sweeter, hollow.

I shouldn't find him first. Not anymore.

But still, my eyes go hunting.

Jake's by the fire, haloed unevenly by the lights. Mom fusses with the garland above his head like Christmas hinges on symmetry. Ava floats between guests, glittery and effortless, narrating the evening like she's hosting a holiday special.

"Okay, Snowdens," Dad calls, clapping once. "Family

Fun Night, round two! Luca, where'd you disappear to, buddy?"

Luca barrels down the hall, curls wild, cheeks flushed. He's hugging a wrapped box almost as big as his torso.

"I found it!" he crows. "It was under the tree. For me!"

In his other hand—held up like evidence—is a small red-edged familiar card.

"I saw this in the calendar too," he says. "The little door was open. It says, 'Be brave, Mouse.' That's you, right, Mom?"

The air shifts—from sugar to smoke.

My fingers numb around the mug.

Across the room, Jake follows Luca's voice, then the card, then me.

My smile feels pinned in place. "That's me."

"Mom says it to me the same way you used to say it to her."

The room doesn't just quiet. It drops.

Jake's head lifts—too quickly—and for a heartbeat he looks like someone cut a wire inside him. His eyes dart to Luca, then to me, and something inside them opens in a way I'm not ready for.

Not anger.

Not shock.

Not recognition—yet. The moment before it.

My pulse kicks. Air sticks halfway up my throat.

Peppermint was the courage Jake gave me for the world; "Be brave, Mouse" was the courage he gave me for the truth, and hearing Luca say it—our son, his phrase—I might as well have placed the truth directly in Jake's hands.

His gaze returns to Luca, gentler now—aching and bewildered—before landing on me with a weight that presses against my ribs.

Harper glances between us, brows lifting in a slow *Oh God* arc.

I force a thin laugh. "He repeats everything. Little mimic."

Jake doesn't smile.

Doesn't blink.

Just sits there, firelight tracing the hard line of his jaw, looking at me like the last chapter of a story he realizes he didn't finish.

One quiet moment—sharp enough to cut—and it ruins me.

Mom swoops in, clapping. "Let's do Truth, Dare, Confess! We haven't played in ages."

"Oh hell yes," Harper slurs. "Vintage Snowden chaos."

"Language," Mom scolds.

"Dang," Harper corrects, winking at Luca.

Ava reappears, settling between Dylan and Jake. "It'll be fun . . . remember, Mia? You invented Truth, Dare, Confess."

How could I forget?

Because of course I invented the one game designed to pry my ribs apart.

I manage a smile. "My crowning achievement."

Jake angles toward the fire, a throw pillow suddenly between him and Ava. His hand rests along the back of the couch, fingers tapping a restrained rhythm.

He hasn't looked at her once.

"Let's do a round," Ava says, bright as a marquee. "For tradition."

"Your version of tradition involves drama and emotional arson," Harper mutters.

"And mini marshmallows," Ava counters, passing a mug to Dylan without looking. *Muscle memory.*

He takes it, fingers brushing hers. His gaze lingers a beat too long. Color rises in her cheeks before she ducks behind her glass.

"Some things don't change," he says quietly.

"Some things get better," she answers, the words curling warm, like ribbon catching light.

My stomach knots.

Mom produces the deck—a stack of homemade cards marked *Truth*, *Dare*, or *Confess* in my teenage handwriting. I'd forgotten how my younger self weaponized cardstock.

"Luca, you're first," Dad declares.

Luca bounces onto the rug. "Truth!"

"Alright, bud." Harper plucks a card and squints. "What are you most excited about for Christmas?"

"Everything," he says immediately. Then, he thinks. "But mostly cinnamon rolls. And maybe if Santa brings a sled. And also . . . skating, but only if Uncle Jake goes with me again."

Jake exhales something close to a laugh. His gaze flicks my way, quick as a spark.

"Strong priorities," Harper says. "Ten out of ten, no notes."

The first few rounds stay light. Mom confesses she once burned a whole batch of cookies and bought replacements. Dad takes a dare and attempts an Elvis impression that makes Luca wheeze and the rest of us cringe.

Then, Harper cuts the deck with a flourish and hands it to Dylan.

"Alright, Florida Boy," she says. "You're up."

Dylan pulls a card. "Confess." He sighs. "Of course."

Harper leans in. "Ooh, good one. Confess a regret. Hit us."

People chuckle. It's a prompt meant for safe admissions.

He doesn't look at the card again.

He looks at Ava. The room tilts.

"I should've fought harder," he says quietly.

The playlist hums. Someone in the kitchen rattles a pan. But here—stillness.

Ava freezes mid-sip. Color climbs her neck. She stares at the floor as if searching for a trapdoor.

"For what?" Mom asks gently.

He doesn't answer her. His eyes stay on Ava—steady, unflinching. "For the thing I wanted," he says. "Instead of letting other people choose for me."

Silence thickens.

Ava's throat shifts once. She takes a gulp of her drink and stares at the tree like it betrayed her.

Instinct has me glance toward Jake.

His head is bowed, gaze fixed on the rug. His jaw locked line. This isn't new to him. It's confirmation.

For a moment, I feel lighter—like the spotlight drifted and found someone else with a messier story.

The relief barely sparks before shame drowns it. I'm not the only one lying here. I'm just the one whose lie has a heartbeat and dimples.

Harper clears her throat. "Well! That was . . . delightfully heavy. Pro tip: Regrets land better if you follow them with a knock-knock joke."

Luca giggles. A few adults chuckle. Dylan still watches Ava.

Finally, she lifts her eyes—one quick, luminous glance I recognize from an ice rink.

Harper bumps Dylan's shoulder, snapping the line stretched between them. It dies out.

"Your turn, hero," she says, offering the deck to Jake. "Save us from group therapy hour."

Jake's fingers close around the cards. He draws one.

"Dare," he says.

Harper leans over. "Ooh—Say something you've never said out loud. Floor's yours, Carter."

He exhales slowly. Then his eyes lift.

They find mine—a thread pulling them there, no matter how he fights it.

Heat coils low in my stomach.

Jake looks away, jaw hardening. When he speaks, his voice is steady but rough.

"There was a time," he says, "when I kept writing to someone who never wrote back."

My pulse stutters.

"I kept waiting for her to open a door she'd left closed." A beat. "I thought she chose silence over me."

His gaze brushes mine—brief and searing—but enough to root me in place.

"Turns out," he finishes softly, "I was wrong about a lot of things."

The room holds its breath.

Then Luca knocks into Jake's knees, giggling. "Uncle Jake! Look at my present!"

Jake's hand slips into his hair without thought. The kind of touch that once steadied me.

My chest caves. It feels like two lives colliding under the same lights: the one I built, and the one I buried.

"Mia!" Harper calls. "Your turn."

A card waits in my hand. I don't remember picking it up.

She reads it. "Say one truth you've never said out loud."

Of course, it's the same dare.

Every face turns toward me—Jake, Ava, my mom, the entire room full of people I cannot tell.

I swallow. Air snags on something jagged.

"I've been carrying something alone for a long time," I say quietly. "And . . . it's killing me."

"Mia . . . " Mom's voice is a fragile warning.

Jake looks wrecked. His hand is still in Luca's hair. Ava sits rigid, knuckles white around her glass. Dylan studies the space between Jake and me like he's finally seeing the outline of something permanent.

It's too much.

"Also," I blurt, "when I was fifteen, I made out with a cardboard cutout of Zac Efron in a Santa hat. It was a rough year."

Luca shrieks. Harper chokes on wine. Dad snorts. Laughter breaks the tension enough to breathe.

It doesn't reach me.

I could've said it. *He's your son. You were never the silence, Jake. I was the one who closed the door.*

The truth claws at my ribs, begging for daylight.

"I . . . need some water."

I stand too fast. The room wavers. Harper watches but doesn't stop me. She knows when someone is already unraveling.

"I've got it," I add when Mom rises. "I'm fine."

Lie after lie.

I set my mug down and head for the hall. Each step feels like crossing thin ice, waiting for the break.

I can feel him behind me—quietly tracking me without moving.

Be brave, Mouse.

Not tonight.

The hallway is dimmer. My heartbeat thuds in my ears as I slip around the corner, out of sight.

I press my back to the wall and drag in a breath that scrapes.

Truth: *Jake saw something tonight I can't undo.*

Dare: *I walked away before I shattered.*

Confession: *Tomorrow, the truth won't stay quiet.*

29

WHERE THE SKY KNOWS FIRST

MIA

The narrow observatory stairs complain under my boots, each creak swallowed by insulation and old dust. When the door closes behind me, the house drops to a distant hum—laughter, carols, Ava's brittle cheer. All of it sounds like it belongs to another version of me I misplaced years ago.

Frost nets across the skylight. The battered telescope leans toward a shard of winter sky that used to feel endless. Now it feels like something I've stepped outside of.

I fold myself onto the window seat, knees tucked tight, trying to shrink into a shape that won't spill. My breath fogs the glass.

I almost said it downstairs. The truth had risen like it wanted to crack my teeth open and speak for itself.

I can't hold in what I've been carrying anymore: *He's not your fiancé, Ava. He was never really yours.*

But I swallowed it. I always do.

I wrap my arms around my shins and lower my forehead to the cold pane. Snow drifts against the glass above me—

soft, relentless. Pretty, if you've never had to dig out from under it.

Floorboards groan below. Someone laughs. Someone misses a note in a carol, and everyone barrels on. Life keeps moving while I sit here, trying not to fracture.

I don't know what counts as bravery anymore—shattering the lie or learning to breathe around it.

I pull the old plaid blanket over my shoulders. It smells like childhood winters. And lies that felt easier back then.

Luca's voice won't leave my head: *Mom says it to me the same way you used to say it to her.*

Jake's face when he heard that—*that* is what unraveled me. Like someone had slid an old puzzle piece into his palm, and he suddenly saw the picture differently.

My breath fogs the glass again. Fades and disappears.

Downstairs, carols rise and fall over the pulse of conversation. A spoon scrapes. A chair drags. Normal life, blissfully oblivious to the fault line up here.

The stair creaks.

Every muscle in me goes still.

"Door was open," Jake says softly. "You always forget to lock it."

His voice reaches me first. His restraint reaches me second.

I turn.

He stands in the doorway, one hand braced on the frame like he needs the anchoring. His hair is damp from melted snow. Firelight doesn't reach this high, so only the string of dim bulbs and the cold moonlight catch him.

He looks . . . contained. Too contained. Like something inside him is splintering, and he's trying to hold the pieces steady.

"You shouldn't be here."

"You shouldn't be up here alone," he answers, quiet but sure. "Not after . . . that."

That.

The dare. The almost-confession.

Luca dropping a live charge in the middle of my family room without knowing it.

"I'm fine." The lie barely holds shape.

One corner of his mouth twitches like he wants to believe me and can't. He steps inside and closes the door with a soft click that lands heavily.

"You left like you were underwater," he murmurs. "Couldn't just sit there and pretend I didn't see that."

"It was a game, Jake. Everyone said something. I said something. End of story."

He shakes his head slowly. "Mia . . . I know the difference between you talking and you bleeding."

Another night, that would've earned a smile. Tonight, it just hits.

Silence settles between us, thin and trembling under the carols.

"What do you want, Jake?"

He exhales through his nose, like the question hurts. "To make sure you're okay."

"I'm not," I say, sharper than I mean to. Softer, "But I will be."

He absorbs the first part and holds on to the second like it's permission to stay.

"You don't have to be okay," he says. "Not up here. Not with me."

A cracked sound escapes me—half laugh, half something else. "Since when?"

"Since always."

No hesitation. No flourish. Just truth. I feel it in places I've worked hard to numb.

"Don't," I whisper.

"Don't what?"

"This." My hands tighten around the blanket. "The remembering. The way you look at me. The offer to be the person I lean on when you're the reason I can't stand."

His breath stutters, like he's absorbing another hit he refuses to dodge.

"Okay," he says eventually. "Then don't lean. Just sit. I'll sit too. No talking. No looking. I can do that."

It's a fragile attempt at humor, but the offer underneath is stripped bare.

"It's safer if you go."

"For who?" he asks.

For you. For me. For the life you're pretending still fits.

"For me."

He nods once, jaw working. He takes the blow without countering it.

"I'm not here to make this harder," he says. "I just . . . couldn't watch you walk out of that room like that and stay downstairs."

"Because of my 'truth'?" I force air quotes. "Great. New record. I embarrassed myself in under ten seconds."

"Because of everything," he says. "Your truth. The way your hand shook. The way your mom looked at you. The way Luca—"

He stops.

Luca's name lands between us like a dropped match.

"What about Luca?" My voice is too quick, too thin.

He meets my eyes then—really meets them. The caution there is almost tender.

"He's a great kid," Jake says. "Brave. Sharp. Too perceptive."

Every muscle in me coils. "Don't."

"I'm not accusing you of anything," he says fast. "I'm not —" His hand curls at his side, like it wants to reach for something he doesn't deserve. "I'm just saying . . . when he read that card and said you say it to him the way I used to say it to you—"

His voice frays. He doesn't finish.

He doesn't need to.

"He parrots things," I say. "You know he does. Mom tells stories. He picks stuff up."

"Yeah," Jake murmurs. "That's what I told myself."

The problem is his voice says he's losing that argument.

He takes a single step toward me—then stops short, like the restraint costs him something real.

"Mia." His voice is low, far too gentle. "Look at me."

"I'd rather not."

"Yeah," he whispers. "I know. But I need you to."

I force myself to meet his eyes.

They're chaos—fear, tenderness, guilt, something deeper he's fighting to cage.

"I'm not asking questions I don't have the right to," he says. "Not tonight. Not when you're already . . . this." He gestures small, helpless. "I just need you to know that when he said it, something in me"—his hand touches his chest, brief and tight—"shifted."

I swallow hard. "I've been carrying something alone for a long time," I say, barely audible. "And I can't keep doing it."

His face softens, and it steals the air from my lungs.

"Then let me take some of it," he murmurs. "You don't have to tell me what it is. Just let me stand with you. Even blind."

"It's not your job to fix me."

A faint, broken smile. "Try telling that to the part of me that still watches the exits for you."

A thin laugh slips out of me—ragged, but real. He eases a fraction, like the sound steadies him.

"Jake . . ."

"I know," he interrupts gently. "I'm engaged. The reasons this can't happen are endless. I'm not asking you to break anything. I'm not asking you to choose me."

He steps one small, ruinous inch closer. "I'm just asking you not to shut me out while you're drowning."

My eyes sting. "Why do you still care this much?"

"Because I don't know how not to," he says. Quiet. Immediate. Unprotected.

It lands like a blow.

He watches my reaction, searching for something he can endure.

I give him none of it.

He lifts a hand. For a breath, I think he might reach for me—steady me, shake the truth loose, do anything reckless enough to end us.

But he doesn't.

He stops an inch from my skin, his fingers hovering near my cheek, close enough to radiate heat.

He holds perfectly still, like moving any closer would break both of us.

His eyes close tight and brief, as if the nearness burns.

When he opens them, they shine.

And then it happens.

Not a sob. Not a sharp inhale.

Just one silent tear slips free before he can cage it.

He doesn't brush it away. He stands there with his hand

suspended between wanting and knowing better, memorizing me without asking a thing in return.

"Jake . . . " My voice fissures. "Why are you crying?"

"Because I'm standing here while the woman I—" His throat locks. He tries again. "—while the person who shaped every version of me is slipping out of reach again."

I sway as the world tilts.

"Mia," he says, voice raw, "whatever you're carrying . . . I'm not going anywhere."

"You might."

"Then that's on me," he whispers. "Not you."

I shake my head, vision swimming. "If this breaks open, it hurts everyone. You, Ava, my family, your parents, Luca—"

His jaw tightens at the name. Just once. Enough to tell the truth he won't ask for is already burning him.

"I know," he says. "That's why I'm not pushing. That's why I'm up here instead of downstairs saying something I can't undo."

He steps back—just enough to give me air. The retreat costs him; I feel it.

"I won't force you," he says. "To talk. To feel. To choose."

"But you want me to," I breathe.

"Yeah." No shame. Only longing. "I do."

The room feels too small. My skin too tight. My secrets too loud.

"I can't do this," I whisper. "Not with you looking at me like that."

"Like what?"

"Like you already know the ending," I say. "And you're waiting for me to confirm it."

Something in him softens. Breaks. Reforms into quiet acceptance.

He nods, surrendering. "Okay," he murmurs. "I'll stop looking at you like that."

We both know he can't.

I move past him, the blanket clutched like armor. My shoulder grazes his arm. A spark shoots through me.

He doesn't stop me. But his hand lifts—just slightly—as if to catch the last echo of me in the room.

Then drops.

I take the stairs slowly, pulse thundering.

Behind me, a floorboard creaks as he crosses to the window seat I abandoned. I can almost hear what he might whisper to the empty room.

Be brave, Mouse.

Truth: *He's closer than I ever meant him to be.*

Dare: *I walked away instead of choosing him.*

Confession: *When this breaks open, none of us walk away clean.*

30

THE ADVENT OF EVERYTHING

MIA

The house sleeps heavily.

Wrapping paper sags under the tree in crumpled drifts. The kitchen smells like ham and sugar, cooling in the dark. Upstairs, the walls hum with soft snores and shifting mattresses—familiar bodies sinking into Christmas Eve.

I should be asleep.

Instead, I'm sitting on the edge of my bed, fingers dug into the comforter, listening to my pulse trying to jack-hammer its way out of my throat.

The night won't let me go.

Jake's voice from the game. Luca's little body wedged between his knees.

That card in Luca's hand. *It says, "Be brave, Mouse."*

That's you, right, Mom? Mom says it to me the same way you used to say it to her.

I squeeze my eyes shut, but that only makes it worse.

And then upstairs.

The observatory.

The almost-touch.

That single tear he didn't wipe away.

My heart hasn't slowed down since.

I stand abruptly. The floor creaks under my feet, loud in the quiet. My room is mostly shadow, familiar shapes smudged into softer darkness. My gaze catches on the one thing that doesn't blur—the Advent calendar propped in the corner, leaning where I tossed it earlier.

It has followed me from room to room since I came home. Like a stray I pretended not to feed.

"Don't," I whisper to myself. "Don't do this."

Because I know exactly what I'm about to do.

Jake's voice from the motel presses in—Door 24, three years of letters, felt and cardboard and words he thought I'd read.

I kept everything from that night. I wrote to you. I loved you. I never stopped.

I swallow against the burn in my throat. "If they're not there," I murmur, "it hurts. If they are, it hurts worse."

Perfect no-win scenario.

I cross the room, anyway.

The cardboard is worn soft under my fingers, edges frayed, felt peeling at the corners. It's lived a life. I set it on the bed in front of me, legs folded underneath, like I'm twelve again and this is the most magical thing in the world.

Now it feels like a bomb.

My hand hovers over the little doors.

"This is insane," I tell the shadows. "He's wrong. Mom would've seen them. I would've. There's no way—"

My fingers land on the twenty-fourth square.

Our door.

I hold my breath and flip it open.

An envelope slides forward into my palm.

My name stares up at me in Jake's handwriting. Not teenage scrawl. Not shaky print. The looped J, the steady line of the S, the way he always pressed a little too hard on the down strokes.

The air leaves my lungs in a single, sharp exhale. "No," I whisper. "No, no—"

But my hands are already moving, tearing gently along the top.

Paper rasps. My heart howls.

Letter One – Truth (Age 18)

Mouse,

You'll probably find this on Christmas morning. I won't be there. Not because I don't want to be—God, you know I do—but because tomorrow is goodbye in a dozen small, stupid ways, and I don't trust myself to get any of them right.

Mom thinks I'm packing. Dad keeps saying this is a mistake. No one knows I'm in here trying to write something that won't fall apart when you read it. I just needed to leave you something before everything gets loud tomorrow.

Here's the truth: I should've kissed you that night in the snow. You probably don't think about it, but I do. That dumb penguin you made, the way you said it had "personality", you bumping my shoulder like you were trying not to smile.

I remember the cold getting through my gloves, your hair frosted at the ends, and then my stupid overbuilt snowman collapsing and you tackling me into the drift like it was my fault. You landed on my chest, and everything just . . . stopped. You didn't pull away. I didn't want you to.

I think about that one second more than I should—the one where it felt like maybe you liked me back, and I almost reached for you. I should've been brave. I wasn't.

If the stars look brighter tonight, it's because they're holding all the things I didn't say. Every one of them has your name on it.

Be good. Be brave. Be mine, even if I never earn the right to ask.

—J.

The words smear before I even finish them.

God. Sixteen. Frost in my hair, snow in my boots, pretending I wasn't watching him watch me. I can see it so clearly now—that exact, breath-held second—on the ground, my arm across his chest, his laugh still caught in his throat.

I remember thinking, *If he wanted me, this is where he'd show it.* So when he didn't reach, I convinced myself he didn't feel it.

But he did.

He felt it enough to write it down.

He felt it enough to carry that moment for years.

A strangled laugh slips out—wet, uneven. I press the letter to my mouth like I'm trying to stop time from moving any further, like maybe sixteen-year-old me can hear me begging her to just *look at him.*

I reach back into the narrow hollow behind the felt door. Another envelope grazes my fingertips.

Letter Two – Dare (Age 19)

Mouse,
They gave us nine minutes of signal and a plastic

tree strung with bullets instead of bulbs. It's midnight here, and cold enough to make your bones ring.

Torres—the guy who kept me laughing through boot camp—is gone. Quick, they said. No pain. That's a lie. I saw it. And when the noise stopped, all I could think about was your laugh. How it used to drown out everything bad.

I'm leaving this letter before I ship out again, same place as always. I tell myself you'll open it—pretend you'll roll your eyes, whisper something about how I'm still impossible.

So here's my dare: Dare me to make it home. Dare me to believe you still look at Orion and think of me. Dare me to keep living in a world that doesn't have your voice in it.

If you can do that, I'll keep my promise.

— J.

My hand flies to my mouth. *Torres.* I don't know him, but suddenly I feel like I do—because Jake does. Because Jake trusted him. Because Jake lost him.

I picture Jake somewhere dust-heavy and dangerous, a plastic tree wired with bullets instead of lights, someone beside him cracking jokes to keep him from breaking. And I was here. Safe. Stubborn. Making up stories about why he didn't try harder.

He asked me to dare him to live.

And I never knew he was asking.

My chest squeezes so tight it almost tips into laughter. The terrible kind. The kind that cracks.

I reach for the next envelope like my hands already know what comes next.

Letter Three – Confession (Age 20)

Mouse,

Another Christmas. Another borrowed room. I got home long enough to slide this into the calendar. I don't know if you look there anymore. If you don't, that's on me, not you. I just can't seem to stop writing.

Things feel different this year. Straighter. Like the noise around me keeps burning off until only the real stuff is left. Time does that out here—it strips things down. And somehow the part that stays steady is you.

Here's what I've been trying to say since we were sixteen and you built a lopsided penguin and told me it had "personality": It was never a phase. Never just friendship. You were the quiet between all the noise. The place I kept trying to get back to without realizing it.

I don't know where you are in your life now. I don't expect anything to come from this. But if you ever open it, even years from now, I want you to know the simplest version of the truth:

You were my once. My always. My north.

Be brave, Mouse.

—J.

Something inside me loosens, like a knot pulled free after years of pretending it wasn't there.

I lean forward, elbows on my knees, the letter folding against my chest as if pressing it tighter might keep everything from spilling out. His words echo in my ribs. Not teenage exaggeration. Not misread signals. Not the story I kept rewriting so it would hurt less.

He loved me.

Not lightly.

Not accidentally.

Not in passing.

Once. Always. North.

The simplicity of it wrecks me.

I think of all the nights I lay in unfamiliar beds—dorm rooms with thin walls, city apartments with radiator heat— telling myself I'd imagined the boy next door. That I'd inflated every look, every moment, every brush of his hand under those cheap plastic stars we stuck to the ceiling.

But I didn't imagine it. He was telling the truth . . . just somewhere I never thought to look.

A tear slips onto the page, then another, and I don't bother wiping them away. The ink blurs faintly, like it's waited years for me to finally understand it.

My fingers shake as they reach back into the hollow of the calendar. They brush one more envelope—newer paper, firmer edges. My name written with a steadier hand, like he'd grown into himself between the lines.

My stomach drops, already bracing.

I open it.

Letter Four – Promise (Age 21)

Mouse,

If you're reading this, I didn't stay long enough to say any of it out loud. You were still asleep—hair everywhere, blanket half off your shoulder. I stood there trying to decide if waking you would make leaving harder or easier. I didn't get an answer before the phone did it for me.

They moved up my deployment time. "Now," they said. No warning. No chance to explain the kind of night we had. No way to tell you that nothing about it was an accident. Not the kiss. Not the way you pulled me close. Not the way I carried you inside like I'd finally been handed the thing I'd been reaching for since the first snowman you built with lopsided arms.

Last night wasn't a mistake. It wasn't too much. It wasn't too fast. It felt like something that had been waiting on the edge of my life for years and finally stepped forward.

You told me not to forget again. I heard you. It cut deeper than anything that's ever been said to me. I wanted to tell you I wouldn't. I wanted to tell you I couldn't. But the words didn't come out, and then the moment was gone, and I was staring at a blank page instead of your face.

I tried to write a note. You probably saw the smudge. I meant to tell you where I was going. I meant to tell you what last night meant to me. I meant to tell you that I would've stayed if I could've taken you with me. But everything I wrote sounded either too small or too selfish, and I couldn't hand you something half-finished and call it goodbye.

So here's the closest I can get to a confession: Every road I've taken—every mistake, every detour, every place with a name you've only read on headlines—brought me back to you last night. I don't know what that means for you. I don't get to ask for anything. But I needed you to know what it meant for me.

If the universe gives me even one chance, I'll come home to you, and I'll earn the right to say the things I couldn't say this morning.

And if it doesn't—if this is the last thing you ever read from me—remember this:

*You weren't a moment, Mia. You weren't a mistake or
a night that got ahead of us.*

You were the part of my life that finally felt true.

My beginning, my middle, my always.

Be brave.

—J.

My breath stutters. My whole body goes strange—hollow
in the center, too tight at the edges. This is the letter I didn't
know I'd been bracing for. The one that rewrites everything I
told myself about that night. About him. About me.

He didn't disappear because it meant nothing.

He didn't leave because I was foolish or forgettable.

He didn't walk out without a word because he didn't care.

He tried. God, he tried.

I see it now—him standing over my bed, torn between
waking me and protecting me. The smudge on that blank
note. The pen dent where he'd started a sentence and buried it
before it could become a promise he wasn't sure he had the
right to make.

He left because someone else said, *Now*, and the universe
stole the rest.

My chest caves around the truth of it.

I press the letter flat against me, like holding it closer
might quiet the ache tearing through my ribs. But it doesn't. It
sharpens. It spills. It breaks open every lie I used to keep
myself upright.

*You weren't a moment. You were the part of my life that
finally felt true.*

It crushes something soft and stubborn in me—everything
I built on the belief that I'd imagined us, that I'd been
dramatic, naïve, a girl reading meaning where there
wasn't any.

But it was *real.*

To him, it was real enough to carry into a war zone.

Real enough to write into a calendar he hoped I'd open someday.

Real enough that he almost stayed.

My throat goes tight. My fingers shake.

I think of that morning—sunlight sliding across the sheets, the dent in the pillow where his head had been hours earlier. I remember lifting the scrap of paper with my name on it, stupidly hopeful, only to find it empty.

It wasn't empty. I just didn't know how to read what was missing.

I smooth the envelopes out on the comforter, side by side, like I'm laying down cards in a game I invented and then ran from.

Truth.

Dare.

Confession.

Downstairs, Harper called it, *Vintage Snowden Chaos.* Say something you've never said out loud. Be a good sport. Don't ruin Christmas.

I almost did.

Now I'm here with the advanced level—Jake Carter's deluxe edition—and apparently the universe isn't going to let me skip my turn twice in one night.

"Christmas Confessions," I whisper, my voice rough. "Fine. My deal this time."

If this were a round, if Harper was waving the deck at me and Luca was watching with those too-knowing eyes, this is what I should've said:

✳

Truth: *I was never the girl who didn't know. I knew. I felt it. In the snow, on the ice, under those stupid plastic stars. I just pretended I didn't because it was easier to survive if I convinced myself I imagined the thing I lost.*

Dare: *Tell him he wasn't the only one writing letters into the dark. That I built a whole life around not answering mine. That every time I told myself he chose silence, what I really meant was, I did.*

Confession: *There is a little boy down the hall who carries your nose and my stubbornness and thinks, "Be brave, Mouse" is just something his mom says when he's scared. He doesn't know he was the moment I stopped pretending you were a phase. You don't know you've already come home to me in the loudest way a person can.*

My throat burns. I press my knuckles to my mouth to keep the words from leaking out and finding him on their own.

Jake left me three years of honesty hidden behind felt and cardboard.

If this is my Truth, Dare, Confession, then the Promise has to be mine, too.

Promise: *I won't let him carry a lie he didn't choose. Not Luca. Not Jake. Not anymore. However this breaks, whatever it costs, I won't keep standing in the doorway pretending I don't see the life on the other side.*

My hand settles over the last envelope, the one that says, *My beginning, my middle, my always.* The one that rewrote every empty space I blamed him for.

"Be brave, Mouse," I whisper back to the page, to sixteen, to twenty-one, to the girl who invented this stupid game and then refused to play it.

This is my Christmas confession: *I'm done hiding.*

31

HARPER'S TRUTH

MIA

The stargazing room is the only place that hasn't tilted under my feet.

Everything else feels off—the hallway too bright, the kitchen too warm, the living room breathing too loudly. But up here, under the sloped ceiling and frost-bitten skylight, the air is the same thin, suspended kind it's always been. The telescope still leans toward the glass like it's ready to launch itself into orbit. The old plaid blanket waits on the window seat. The heater ticks like it's nursing a wound.

Luca sits cross-legged on the rug, surrounded by a debris of crayons. He's humming to himself, tongue caught between his teeth, dragging stars onto the page with the determination of someone trying to redraw the whole sky. Every few seconds he checks to see if I'm looking.

I am.

I nod.

I try to smile.

It barely lifts.

The letters sit in my pocket, edges pressing through the fabric like teeth. Four little ghosts. Four detonations I didn't know I'd been building my life around.

I thought he had forgotten me.

He never did.

I thought I was the only one bleeding.

I wasn't.

It's like realizing the roof you've slept under for six years has been missing the whole time.

Footsteps in the hall. A knock. "Snowden?" Harper's voice. "You in here?"

My reply scrapes out thin. "Yeah."

Harper steps inside—eyeliner smudged, hair twisted with a pen, hoodie half-zipped. One glance at me and the tease she's ready to throw evaporates.

She shuts the door. Looks at Luca, then back at me. "Hey, starboy," she murmurs. "Permission to enter the galaxy?"

Luca doesn't look up. "Only if you brought snacks."

She digs into her bag and pulls out a candy cane like she planned this entire interaction. "One certified astronaut fuel cell."

He beams. "You may enter."

He catches the candy midair without even aiming. My heart clenches the way it does every time he does something that feels like Jake.

Harper drops beside me on the window seat. Our knees bump. She takes one long look at my face. "You look like you just found out Santa's been running a Ponzi scheme."

A sound escapes me—half laugh, half injury. "Feels about that catastrophic."

She lets it fall. No coddling. No pity. Just presence. Her gaze flicks to the skylight. Snow smears across the glass in streaks, washing the sky to silence.

"There were letters," I say.

Her head turns slowly. "From him?"

I nod. Tension tightens my jaw until it aches. "Every Christmas. Door 24. Three years straight. He wrote to me and hid them in the calendar and I never—"

The sentence snaps. "I never opened a single one."

Something in Harper softens—not pity, just recognition. "What did they say?"

Everything. Every goddamn thing.

"That he should've kissed me that night in the snow. That he was scared to live without me. That he wrote to me from . . . " I gesture vaguely at the world beyond this one. "Over there. That I wasn't some teenage fling. That I was his once and always and North. That I wasn't a chapter—I was the whole damn book."

My voice breaks on *book*.

Luca hums louder, dragging a blue crayon with ferocity.

"I thought he walked away," I whisper. "I thought he forgot. I thought he replaced me and moved on and didn't look back." My throat burns. "And he was coming to this house every Christmas, writing to me, begging me in handwriting to see him."

"You didn't know," Harper says.

"I didn't look." It comes out too sharp, too loud. "I told myself we were over. I told myself opening Door 24 would make me pathetic. Turns out my pride cost us six years."

The guilt is a physical thing. A weight. A bruise blooming under the ribs.

"And now?" she asks.

"Now it's too late." My voice shreds. "He loved me that whole time, and I spent years hating him for abandoning me while he was literally leaving bread crumbs in felt, waiting for me to find them."

My chest twists. Hard.

I see his face in the motel—how he couldn't look at me when he mentioned the letters. I see the tear he didn't hide in the observatory. The way he held my hand like it belonged there.

God, I still want him. The wanting is the rot underneath everything else.

"There's more," I whisper.

Harper straightens. Zero blinks. Full alert.

I look at Luca. He's drawing a cluster of three large stars and one smaller one. My heart drops into my stomach.

"There's something else I never told him," I say. "About Luca."

His name cracks me open.

Harper stops breathing. Her gaze travels from his curls to his determined little mouth to the way he sits—legs folded, shoulders squared. Then she looks at me.

"Oh," she says quietly.

Tears surge up before I can stop them. "I thought I was doing the right thing," I choke. "He was gone. He was in danger. I had no way to reach him. I told myself dragging him into it when I didn't even know if he'd come back was cruel. That if I told him and he didn't want us, I'd break before he left."

"And if he did want you?" Harper asks, deadly soft.

"That was worse," I snap, voice cracking. "Because then he'd have something else tying him here. Another weight. Another reason to feel torn. I told myself I was protecting everyone—him, Ava, Luca, me."

"How's that going?" she asks flatly.

"Terribly." I wipe at my face, uselessly. "I'm drowning in a secret I convinced myself was noble."

Shaking, I say, "If I tell him now, I blow up everything.

He could be furious. He could demand everything. Or he could walk away because it's too much." My voice splinters. "I don't know which one terrifies me more."

"And if you don't tell him?" Harper says.

"Then I lie to my son forever," I whisper. "And to myself every time I look at him and see Jake's eyes."

The words taste metallic. Shameful.

Harper inhales, slow and sharp. "Mia, you aren't protecting anyone anymore. You're just clinging to silence because it's familiar. It's easier to hold a wound than to risk healing it."

I flinch like she slapped me.

Because it's true.

Because she knows exactly where to cut.

"You love him," she says—not a question. "And you're terrified he still loves you back, and if he does, then you don't get to pretend this was one-sided, or simpler, or safer than it actually was."

Tears spill again, faster now. I don't wipe them.

"I look at him and I can't breathe," I say. "The way he watched Luca skate. The way he held my hand. The way he kept that cocoa packet like it meant something. I still—" My voice breaks. "I still want him. And I hate that."

"Of course you want him," Harper says. "The man is terminally loyal and, unfortunately, hot. And you've been in love with him since before you grew actual hips."

A strangled laugh escapes me. It hurts.

"What if I tell him," I whisper, "and I lose him?"

"You already lost him," Harper says. "Six years ago. The question is whether you honestly want to lose him this time."

The truth detonates. Quiet. Total.

My eyes drift to Luca. He's holding up his drawing—three stars clustered tight, one small star tucked beside them.

"These are us," he announces. "They're friends."

My vision blurs. "They're perfect," I manage.

He beams and returns to his universe.

Harper stands, swinging her bag over her shoulder. She looks at me—sharp, loving, unyielding. "You don't have to be strong. Just brave."

The door clicks shut behind her.

Snow presses hard against the skylight. The heater ticks. Luca hums as he draws whole galaxies because he doesn't know the one in this room is about to shift. I curl my fingers around the letters in my pocket—the bend in the paper where I've gripped them too tight.

I don't say it aloud. I don't need to.

The decision is already there, heavy and done.

I'm going to tell him.

32

EXIT WOUNDS IN TINSEL LIGHT

JAKE

Christmas Eve looks perfect on paper.

Tree lit. Stockings straight. Presents lined up under the branches like they attended a briefing. Ava's touches are everywhere—garland fluffed, ribbons tied in the exact same bow, cocoa mugs waiting on coasters no one is allowed to actually put cocoa on.

Once, that order calmed me. Now it feels like staging. A set waiting for actors who never show.

I sit on the couch with a cooling mug in my hands, staring at the lights until they blur. Every ornament is in its assigned position, every strand of tinsel in compliance. And all I can see is a different tree in a different living room—Mia on a stool, laughing too hard as she drops the star, me fixing the bent tip with tape and pretending it was all part of the plan.

That tree was crooked and uneven and alive. This one looks right and feels wrong.

Since Mia came home, the silence between Ava and me has gone from easy to sentient. It waits in the corners, under the bed, between sentences. I've followed the checklist—wrap the gifts, show up for the parties, stand where I'm told in photos—but every time I blink, I see dark hair and a peppermint wrapper between someone else's fingers.

A five-year-old's laugh that sounds too familiar.

A motel room.

A tear in an observatory I pretended not to wipe away.

I set the mug down before my grip rattles it to the floor and push myself off the couch. My legs feel like I'm walking toward a debrief where I already know the report won't be good.

The bedroom light spills in a neat rectangle across the hall. Ava stands in the middle of it, back to me, already halfway through some project no one asked for. The weekender bag sits open on the chair, a contained explosion of sweaters and folded jeans. On the bed, she's sorting ribbons into strict little color lines—red, gold, silver.

Her version of triage.

"Ava," I say.

"Hmm?" She doesn't look up. "If you're here for the tape, it's in the top drawer. Again. Labeled. Like a civilized human."

"We need to talk."

Her hands still on the ribbon. The smallest pause, then an exhale through her nose. "You know that phrase should come with a hazard warning."

"It won't end well," I say. My throat feels raw. "But you deserve the truth."

That gets me her face. She turns slowly, like she already knows what's on the table and is just taking her time getting there. Her expression is smooth—too smooth. I've seen this version of her in hospital waiting rooms and at her parents'

Easter dinners when the conversation went off the rails. Controlled. Contained.

"The truth about what?" she asks.

"About me." My fingers rake through my hair, stalling for seconds I don't deserve. "About before you and I, and about what's been happening in my head since Mia came home."

There it is. Out. No way to pull it back.

Something moves in her eyes—relief, almost, folded into something harder. Like a test result she's been expecting finally came in.

"Mia," she says. Not a question.

I nod once. "I thought I could . . . manage it. Put it in a box. If I stacked enough plans on top—parties, holidays, lists —I figured eventually it would just . . . flatten."

"And how's that strategy working out for you?" she asks.

I huff out something that wishes it were a laugh. "It's not."

She folds her arms over her chest, hugging herself instead of me. "You don't think I've seen you?" she says quietly. "The way you look at her?"

My stomach twists. "Ava—"

"Don't." She holds up a hand, but there's no heat in it. Just tired. "That first day? In my parents' living room? You watched her like you'd been shot and were checking to see if you were still bleeding. I was standing right there, Jake."

I wince. The only thing to say to that would be a lie.

"And the gingerbread thing?" she goes on, a little sharper. "You two kept . . . circling. Like there was a joke, and you were the only punchline that made sense to each other. Everyone else was decorating houses. You were trying not to collide."

"It wasn't—"

"It wasn't subtle," she finishes. "I think the only accident here is how long we pretended not to see it."

She laughs once, short and cracked. "Honestly? I think everyone clocked it at the engagement party. You, staring down the bartender every time he made her laugh? That wasn't nostalgia. That was you trying not to put a target on another human soul."

She's not wrong. I remember that night too clearly—the way Mia avoided my eyes, the way I watched her, anyway.

I exhale, slow. "I won't lie to you. Not about this."

"Then don't." Her gaze doesn't waver. "Say it."

The air in the room gets dense. The distance between us feels measured in years, not feet.

"One Christmas Eve before I deployed again," I start, my voice lower, "she and I . . . stopped pretending we were just friends."

Ava's jaw tightens. Color fades, then rushes back. She doesn't speak.

"We kissed," I say. "And more than kissed. The next morning, they moved my orders up. I left without explaining. I tried to write a note. I didn't leave one."

Her fingers curl in the edge of the comforter until her knuckles go pale.

"The letters weren't after that night," I add, because it's all or nothing now. "They were from the years before—every Christmas I made it home. Three of them. I hid them in her Advent calendar. She never opened the doors."

"She knows now," she says quietly.

I blink. "What?"

"The letters . . . " Her gaze flicks past me. "She found them last night. Early this morning, technically."

Something in my chest lurches. The room tilts for a second. Of course she did. Of course it's tonight.

Ava swallows. "You two have been living in different versions of the same ghost story for six years," she says. "At least now you're both reading from the same page."

Guilt stings so sharp it's almost clean. I picture Mia in that old room with that old calendar, my handwriting in her hands. I picture tears I don't get to see.

"And this week," I go on, because I can't ask for mercy and still hold back, "at the motel . . . we kissed again." The memory flashes—her hand in my shirt, the way everything in me surged like a muscle remembering how to work. "I pulled back. It doesn't matter. The line didn't start there."

I stare down at my hands, flexing them like I can shake off the history baked into them.

"It started way before any of that," I say. "I've been in love with her longer than I know how to say. I thought I could build a life on top of it and eventually it would stop being true."

Ava takes that hit the way she takes all of them—upright, breathing, no dramatics. Just one long inhale, like she needs the extra air to hold the words.

"How long have you loved her?" she asks.

She looks away for a second, staring at the weekender bag like she's trying to remember why it's open.

"Timeline," she says suddenly.

I frown. "What?"

"Give me numbers," she says. "Not feelings, Jake. Those are unreliable."

I nod once. Orders. I know how to take those.

"You and Mia," she says. "That night. The one that wasn't *just friends*. That was . . . Christmas Eve. Six years ago."

"Yeah." I can still see the snow, her hair damp at the ends, the way she looked at me like I was something she'd already chosen. "Six years."

"You shipped out—"

"Christmas morning." I could tell her the time down to the minute.

She tracks it, eyes narrowing as she lines it up. "And Mia left town that May for college."

"Yes."

"You kept coming back for Christmases after that," she goes on. "In between deployments."

"Yes."

"And you and I . . . started whatever this is . . . " Her mouth presses together, then flattens into something like a smile that didn't quite make it. "About a year later."

"Yeah." I swallow. "About a year after that Christmas Eve." Gutted from silence, dumb enough to think starting over with someone kind and steady would fix the part of me still turned toward Mia's house across the street.

She nods slowly. "So you and I have been . . . us . . . for almost five years."

"Five," I confirm. The number tastes like someone else's story.

She glances over my shoulder toward the hallway, toward the rest of the house, like she's checking that it's still standing. "Luca's five," she says lightly. Too lightly. "He turned five in September."

Something sharp flickers at the edge of my thoughts. I shove it away before it can take shape. I've been doing that since I watched him skate, since I heard him say *Mouse* like he'd been born knowing how. There's a question I haven't let myself look at straight on. I don't look at it now.

"Yeah," I say carefully. "He's five."

She studies my face like she's looking for an admission I'm not giving. Then her gaze drifts past me, somewhere over my shoulder, like she's replaying old footage.

"December to September," she murmurs.

I watch the math land. Her eyes unfocus for a heartbeat, then snap back.

"Ava?" I step closer.

Her lips tremble. "I told myself it was just . . . habit," she admits. "Old history. That you'd grow out of it once we built enough new memories. If I made everything here perfect— every holiday, every plan, every plate in the cabinet in the right spot—eventually you'd look at me the way you look at her."

She glances toward the doorway, toward the tree I left glowing in the living room.

"But even my color-coded Christmas couldn't compete with what you have with her, could it?" she says, quieter now. "Messy and loud and . . . alive."

"Ava—"

"Don't apologize for finally saying it out loud," she cuts in gently. "Just don't pretend you didn't know. You've known, Jake. Since she walked back in. Probably since before you slid that ring on my finger and hoped it would act like a tourniquet."

She's not wrong about that either, and the shame of it hits hard.

"I didn't want to hurt you," I say. It sounds thin even to my own ears. "I told myself I could make the feelings line up later. That if I kept being the man you needed, the rest would . . . follow."

"You can't schedule your way into loving someone more," she says. "You can't spreadsheet your heart into compliance."

I scrub a hand over my face. "I told myself you were the right choice," I admit. "You are. You're smart, capable, and kind. You make things better just by walking into them. I thought if I built a life with you—this house, these traditions —I could outrun what I left with Mia. But every room I walk into, I still look for her first. That's not fair to you. Or her. Or anyone."

She flinches at that, like even the truth she expected still manages to cut.

Her eyes shine, but her chin stays up. "You should've told me."

"I know." The words scrape on the way out. "I kept thinking I could handle it. That I could be your fiancé and also . . . carry this thing with her quietly until it burned itself out. Like I could muscle through loving two people in different ways and somehow no one would get crushed."

"And?" she asks.

"And I was wrong," I say. "So wrong it's almost funny."

Ava moves then, walking around the bed to sit on the edge, leaving a space beside her. She doesn't gesture for me to join, but she doesn't push me away either.

"Can I ask you something?" she says.

"Yeah."

"When you picture the future—the real one, not the Pinterest board we've been living on—who's there?" Her voice is gentle, but it lands like a gavel. "When you think about bad days, or coming home from a deployment, or being old and cranky about the neighbors' music . . . who's beside you?"

The answer is instant and merciless. It stalls in my throat anyway.

I don't say anything.

That's enough.

She nods, like she's checking off a box. Her eyes close briefly, and when she opens them again, something has settled.

"You love her," she says. "Not like a ghost. Not like a mistake you wish you hadn't made. Like a fact. Like gravity."

My chest feels too small for my lungs.

"And she loves you back," Ava adds. "You know that, right? You both finally said it with your faces if not your mouths. I've seen people in love, Jake. I grew up with you. I know what you look like when you're trying not to touch something that already belongs to you."

I swallow hard. The room tilts.

Ava wipes at a tear with the heel of her hand, shaking her head like she's annoyed at herself for leaking. "I deserve someone who doesn't have to grind his teeth to get through loving me," she says, voice fraying. "And you deserve to stop pretending the person who makes you feel like yourself again is some kind of moral failure."

"I thought I could get over her," I say, barely above a whisper.

"You never tried to get over her," she replies, almost kind. "You tried to bury her. That's not the same thing."

Silence stretches, thick and humming. I can hear the heater kick on in the hall, the faint rustle of the tree in the draft.

"You know what hurts the most?" she asks.

I brace. "What?"

"You asked me to move into a life that was basically one big exercise in not saying her name." Her words are sharp, but her tone isn't. "Every choice you made—the town you stayed in, the nights you volunteered for extra shifts, the way you dodged certain streets—it was all about avoiding the person you actually wanted. And you still held out your hand and said, 'Come stand in this with me.'"

I close my eyes. There's no defense.

"I believe you didn't wake up thinking, 'How can I

wreck Ava today?',", she says. "I believe you were trying your best with what you had. But intent doesn't erase impact."

She turns away then, reaching for the weekender bag. The zipper rasps through the quiet, decisively.

"Ava . . . "

"I can't stay here tonight," she says, still focused on the bag. "I can't lie next to you in that bed and pretend there isn't someone else between us. I'm not that girl. I won't make myself into her."

"You don't have to go," I say, even though every part of me knows she does. "We can—"

"Please don't make this harder," she says, facing me fully now. Her cheeks are wet. Her posture is perfect. "You don't get to finally admit you're in love with my twin sister and then ask me to stay and drink cocoa under the tree."

The word hits like a physical blow. She grabs her phone off the nightstand, thumbs moving fast. A second later, it buzzes. She glances at the screen, then locks it.

"Dylan's on his way," she says.

Of course he is. Part of me is grateful. Part of me wants to tell him not to come within ten miles of the mess I made.

"Ava," I start, because there's so much I want to rewind and none of it is available. "If I'd handled this differently—if I'd told you sooner—"

"If you'd told me sooner, it still would've landed here," she says. "We just would've saved ourselves some time. Maybe I wouldn't have spent so long trying to peel parts of myself off and glue on pieces I thought you could love more. And maybe you wouldn't have wasted so much energy pretending you didn't already know exactly who you belonged to."

We stand there, a few feet and six years apart. The only

sounds are the heater and the faint muffled jingle of some neighbor's music outside.

"You're a good man, Jake," she says quietly. "You are. But you're not my future. And I'm not yours. I think we both knew that a while ago and were too scared to say it in case speaking it made it real."

I step closer on instinct. "I'm sorry," I say again, because it's the only thing left. "I am so damn sorry."

She nods, pressing her lips together. "I know," she says. "For what it's worth, I don't think you're the villain here. I think you're just a guy who tried to make the honorable choice without being honest about what his heart was doing. But that doesn't make this any less over."

She swings the bag onto her shoulder and walks past me. Her shoulder brushes my arm. It feels like a goodbye. At the doorway, she pauses, looking toward the living room—the tree, the stockings, the carefully arranged future.

"You should go find her," she says, still facing away. "Whatever this is between you and Mia? It already shattered us. Pretending it doesn't matter won't un-break anything."

The front door opens. Cold air cuts down the hall.

I follow her out onto the porch but don't reach for her. I've taken enough from her without asking.

Snow dusts the railings and the steps. The sky is a flat, heavy gray, sagging over the street. Dylan's truck idles at the curb, exhaust puffing in fat bursts. He steps out when he sees her, jaw tight, eyes running over her like he's counting injuries.

He takes the bag from her without a word and opens the passenger door.

Ava looks back at me once. No theatrics. Just a woman who finally decided she doesn't have to live in the smoke of someone else's fire.

"Merry Christmas, Jake," she says softly.

My throat burns. "Merry Christmas, Ava."

She gets in. The door shuts with a dull, final sound. Dylan gives me one long, measuring look, then circles the hood and climbs behind the wheel. The taillights flare red, then shrink, then disappear around the corner.

I stay there until the cold finds my skin through the thin cotton of my socks, until my fingers sting.

The life I built is gone. The script I've been following just burned.

Truth: *I'm done pretending I don't love her.*

Dare: *Face what comes next without running, lying, or burying the pieces.*

Confession: *When I pictured the future . . . Mia was already standing in it.*

33

FIFTEEN, SANTA, AND YOU

MIA

The cold hits first. Clean, biting, the kind of cold that hushes whatever chaos you're still carrying.

I shut the front door behind me and lean on it for a breath. Pine and smoke cling to the wood—childhood Christmas, safety, everything I don't feel anymore.

Luca's mitten slips into mine. "Come on, Mom! Santa!"

He's practically vibrating, a human sparkler in a red hat. His curls bounce as he pulls, unbothered by gravity or the weight in my chest.

"Slow down," I say, breath fogging. "He'll wait."

Unlike other things.

We reach the porch steps—and stop.

Jake stands at the bottom, shoulders dusted in snow, hands jammed in his coat pockets like he doesn't trust them not to shake. He looks like he hasn't slept in days. Or like sleep tried to come for him and he outran it.

When his eyes find mine, something in him softens. Breaks a little.

"Mia," he says, and my name sounds like an apology swallowed halfway.

"Jake." My voice is thinner than I want it to be. "It's . . . not a good time."

"Maybe not," he says quietly. "But I needed to see you."

Luca's delighted shout splits the tension. "Jake!" He barrels forward, mittens flapping.

Jake drops to one knee and catches him with a familiarity that shouldn't undo me—but it does. It always has. "Hey, little man." Jake's voice warms around the words. "Where to?"

"Santa! In the square! Come with us?"

Jake looks up at me. Snow clings to his lashes, melting down the tired edges of his face. "If your mom's okay with that."

"You don't have to," I say.

"Maybe not." A faint smile curves his mouth—tired, crooked, too honest. "But I'd like to see him try to out-jolly you."

It slips a startled laugh out of me. Tiny. Uncontrolled. Dangerous.

Luca grabs both our hands and pulls us down the walk-way, his joy filling the spaces we've both been avoiding. For a moment, the three of us move in sync—shadows overlapping on the snow like a memory that's been waiting for its moment.

Jake's thumb brushes the back of my hand as we walk.

A graze. A ghost. Definitely not an accident.

The question rises like a tide: *Am I really going to do this?*

The snow answers in soft yeses.

The silence between us isn't empty. It's crowded—with

things unsaid, truths circling the edges, the weight of every year we didn't speak.

The town square is lit like a snow globe someone shook too hard. Gold and white lights drip off lampposts, laughter swirls through the cold, and Christmas sweetness hangs heavy in the air.

It should feel festive. Instead, we're standing on a fault line.

"This place hasn't changed," Jake murmurs. "Still feels like it's holding its own heartbeat."

"You haven't visited?" I ask.

His smile tips ruefully. "Haven't been here since . . . us."

Us is a spark on dry tinder.

"All these years?" I press. "Not once?"

He shakes his head. "Didn't want to."

"Why not?"

He looks at the lights instead of me. "Because it wouldn't be the same without you."

My throat tightens. He keeps talking, softer now, like he's afraid the cold will steal the words.

"Remember the time I made you sit on Santa's lap? You were fifteen and furious at me."

I laugh before I can stop myself. "Mortified."

"You were radiant." His shoulder nudges mine. "And I was right. We were the last ones. No harm done."

"You're impossible."

"You loved it."

"Maybe."

He glances sideways, smiling gently in the way that used to unravel me. "It had just turned Christmas when it was my turn."

"You took forever," I tease.

"Do you want to know what I wished for, Mouse?"

But Luca bursts through the moment. "Santa's here!"

Jake's mouth curves, something knowing underneath. "He's always early. Dad never could resist the spotlight."

The way he says it makes something warm flicker under my ribs. A familiar expression flashes across his face—the one that came right before trouble, right before a dare, right before everything between us shifted.

God, I missed that look.

Darren—Santa—greets us like he's been waiting. His eyes soften when they land on me. Then on Jake. Then on Luca.

He knows something. Not everything. But enough that the air around us shifts a degree, like someone opened a door to a different kind of truth.

Luca clambers into his lap, all hat and mittens and breathless excitement. Darren leans in, gloved hand cupped to Luca's ear.

"Tell me what you're wishing for this year," he says, voice all jolly rumble with a seam of something real under it.

Luca whispers. I can't hear the words, but I don't need to. I see it land on Darren's face—surprise first, then understanding, then a sadness too kind to live out in the open.

Beside me, Jake goes very still. His hands disappear deeper into his coat pockets, shoulders tightening like he's bracing for impact he can't stop. I can feel him watching the two of them—his dad in the red suit, his son on that lap—and then, almost visibly, I feel him look away.

Not because he doesn't care. Because he cares too much. Because if he watches this moment straight on, it might knock him flat.

Darren reaches under the chair and pulls out a small red box. He presses it into Luca's hands with a ceremony usually reserved for crowns or rings.

"For your tree," he says quietly. "So you remember this wish."

Luca pops the lid before we even step aside. Nestled in the tissue is a red glass ornament, deep as cranberries and lit from the inside by every strand of light in the square.

One word curls across the front in white script.

Daddy.

The ground tilts. Just a fraction. Enough to rearrange my bones.

My fingers close over Luca's before the ornament can slip. The glass is smooth and cold and heavier than it has any right to be. For a second, I swear Darren's gaze is on us like a hand at my back—steadying, apologizing, blessing, all at once.

"Can we put it on our tree tonight?" Luca asks, looking up at me like he's already decided the answer is yes. His eyes are bright and hopeful, and so much like Jake's that it hurts to breathe.

I find my voice somewhere past the tightness in my throat. "Yeah, baby," I manage. "We can."

I slip the box closed again, tucking the ornament safely into my pocket before Jake can get close enough to read the word. He's still a few paces away, head tipped back, staring hard at the lights strung over the square like they're the only things holding him together.

He misses the fault line opening at our feet because he's busy surviving the sight of his father and his son in the same frame.

Time curls, stretches. The crowd thins. Music softens. Snow swallows footsteps. By the time we find a bench, Luca is half-asleep against my shoulder. Jake sinks down beside me, close enough that our coats brush when we breathe.

"You always said the last wish was the most important," he murmurs.

"You remember that?"

"Every year. Even when I didn't want to."

I smile, aching. "Looks like we made it to the last kid."

"Looks like we did."

He exhales, looking at the lights. "My wish that year, Mia . . . I wished for a way back."

The world tilts.

Just slightly.

Enough.

"I didn't know it'd take this long," he adds.

"You were always terrible with directions," I whisper.

"Only when I was trying to get somewhere that mattered."

My pulse skids. "You make it sound like you got lost on purpose."

"Maybe I did." His voice drops. "Every road looked wrong without you at the end of it."

"You don't get to say things like that anymore," I breathe.

"Then don't ask why I stayed away," he replies, low. "This is where I said it for the first time."

"Said what?"

He looks at me. *Really looks.* Firelight glints off the snow and catches in his eyes.

"I didn't tell you," he murmurs. "I asked."

My brow folds. "Asked who?"

His gaze shifts toward the gazebo—toward Darren in the red suit.

"Santa," Jake says softly. "I asked Santa if what I felt for you . . . was love."

My breath catches like it hit ice.

"I was fifteen," he goes on, voice thickening. "I didn't

know what to call it. I just knew when you laughed, my whole chest felt too small. I knew I couldn't breathe right when you looked at me too long. I knew nothing else in my world fit unless you were in it."

A stunned sound slips out of me. Barely a breath.

He swallows. "So I asked my dad—without knowing I was asking my dad—if that feeling meant I was already gone for you."

I stare at him, heat rising in my face despite the cold. "Jake . . . "

He shrugs one shoulder, helpless. "Guess he knew the answer before I did."

Luca stirs, half-asleep. "Can we stay with Jake tonight?"

Jake freezes, and my heart falls straight through me.

He looks at me, something fierce and breakable in his eyes. "It's just one night," he murmurs. "I've got the room."

I say nothing.

"It's late," he adds. "Come to the cabin. Just for tonight."

Harper's voice echoes in my ribcage: *You don't have to be strong. Just brave.*

I stand, brushing snow from my jeans. "Okay," I say quietly. "Yeah. Fine."

Jake exhales like something inside him finally unclenched. Then, he looks over to Luca. "Let me carry him."

"I got him."

I don't.

He reaches before I can argue, lifting Luca with a gentleness that breaks something inside me. Luca melts into him like he's been doing it forever.

We start walking.

The town glitters behind us.

The road ahead is dark and waiting.

Truth: *I didn't say yes because it was practical. Or because Luca asked. I said yes because I wanted to go. Because some part of me has been walking toward him for years.*

Dare: *Each step toward the truck feels like crossing a threshold I can't uncross. I take it anyway.*

Confess: *Not aloud. Not yet. But the truth is a live thing in my throat—and if Jake turns to me in the dark and asks anything real, anything at all, I won't be able to lie.*

34

NORTHLIGHT

MIA

The road shrinks as we climb—just two tire tracks cut through white, pines crowding close like they're keeping secrets. Headlights slice between trunks, catching on frost, on low stone walls I remember from a lifetime ago.

Jake drives like he always does in bad weather—steady, careful, reading the road the way he reads people. Hands loose on the wheel, shoulders tight. He hasn't said much since the square.

Neither have I.

Luca is dead weight in the backseat, hat askew, mouth parted. Every time we hit a bump, he makes a tiny sound and burrows deeper into the blanket. Jake keeps glancing at him in the rearview like he's memorizing each twitch.

My heart hasn't picked a rhythm since I said yes.

Yes, we'll go.

Yes, I'll walk into his space.

Yes, I'm done pretending I don't want to.

Ahead, the trees thin. A dark shape materializes between them as a cabin appears.

It's like the woods just . . . open. A small clearing, roofline cut against the dark, snow thick on the eaves. A chimney threads smoke into the sky. Warm light beads behind the front windows—like the house is lit from its own heartbeat.

My breath catches.

Not because it's cute.

Because I *know* this place.

Not in the, *I've-been-here* sense. In the, *Oh God, it's you* version. The shape of it. The way it sits against the line of trees. The angle of the hill behind it, sloping up to where the town lights used to look small enough to pocket.

Northlight.

Before I can grab the thought, a memory rises, sharp as cold air.

We were eighteen, wrapped in every hoodie we owned, the ancient truck protesting each turn as we climbed out of town.

The cabin hadn't been his then. It wasn't even really the point. It was just a warm square of light in the distance—the landmark I pointed to when everything else felt like it was sliding.

We parked at the top of the hill above it, engine ticking in the cold. Our breath fogged the cab; the radio hummed something soft and crackly. The stars were ridiculous—too many, too bright, like someone had overcommitted.

"It's not about the stars," I said, forehead against the glass. "It's perspective. When something's far enough away, your problems shrink."

Jake snorted. "Perspective. That what you call drag-

ging me out here in twenty-degree weather when sane people are inside with cocoa?"

"You're just upset I'm smarter than you."

He bumped my shoulder. "Not upset. Just trying to understand how staring at dots makes you profound."

I rolled my eyes, but the air between us felt thin and alive. "You feel something when you look up there. You can't deny it."

"Oh, I feel something," he said, shifting closer. Our sleeves brushed. "Not sure it's about the stars."

Heat crawled up my neck. I pretended to ignore him. Failed.

"You like it," I said.

His voice went softer. "Maybe. When everything feels like it's shifting, this makes it easier to breathe."

The duffel bag in his room. December 26th circled on his calendar. The future somewhere we couldn't see yet.

"Hey, Mouse?" he asked.

"Yeah?"

"When you're famous for decoding brains, don't forget this place."

I smiled at the windshield. "Only if you buy me a telescope."

"A telescope?" he scoffed. "Planning to name a star after yourself?"

"No." I nudged him back. "I want to see what you see when you look up there."

Something in him went quiet. Not empty. Focused.

"Then I'll find you one," he said. "Strong enough to find home from anywhere."

My throat did that tight, traitorous thing. "And you'll write?"

"I'll write," he promised, just like that. No hesitation.

"Even if it's just to tell you what the stars look like from the other side of the world."

I swallowed. "Then maybe I'll keep looking. So I don't miss you."

The cab held the words between us, bright and break-able. Outside, the cabin we now call Northlight glowed like a dot on a map we both pretended not to be drawing.

The truck bumps back into the present as Jake eases off the gas. Snow crunches under the tires; the porch lamp grows, haloing the steps in warm gold.

He cuts the engine. Silence drops thick and soft. For a second, neither of us moves.

"You bought it," I say, voice thin.

He looks at the cabin, then at me. There's a whole story in the way his mouth curves. "Yeah."

"How long have you . . . ?"

"A few years," he says. "Paperwork went through the year after my last long deployment." His hand tightens on the wheel. "It came up for sale, and I . . . couldn't let it be someone else's."

My heart stutters. "The hill. The lights. This is—"

"Northlight," he finishes quietly. "Our spot. Just . . . closer."

Our.

"And you and Ava . . . ?" I can't quite finish the thought. I don't want her ghost in this room I've carried in my chest.

"We had the rental by the school," he says immediately. "She never came up here." His gaze searches mine, making sure I hear it. "This place was always . . . "

Us.

He doesn't say it, but I hear it anyway.

Luca mutters in his sleep, fingers clutching for something.

The sound breaks whatever spell we're in. Jake's hand goes to the backseat, steady at Luca's shoulder until he settles.

"Come on," he says, voice gentler. "Let's get him inside before he turns into a popsicle."

I open my door. The cold hits first—sharp, honest. Snow squeaks under my boots. The cabin looks even more like a memory from out here, smoke threading into the dark, windows glowing amber.

Jake rounds the truck, opens the back door, and lifts Luca into his arms. Luca's head tips onto his shoulder, hat sliding back. Jake adjusts it automatically, thumb lingering at Luca's temple.

Something inside me twists hard. Still, I follow them up the steps.

The porch boards creak under our weight. Jake shoulders the door open, flicks on a lamp with practiced ease.

Warmth wraps around me.

Cedar and smoke and something that's just . . . *him*. The space is small but open, all wood and light and clean lines. A stone fireplace at one end, fire banked low but steady. Books stacked in uneven piles. A worn leather couch. No random decorative sign screaming, *LIVE LAUGH LOVE*. No trace of Ava's taste. No trace of anyone else's, really.

Just Jake.

My lungs work around it slowly.

He toes his boots off without jostling Luca and nods toward the short hall. "The bedroom's made up," he says. "He can have the bed. There's plenty of room for you too, if you want to stay in with him. I'll—"

"Where will you sleep?" I ask, because the couch is right there, and I hate that I already know the answer.

He huffs something like a laugh. "I've done worse than a couch, Mouse."

Relief and guilt braid tight in my chest. "Jake—"

"Later," he says, not unkindly. "Let's get him down."

I follow him down the hall. The bedroom is small and warm, lamplight turning the plaid quilt into something from an old Christmas card. The window looks out onto darkness and snow.

Jake lays Luca on the bed, careful hands undoing boots, easing off mittens. Luca flops once, mumbling about rockets. Jake smiles—just a twitch at the corner of his mouth—and tucks the blanket up under Luca's chin.

"Sleep easy, space ranger," he whispers, fingertips brushing Luca's hairline.

I stand in the doorway, every muscle trying not to give me away. Watching him tuck our son in feels more intimate than anything that's happened between us so far. Like walking in on a dream I never let myself have.

He straightens and turns, catching me mid-stare.

For a moment we just look at each other. No jokes. No deflection.

He's the one who looks away first.

I step into the room. Tug the blanket one millimeter higher. Press a kiss to Luca's curls. "I'll be right down the hall," I whisper, even though he's too far gone to hear.

Jake waits in the doorway, giving us space. When I move past him, the hallway feels too narrow. My shoulder brushes his arm. Heat zips through me at the contact.

"Come sit by the fire," he says, voice low. "You look like you're one thought away from shaking apart."

"I'm fine," I lie.

He doesn't argue. Just leads the way.

35

LETTERS, EMBERS, AND ALMOSTS

MIA

The fire's mostly ember now, a low orange glow more than flame. Jake tosses on a log, nudges it into place with the poker. Sparks jump, then settle. The light shifts, stretching farther across the room.

He nods toward the couch. "Sit. I'll make something."

"I don't need—"

"Mia." He glances over his shoulder, voice gentle but not asking. "Humor me."

I sit.

He disappears into the kitchen, moving like he's done this a hundred quiet nights in a row. Cupboard. Mug. Kettle. The soft clink of ceramic. I shouldn't know the shape of him in a kitchen this well. I do anyway.

I let my gaze wander because looking at the hallway feels dangerous.

No framed engagement photos. No forgotten earrings on end tables, no blush throw pillows. Just a mug on the table with a permanent ring, a stack of paperbacks on the floor, a sketchbook half-tucked under the couch.

Northlight isn't a love nest.

It's a held breath.

He comes back with two mismatched mugs and passes one to me, careful not to brush my fingers more than he has to.

Tea. Honey. Whiskey.

"Nothing fancy," he says. "But it's not the cheap stuff that tastes like bad decisions."

"Didn't peg you as a moderation guy," I say.

He tips his mug toward the hall. "Five-year-old sleeping down there. I'd like to be able to walk in a straight line if he needs something."

I picture Luca padding out, finding Jake zoned out on this couch, too far from us and everything he's finally letting himself want.

I wrap both hands around the mug. The heat seeps into my fingers, my wrists, the places that won't stop shaking.

"You're quiet," he says after a beat.

"You used to like that about me."

"I used to think it meant you were content." He watches the fire instead of my face. "Tonight it feels like you're trying to hold a door shut."

He's not wrong.

"It's safer than opening it," I say.

He lets that sit. The log catches slowly; one corner blooms into flame.

"I'm sorry about Ava," I add, the words scraping up my throat. "I keep thinking I should have . . . said something. Done something. So none of this—"

"She deserved better than what I gave her," he says quietly. "That's on me, Mouse. Not you."

"You were trying to be good," I murmur. "To everyone."

"Good men still wreck things." He takes a sip, winces. "I told her the truth. All of it. About you. About that night. About the letters. About how I've been trying to live in the middle and pretending that was honest."

Letters hits like a pebble thrown at glass. Doesn't shatter anything. Just makes a crack.

"I found them," I say.

His head turns. Slowly. Carefully.

"Door 24," I go on. "Last night I ripped the calendar apart like maybe time had a loophole."

He blows out a breath, like he's been holding it since the observatory. "Mia . . . "

"I read everything," I say. "The snowman. Torres. That plastic tree. The way you left that morning." My voice thins. "I walked around for six years furious that you just . . . vanished. Like it cost you nothing. And the whole time you were—"

"Writing to you from the other side of the world," he finishes, rough. "I know. I used to picture you rolling your eyes at the metaphors."

"I never opened the calendar," I admit, shame rushing in hot. "I didn't even know there was anything inside. I told myself opening it would make me pathetic—like I was still hoping for something that wasn't real. If you cared, you would've said it out loud. That was my rule." I swallow hard. "Turns out the coward wasn't you."

"Hey." His voice cuts through, low and firm. "Don't do that."

"Do what?"

"Turn every angle so you're the villain." He shifts closer, mug balanced on his knee. "I hid instead of speaking. You shut a door that looked empty from where you stood. We were two idiots trying not to bleed on each other and still managing to leave marks."

A broken little sound escapes me. "That's one way to put it."

His mouth twitches. "Not the poetic version?"

"There was plenty of poetry," I say. "You really committed to the stars. You called me your 'once and always and North.'" My chest tightens around the words.

He groans and lets his head fall back against the couch. "Of course you'd quote me."

"You don't get to be embarrassed now."

His eyes close. When he opens them again, they're brighter, unguarded in a way I remember from high school trucks and almost-kisses.

"You weren't supposed to find those while I was engaged to your sister," he says.

"I wasn't supposed to be raising your son alone," I fire back.

The sentence lands between us like a dropped match.

We both go still.

His gaze locks on mine. The room shrinks down to fire-light and the sound of my own heartbeat.

"Mia," he says, barely sound. "What are you saying?"

My hand shakes around the mug. I set it down before I baptize his floor in hot whiskey tea.

"I've been carrying something by myself for a long time," I say, echoing the words from the game without hiding behind Zac Efron this time. "It's heavier than I thought it would be."

The muscle in his jaw jumps. "Let me carry some of it."

"You don't even know what it is yet."

He turns his whole body toward me, forearms planted on his thighs, hands open. "You've been holding up a life meant for two people," he says quietly. "If I drop what you hand me, that's on me. But I can't stand here and watch you fold under it alone."

The simple sincerity of it slices something open in my chest.

"Is it about Luca?" he asks.

The question hits like a physical thing.

The fire pops. The heater ticks. Outside, wind scrapes along the eaves. Inside, everything in me presses against my skin like it's trying to get out.

"I'm not asking for a dossier," he adds quickly, palms up. "I'm not trying to corner you. I just—when he said that thing at your parents'—"

"Be brave, Mouse," I whisper.

His eyes close briefly, pain cutting through his features. "Yeah. That."

"He repeats everything," I say. "Mom's stories, Harper's oversharing, the internet. He collects phrases like Lego bricks."

"Maybe." His gaze meets mine again. There's no accusation in it. Just ache. "But when he said it, something in here" —he taps his chest once—"shifted. Like a camera finally focusing."

I stare at the pattern in the rug because looking at him feels like stepping off a cliff. "Jake . . . "

"You don't owe me absolution," he says. "Or a second chance. Or an explanation that rips you open if you're not ready. I just—" He swallows, like the next part hurts going past. "I just don't want you breaking yourself trying to protect me from something I'm already standing in."

One tear slips out before I can stop it. Then another. Once they start, it's over.

He sees. Of course he sees.

He moves in slow increments, like he's trying not to

startle a skittish animal. One shift closer along the couch. Then another. He waits until I don't flinch before he lifts a hand.

His fingers settle against the side of my neck, thumb resting just under my jaw. Not grip. Not claim. Just a point of contact.

"Mia." His voice is soft but anchored. "You don't have to unload everything tonight. You don't even have to say the words out loud. But you need to know this."

He waits until my eyes drag up to his.

"I'm here," he says. Each word lands heavy. "I'm not going back to Ava. I'm not shipping out. I'm not hiding behind blank notes and numbered doors. Whatever comes next, I'm in it. With you. Even if it means listening to every way I failed you."

My exhale stutters. "You might change your mind."

His thumb brushes away a tear like it has some personal vendetta. "I've had nine years and three continents to change my mind about you," he says. "Didn't take."

Something inside me tilts hard.

"I thought I was protecting you," I whisper. "By keeping you out of it."

His mouth twists. There's hurt there, yes—but also something unbearably tender. "You've been standing in a burning house and shoving everyone else out," he says. "Meanwhile, you locked yourself inside and called it noble."

"I wasn't ready," I say. "For what it would mean. For what you'd say."

"I know." His hand slips up into my hair, fingers resting at the base of my skull. Not pulling. Just holding. "You don't have to be ready, Mouse. Just honest."

The last of my grip on myself slides.

I lean into him—not gracefully, not like a movie, a slow

collapse toward the one place that has always felt like *center.* My forehead finds the angle where his neck meets his shoulder. His arm folds around me as if waiting for the command.

My hands bunch in the front of his sweatshirt. His heart thuds against my palms, strong and erratic, like mine.

We sit like that. Fire. Heater. Wind. His breathing under my ear.

I feel his lips press into my hair. A quick, reverent touch, gone almost as soon as it lands.

"Truth," he murmurs against my crown. "I've been in love with you my whole damn life."

The words move through me like heat after a long time cold.

"Dare," he adds, a little rougher. "I'm done pretending *that* isn't true."

I pull back an inch, eyes searching his. "Confession?" I ask, because of course I do.

His gaze steadies, bracing. "Confession," he agrees.

"I'm terrified," I say, "of what happens when I stop lying. Of who I hurt. Of what you'll see when you look at the last six years and realize what I kept from you."

He doesn't flinch. "Okay."

"Okay?" I echo. Ridiculous. Not enough.

"Okay," he repeats. "You're terrified. That's allowed. I'll be terrified with you." His thumb traces the line of my cheek slowly. "I'm not asking you to stop being scared, Mia. I'm asking you to stop running away from me because of it."

Something that's been knotted under my ribs since I stared at a plus sign on a stick loosens a fraction. There's still a boulder. There's still a cliff. But there's also a rope.

"Not tonight," I say.

His brows pull together. "Not . . . telling?"

"Not detonating," I clarify. "I need one night where the

world doesn't tilt. Where Luca just sleeps and we just . . . exist. I'll tell you. I will. I just—" My throat closes for a second. "I need to catch my breath first."

Disappointment flickers across his face—real, sharp, gone. He nods anyway.

"One night," he says. "No explosions. Just . . . sleep."

"Just sleep," I echo, trying to believe it.

"You take the bed with Luca," he says. "I'll take the couch. I'll pretend I don't notice every time I hear you shift down the hall."

A startled laugh coughs out of me. "Don't get sentimental, Carter. Might tarnish your taciturn recluse image."

"Pretty sure that died the second he demanded I be his designated fun fact repository," he says.

The way he says *he* cracks something open all over again.

I stand before I can do something like straddle his lap and confess my entire soul. My knees wobble; his hand hovers near my elbow like a spotter who's trying not to touch.

"I should check on Luca . . . "

"Yeah." He leans back, giving me space. "I'll put the fire down and try not to run through every scenario where you change your mind about telling me tomorrow."

"That sounds deeply healthy," I deadpan.

He huffs a laugh, but his eyes stay locked on mine. "Hey, Mia?"

I stop in the doorway, pulse tripping. "Yeah?"

His voice drops, low and unguarded. "Thank you for coming tonight. You could've walked away. You didn't."

My fingers curl into the wood, holding me up. "Truth?"

His nod is slow. "Truth."

"I didn't say yes because it made sense," I admit.

His grip tightens around his mug. "Then why?"

My throat goes tight—but the words come anyway, soft

and unguarded in a way that terrifies me more than any confession I've made tonight.

"Because every part of me wanted to walk in here," I say. "Because it's you. And wanting you has never once been logical."

Jake's breath catches. His eyes—God—his eyes go soft and stunned all at once, like I just put something breakable and holy in his hands.

I keep going, because I'm reckless or brave or both.

"And because the second you opened the door," I whisper, "I remembered what it feels like when wanting you doesn't feel like a mistake."

He doesn't speak.

Doesn't move.

Doesn't even blink.

He's just *there*, looking at me like the truth rearranged the room.

Heat crawls up my throat. If I stay, I'll say the rest—the *dangerous* part, the part I'm not ready to survive.

So I turn—one heartbeat, two—before I can talk myself into more.

—

The bedroom is dim and faintly golden. Luca has taken over most of the bed, limbs thrown in all directions, curls a riot on the pillow. One hand is open like he fell asleep mid-wish.

I stand there a second and just look at him. Every piece of him hurts a little: the line of his nose, the pattern of his lashes, the way he talks in his sleep.

The letters in my pocket feel like they weigh a pound each. The secret in my chest weighs more.

I slide under the covers and curve my body toward his. He immediately shifts toward me, nose scrunching, then relaxes again, breath evening out. My palm finds the space between his shoulder blades and rests there.

"Be brave, Mouse," I hear in two voices at once—one from a truck cab full of stars, one from a living room full of plastic snow.

Down the hall, the couch creaks. A soft thud. The whisper of a blanket. The cabin settles.

I try to match my breathing to Luca's. It works for maybe three seconds before my brain starts sprinting—through letters, through nine missed Christmases, through the way Jake looked at me when I said I wanted to be here.

At some point, the couch creaks again. Footsteps pad down the hall, careful.

A shadow fills the doorway.

"Just checking you're both still here," Jake says, voice a low scrape. Like he's talking to the dark more than to me.

"I'm awake," I murmur. "Barely."

He hesitates. I can feel it, like a shift in air pressure.

"Couch is giving up," he admits. "Didn't mean to wake you."

"You didn't." I swallow. "You don't have to stand there like a horror movie extra."

Very soft laughter. "Didn't want to intrude."

I pat the empty space on the other side of Luca before my sanity catches up. "You're already in the house, Jake. Damage done."

"Mia . . . " His name for me this time is all warning.

"Top of the covers," I say. I have to draw a line some-where, even if it's made of hope and bad choices. "So you don't fold yourself into origami and I don't lie here wondering if you've paralyzed your spine to prove a point."

There's a long, suspended second.

Then the mattress dips opposite me. The blanket tugs as

he eases onto the very edge, careful not to jostle Luca. He stays on top of the quilt, one arm folded under his head, the other hovering uncertainly in the space between them.

"This okay?" he asks the ceiling.

"No clue," I whisper. "But it's what we're doing."

Luca sighs in his sleep and immediately rolls toward the new heat source, flinging an arm across Jake's middle like this is old habit. Jake goes rigid.

I hear his inhale, then the long exhale he forces out.

The three of us lie there in the dark, bodies not exactly touching and somehow touching everywhere. The cabin hums around us—old wood, quiet pipes, the distant tick of baseboard heat.

My eyes sting.

Truth: *I stepped into the cabin born from a place that started as ours, became his, and somehow feels like home for all three of us . . . even though I keep pretending it can't be.*

Dare: *Tomorrow, I hand him the last piece and let our story break in the honest direction.*

Confession: *I don't know if I'm more afraid he'll fall apart . . . or that he'll stay standing and walk away.*

36

FIRST LIGHT
JAKE

Heat is the first thing I feel.

Not from the baseboards or the dead fire, but from two bodies pressed in close. One small, all elbows and soft snores. One longer, curved toward my side like she forgot how to sleep any other way.

I don't move.

I lie there and let memory click into place.

Northlight.

Christmas Eve.

Her voice drifting into the doorway, telling me the couch didn't need to be a martyr.

Luca rolling into me the second I laid down.

Mia falling asleep on his other side, hand near his back like she was keeping watch even in her dreams.

That's the last frame I remember.

At some point in the night, things shifted. Luca sprawled diagonally across the mattress, one foot lodged against my hip. Mia drifted toward the space I left, head landing on my upper arm, fingers tangling in the hem of my shirt like her body didn't trust me not to vanish.

I'm still on top of the quilt, one arm extended over Luca to keep him from hitting the floor. I must have moved on instinct, bracing the edge. She must have followed without waking.

A sharp pull goes through my chest.

I've pictured her beside me in a hundred rooms—cramped barracks, bare rentals, the back of a transport plane when I couldn't sleep. None of those versions were this: all of us fully clothed, kid between us, no violins.

Just rightness.

Just inevitability.

Don't disappear, I think, staring at the ceiling. *Not this time.*

Luca kicks in his sleep, mumbling about rockets and syrup. His heel clips my thigh. I smother a laugh and let my free hand rest lightly between his shoulders.

I have exactly zero rights to this. To him. To her. My body has not gotten that memo. It's already taken a position: her on one side, him on the other, me between them and whatever comes next.

Easy, Carter.

I force a slow inhale. Exhale. My brain starts making lists because that's what it knows: call my parents, talk to hers, logistics with Ava, the house, the cabin, the job. That track feels familiar.

What doesn't is the fact that a small, sleeping five-year-old might be my son.

Mia shifts. Her grip on my shirt tightens, thumb brushing once against my ribs. Then she goes still again, lashes fluttering as she climbs toward awake.

Her gaze lands on the ceiling, then on Luca, then on where her cheek is resting on my arm.

"Hey," I say quietly. "Merry Christmas."

She blinks like the words have to travel from the doorway to her ears. "Already?" she whispers, voice rough.

"Been 'already' for a while," I answer. "You two went down hard."

Color rises in her face as she takes in exactly how all three of us are arranged. She lifts her head an inch, then stops, like she's afraid moving too far will crack something fragile.

"Sorry," she murmurs. "I didn't mean to—"

"To sleep?" I shift my arm just enough to give her more room without letting it fall away completely. "You can do that here. It's allowed."

A tiny huff escapes her. Almost a laugh. Almost not.

She pushes up on an elbow, scrubbing at her face with the back of her wrist, hair falling forward. Her shirt's skewed at the collar; she tugs it straight like she'd rather fix cotton than make eye contact. The completely ordinary gesture hits me harder than anything else.

"How's your arm?" she asks suddenly. "You're going to say fine, and it's going to be a lie."

"If this is what it aches from, I'll take it," I say.

Something in her expression softens. Not forgiveness. Something like understanding.

She notices the blanket half off Luca and automatically tugs it up under his chin. His mouth moves around a dream word. He rolls toward her, then back toward me, like he can't decide which orbit to choose.

Our eyes meet over his curls.

A lot lives in that look—gratitude, terror, guilt, longing. None of it named yet.

"I should . . . " She jerks her chin toward the doorway. "Bathroom. Coffee. Something upright."

"Okay." I hold her gaze. "Just . . . go slow. I'm not done looking at you."

Her face goes bright red all at once. If the world were fair, that would be funny. It's not. It's lethal.

She bolts.

The second her weight leaves the bed, cold slides in. I try not to react like someone yanked an IV.

As soon as I hear the bathroom door click, I ease my arm out from under Luca, settle him in the middle of the mattress, and slip off the edge. He sighs, flips to his other side, still somehow taking up ninety percent of the room.

I trade my T-shirt for a sweatshirt, set the coffee going, and open the curtains an inch. Gray morning, slow snow. The kind of quiet that feels like it's waiting.

By the time she comes back, the cabin smells like caffeine and toast from somewhere in my past. She pauses at the end of the counter, fingers wrapped around a mug like it's the only thing keeping her here.

Her hair is twisted up, one damp curl escaping by her ear. The sweatshirt she slept in hangs wide at one shoulder. She doesn't seem to notice.

"You have actual food," she says, eyeing the open fridge like it just confessed a crime. "Eggs. Bread. Produce that isn't in a can."

"Rations," I correct. "Eggs, bread, cheese that might be fine. Peak elite-operator cuisine."

She snorts. A real sound. Quick. "And here I thought you were living on nostalgia and bad coffee."

"Don't knock bad coffee," I say. "It got me through more nights than I care to admit."

She leans a hip against the counter, studying me as if

she's trying to reinstall the version of me she thought she knew. "When did you start staying out here?" she asks.

"Whenever I could," I admit. "After I bought it. Between drills, after rotations. When town felt too full."

"Full of what?"

"Expectations," I say. "Ghosts."

She absorbs that in silence. The coffee maker gurgles. Snow taps the window. The cabin feels like it's holding its breath with us.

"Mia, I just need you to know, Ava and I both knew it was over. I just finally stopped pretending I could build a future while pointing at someone else."

"That doesn't stop it hurting her," she whispers.

"I know." I make myself hold her gaze. "I'm not asking you to excuse any of it. I just don't want you thinking I'm trying to live two lives at once. I chose. I should've done it sooner."

Her shoulders drop a fraction, then hitch again like something heavier just climbed on.

"You should probably hate me," she says, knuckles white around the mug. "For how messy this is. For what it cost her. For what it cost you."

"I don't hate you," I say, immediately. "I hate the years. I hate that we kept choosing fear over truth. I hate that somewhere between fifteen and now, we both learned to expect the worst version of each other."

Her lips press together, fighting tears. Luca mutters in the bedroom, says something about comets. We both pause, listening. He quiets again.

"He's going to wake up and ask about Santa," she says, voice thin. "And pancakes. And I'm standing here like I forgot how to breathe."

I step around the counter, slow enough she can stop me.

She doesn't. I leave a half-step between us, close enough she has to feel the heat coming off me, far enough not to crowd.

"What's going on in there, Mouse?" I ask softly.

She flinches. "Don't call me that."

"Why not?"

"Because it makes me want to tell you," she says. "Everything."

"Maybe that's not the worst thing," I say.

"It is if the truth breaks you," she snaps—not at me, exactly, but at the universe for lining us up like this. "This isn't some bar confession. It's my entire life. It's his entire life."

She nods toward the bedroom door.

"Then let me help hold it," I say. "I meant what I said. I'm done running. I'm done lying. I'm done letting you do all the carrying."

Her shoulders start to shake. Not big sobs. Small tremors, like something inside her is cracking along old fault lines.

"Mia." I move closer, enough that my hands could fit on her arms if she lets me. "Look at me."

She does, finally. Her eyes are wet and fierce at the same time.

"You remember the high rock?" she asks. "At the creek?"

"Yeah."

"You'd jump first," she says. "Every time. Make it look easy. I should've known you'd be the one person I couldn't bring myself to jump toward."

"To tell what?" I ask, even though some part of me already knows.

Her fingers twist in the hem of her sweatshirt, like she needs something to anchor them.

"I told myself I was protecting everyone," she says. "You. Him. Ava. Your parents. Mine. The whole town, like I was some kind of human dam." Her laugh is small and vicious, aimed at herself. "But mostly, I was protecting myself from watching you look at me and decide we were too much. Too late. Too wrong."

The cabin seems to narrow. The only sound is the heater's tick and the hum of my own pulse in my ears.

"Mia," I say. It comes out like a prayer and a warning.

She drags in a breath. "Luca is yours," she whispers. "He's always been yours."

Everything in me goes quiet.

The heater clicks off. The fridge hums. A log in the dead fire shifts.

All I hear is that sentence, replaying behind my eyes.

Luca is yours.

He's always been yours.

My throat works. Nothing moves out.

How long have I known? Some part of me probably started putting it together the first time I heard him laugh. The first time he echoed a phrase I said years ago like it lived in his bones. The first time Ava said *December to September* and went quiet.

Knowing and being handed the truth are not the same thing.

"How long have you known?" I manage. My voice sounds like it belongs to someone a room away.

"After you left. I was late. Then I wasn't. Then it wasn't hypothetical."

Six years.

"How many people know?" I ask.

"My parents," she says. "Harper. That's it."

"You never—" I have to unclench my jaw to get the next part out. "You never tried to reach me."

"I tried," she says, and her laugh this time is poisonous. "I wrote your name in a dozen emails I never sent. I checked headlines so much the news apps started sending me alerts. I stood in your parents' living room while your mom cried over you at the tree farm, and I was hiding the fact that her grandkid was on the way."

Tears spill over. She lets them fall.

"I told myself you deserved to focus on staying alive," she whispers. "Not on some girl who might not want you anymore and a baby you didn't ask for. I told myself if I told you and you did want us, I'd be responsible for making you feel torn between here and there, between us and everyone you were trying to keep breathing. I didn't know how to live with that kind of fear on purpose."

I grab the edge of the counter behind me harder than I mean to. The pain in my hand is the only thing that keeps me anchored.

"You thought I wouldn't have wanted him," I say. Not accusing. Just naming the wound.

"I thought you wouldn't get to know him," she corrects, voice shaking. "And I didn't know if I was strong enough to survive you loving him and then dying, anyway. I didn't know how to walk around with that kind of grief loaded in advance."

I close my eyes for half a second.

Images flash like a slideshow I didn't know I'd been compiling:

Luca wobbling on the ice, reaching for my hand.

Luca at the Christmas market, standing on tiptoes behind the folding table, smearing icing everywhere during the "official" gingerbread contest while vendors pretended not to judge us.

Luca at the rink rail, shouting planet facts with the confidence of a kid who thinks he can out-talk NASA.

And Luca on my dad's lap, small fingers curled around the red ornament my dad had slipped Luca like it was some heirloom meant just for him.

Every moment I shoved into the "impossible" box.

None of this was impossible.

None of this was hypothetical.

"Mia." My voice is ruined now. "I missed everything."

Her face folds. "I know."

"His first word," I say. "His first steps. First time he saw snow. Every Christmas he asked about the sky, and you had to answer alone."

"I know," she chokes. "You're allowed to hate me for that. I do."

"I don't hate you," I say, because that's the only thing I can say with absolute conviction. "I hate that we were both drowning and convinced letting the other one in would make it worse."

A wild sound escapes her—somewhere between a sob and an exhausted laugh.

"You make it sound inevitable," she says.

"Feels like it," I answer. "Like every bad turn still kept pushing us back to the same spot."

She wraps her arms around herself. Her next words are so small I almost miss them.

"If you want to walk away," she says, "I'll let you. If this is too much, or too late, or you decide I'm too much of a coward to forgive, I'll sign whatever you want. Say whatever you need. I won't let you feel trapped."

There it is. The real fear. Not my anger.

My absence.

I let go of the counter and cross to her in two strides. I don't grab. I just step close enough that she has to tilt her head back to keep looking at me.

"Do I look like I want out?" I ask, rough.

"You look like I just told you the ground is lava," she says.

"That's accurate," I admit. "But I also feel like somebody just told me the kid who keeps putting his hand in mine is my son and I'm trying not to fall to my knees about it."

Her eyes blur again. She shakes her head like she doesn't know what to do with that.

"I'm not okay," I say. "I'm not neat or calm about missing five years. I'm not pretending it doesn't gut me that you did this alone." I swallow. "It hurts, Mia. In every place I didn't even know I had."

She flinches. I hold up a hand before she can start blaming herself all over again.

"But," I add, and the word feels like stepping onto a bridge instead of off a ledge, "none of that changes this: I would've wanted him. I still want him. I want the scraped knees and the midnight fevers and the dumb school projects. I want the parent-teacher conferences and the dinosaur phases and the way he looks at a sky full of stars like it owes him answers."

The tears spilling down her face don't stop. They shift. Less shame. More grief.

"You missed his first word," she says, like she owes me every cut. "It was *up*. He'd stand in his crib and yell it until someone came. You missed him swearing the vacuum was an evil robot. You missed how he used to clap every time someone turned on the porch light because he thought it was magic."

Something in my chest actually aches, like a pulled muscle.

"Tell me," I say. My hand finds her arm, thumb moving

back and forth once, twice. "Tell me everything. We have time to catch up."

Her face crumples. For a second, I think she might drop. "I don't know how to do this with you," she says. "I only learned how to do it without you."

"Then we start now," I say. "Badly. Messily. Together."

She stares at me like she's trying to find the trapdoor. "You're allowed to be angry with me," she insists, one more time, like it's a debt she needs collected.

"I am angry," I say. "I'm furious you thought so little of my capacity to love you that you made this call alone. I'm furious at the version of me who made you doubt I'd stay. I'm furious at every younger version of us that chose silence instead of one terrifying conversation."

Her gaze drops.

"And I still don't want out," I finish. "If anything, I want further in. On his life. On yours. On ours."

The cabin holds the words like they matter.

From the bedroom, the faint rustle of blankets. Luca rolls, mutters about reindeer. We both go still, listening. He settles again.

When I look back at her, something has shifted. Not fixed. Just decided.

She steps into me so fast it knocks my balance for half a second. Her forehead lands against my chest. Her hands fist in the front of my sweatshirt.

I catch us both automatically, arms wrapping around her, palms spreading between her shoulder blades. She fits there like she's been fitting there since she was fifteen, and I just didn't get to hold her this long at a time.

"I'm so sorry," she whispers into the cotton. "For all of it. For making you miss him. For making you think I didn't want you. For choosing silence because it felt safer than asking you to stay."

My hand finds the base of her skull. My nose brushes her hair. "I'm sorry too," I say. "For leaving you with nothing. For making you guess. For being such a coward at eighteen that it set a pattern we're still crawling out of."

Her shoulders shake. I hold on.

We stand like that until our hearts stop trying to sprint out of our ribs.

Eventually, she tips her face up, eyes red, mouth unsure.

"What now?" she asks. "We can't just . . . pretend. We can't walk into my parents' house like we didn't just light the last six years on fire."

"We don't pretend," I say. "We just don't tell every person in town before we tell the one who actually deserves the truth first."

Her eyes widen. "Jake, he's five."

"And sharp," I say. "He already feels something. Kids know when there's a missing piece even if they don't have the word for it."

She swallows. "What if I blow up his world?"

"What if you finally make it make sense?" I ask gently. "What if all the tiny questions in his chest finally line up?"

Her fingers twist in my sweatshirt again. "I don't know how to say it."

"I'll start," I say. "You jump in when you can. Like always."

She searches my face, looking for doubt. I let her find the fear, because it's there—but I make sure she also finds the part of me that's already moved.

"So . . . we tell him today," she says slowly, "after presents. After my mother is drugged by carbs. After he's not vibrating like a hummingbird."

"Today," I confirm. "No more Christmases where we all act like we don't see what's right in front of us."

She nods once, like signing a contract. Then, she leans her forehead against mine for a heartbeat, eyes closing.

"Be brave, Mouse," I say before I can stop myself.

This time, the nickname doesn't make her flinch. Her mouth curves, small and shaky.

"I'm trying," she says.

Feet thump against the bedroom floor. A yawn. The squeak of the door.

We step back, not guiltily—just enough to make space.

Luca appears in the hall, hair pointing in six directions, pajama pants twisted, one sock MIA.

"Santa came," he announces, eyes still half-asleep. "I heard him."

Mia swipes quickly at her cheeks. I brush my knuckles against her hand—quick, grounding—then turn toward him.

"Yeah, buddy," I say. My voice stays steady. "I think he did."

He blinks between us, the tilt of his head saying he feels the shift even if he can't name it. Then, Christmas brain wins.

"Do we have pancakes?" he asks.

Mia exhales a sound that's half laugh, half gasp. "We can," she says. "If your Uncle—" She stops. Swallows. Tries again. "If Jake doesn't burn them."

She looks at me when she says my name. It's a small thing. It hits like a bell.

"I make excellent pancakes," I lie.

Luca beams. "Christmas pancakes!"

He rockets at me, arms wrapping around my leg. I catch my balance with one hand on his head and the other on the counter.

Mia meets my eyes over the top of his curls.

We're not okay. Not yet. The hardest conversation is still waiting.

But for the first time in six years, it feels like we're going to walk into it facing the same direction.

Together.

37

FRONT AND CENTER

MIA

By the time we turn onto my parents' street, the day's already loud.

Every house is lit—blinking reindeer, lopsided stars, one inflatable snowman that looks like it's questioning its life choices. Mom and Dad's place glows the brightest. Warm windows. Wreath on the door. Smoke curling from the chimney like the house is sighing out joy.

I used to walk into this picture without thinking.

Today, it feels like stepping onto a stage I've been rewriting backstage.

Luca kicks the back of my seat. "We're here! We're here we're here we're here—"

"Seatbelt," I warn automatically.

He huffs, but the buckle clicks. Jake's mouth curves, the corners soft with amusement and something deeper. His knuckles tap once against the steering wheel, like he's grounding himself.

"You ready?" he asks quietly.

No.

"Yes," I say.

Because we promised.

Because a five-year-old with his eyes deserves the truth more than I deserve another day of safety.

We climb out into the sharp cold. Snow scrunches under my boots. Luca bolts ahead with his new hat sliding down over one eyebrow, the *Daddy* ornament clutched in his mittened hand like treasure.

"Careful on the steps, Lu," Jake calls.

Luca doesn't slow, just throws a hand back in a vague *I-hear-you* wave that looks exactly like Jake when he was sixteen and late.

My throat tightens.

Jake falls into step beside me. Our shoulders brush. The contact is small, steadying.

"You sure you want to tell him here?" he murmurs. "We can wait. Take him for a walk later. Cabin. Anywhere that isn't . . . " He nods toward the front door as it bursts open in a blast of sound and light.

"WELCOME, YOU BEAUTIFUL PEOPLE!" Harper bellows, already in an apron that says, *Baking Is My Cardio.* "You're late. We're on our second cinnamon roll offensive."

Mom appears behind her, cheeks flushed, dish towel over one shoulder. "You're not late," she scolds. "You're exactly on time. Come in—it's freezing."

Heat and noise hit us at once.

Cinnamon. Pine. Wrapping paper rustling. Mariah Carey wailing faintly from somewhere in the back of the house, probably against Dad's will.

Luca launches himself at my mother like a cannonball.

"Nana! Look what Santa gave me!" He brandishes the orna-ment. "It says *Daddy*. For me."

Mom's gaze flickers—ornament, Luca, me. Her face soft-ens, then does that thing where she tucks too much knowing into one small smile.

"That's very special, sweetheart," she says. "We'll find the perfect spot for it."

She squeezes my arm as I pass. Once. Firm. *We'll talk later.* No judgment. Just a quiet, *I see all of you.*

Dad swoops in to hug me, then claps Jake on the shoulder like he's always belonged here. "You staying for dinner, son?" he asks.

Jake hesitates for half a heartbeat.

I feel it—the old instinct to make it easy for him, to say no for both of us, to keep things simple.

"Yes," I say instead. "He is."

Jake glances at me—surprised, then steady. "If the invite's real," he says.

Dad snorts. "We've got more ham than sense. Get in here."

We shed coats in the hallway chaos. Gloves. Hats. Layers. Jake's hand brushes mine, fingers catching briefly on my sleeve. The look he gives me says *thank you* and *holy shit* and *I'm here* all at once.

Inside, it's everything Christmas has ever been—too much and somehow not enough.

Luca and Dad are already on the floor by the tree, exca-vating Lego sets. Harper steals bacon off a plate. Houston appears from behind the couch with a mug and a suspiciously innocent face. Cherie and Darren sit on the loveseat, their heads close, cheeks pink from the walk over. The Carter laugh—loud, warm—twines through the Snowden hum like it's always been part of the soundtrack.

It should be comforting.

It feels like watching a fragile mobile spin, knowing one wrong touch could tangle everything.

Jake stands for a second just inside the living room, taking it all in. His shoulders ease—the barest fraction—at the sight of his parents on the couch, my parents flustering over coffee refills, Luca already insisting that everyone admire the same three rocket pieces.

He glances at me.

I see it hit him—*I could have missed this. I almost did.*

My chest squeezes.

"Jake!" Luca hollers. "You gotta help! It's a four-plus and I'm only five, so I need supervision."

"That's . . . not how numbers work," Harper says, squinting at the box. "But excellent emotional manipulation, kid."

Jake huffs a laugh and drops down beside him. "You heard the man. Supervision."

He rolls his sleeves up, forearms all efficient competence and a faint burn mark I don't recognize. Luca scoots closer, hinging himself against Jake's side like it's muscle memory.

I stand very still and try not to cry about something as stupid as a Lego set.

Houston slides in next to me, offering a mug. "Cocoa?" he says. "Or is it too early to spike things?"

"Emotionally?" I ask. "We're already at New Year's."

He snorts. "That bad?"

I look at the couch—Cherie watching her son with Luca, Darren laughing at something Dad says, Mom pretending not to be tracking every micro-expression on my face.

At the tree—Jake bent carefully over the instructions, Luca narrating step eight like it's a classified briefing.

"It's that . . . much," I say.

Houston follows my gaze. "Yeah," he says, softer. "It is."

He doesn't ask. He doesn't make a joke. Just clinks his mug gently against mine and leaves me with the cocoa and my own heart to figure out.

We almost make it to the second round of cinnamon rolls before the ornament comes back.

Luca digs through the wrapping paper drift and emerges with the red glass sphere held aloft. "We forgot this one!"

The room quiets—not all the way, but enough.

He holds it out to Jake. "You should put it on. Santa said."

Jake takes it like it's made of something more breakable than glass. His thumb rubs over the gold word once. *Daddy.* Then he goes very, very still.

I feel it in my bones.

Cherie is watching. Her eyes shine, but she doesn't speak. Darren's hand tightens on her knee. Mom is frozen by the coffee table, dish towel in mid-air. Dad suddenly finds a spot on the wall completely fascinating.

Luca bounces. "Front and center," he instructs. "'Cause it's new."

Jake swallows. "Yeah," he says hoarsely. "Front and center sounds right."

He glances at me. It's not a question. It's a, *How are we doing this, Mouse?*

My heart pounds. "Come on," I say. "We'll all help."

We move as one—Jake lifting Luca, me steadying them both at the base of the tree. Pine needles prick my wrist. The lights hum quietly.

"Right there," Luca decides, tapping a branch near the middle where the glow is warmest. "So Santa can see it."

Jake hooks the ornament carefully, fingers shaking enough that I feel it through Luca's boot and my own skin.

When they let go, it swings once, catching every color in the room, and settles.

It looks . . . right.

Which is somehow worse.

Luca wriggles, trying to see. Jake lowers him, hands planted wide on his sides, anchoring.

My mother exhales—a tiny sound, like something finally landing where it's been circling for years.

I feel it: A shift. Not dramatic. Not explosive. Just a quiet click as the picture in this room rearranges itself around what's always been true.

Jake straightens, his hand brushing Luca's hair, thumb pausing just long enough to memorize the weight.

He meets my eyes. *We have to tell him.*

The thought is so loud it might as well be spoken.

My palms go slick. "Hey, buddy?" I say, somehow finding my voice. "Can you pause your rocket mission for a little while?"

Luca groans. "Mooom."

"It's important," Jake adds gently.

Luca squints between us, suspicion flaring. "Are we doing feelings?"

Harper snorts into her coffee. "Whose child is this again?"

"Mine," I say, too fast.

Jake's mouth twitches. "Definitely yours."

Cherie steps in then, bless her. "Why don't you use the den?" she suggests lightly, smoothing my hair back like I'm eleven again. "We'll keep the troops occupied out here. No sneak attacks."

My dad nods, clearing his throat. "We'll, uh, run interference. Comes with the grandparent package."

Mom squeezes my hand. Her eyes say everything. *You can do this. You're not alone.*

My knees wobble, anyway.

I take a breath too sharp and murmur, "Give me one second," before anyone can notice the way my voice cracks. I slip into the kitchen under the pretense of refilling the cocoa pot. Really, I just need a wall to lean on.

Mom follows me into the kitchen without being asked. She always has—ever since I was small and hid in pantries to cry about scraped knees or school plays where my antlers fell off.

Now, she just stands beside me as I grip the counter.

"You're trembling," she murmurs.

"I'm fine."

"Mia." Just my name. Soft. Surgical.

I exhale shakily. "I keep thinking about Ava. I feel like I tore apart her whole Christmas."

Mom's hands still. For a second, she just breathes, then nods toward a small stack on the sideboard—three wrapped packages, neat corners, perfect bows.

"She left those this morning," Mom says. "One for Luca. One for you. One for Jake."

My stomach flips. "She came here?"

"Briefly." Mom wipes her hands on a towel, choosing her words with care. "She didn't want a scene. She just wanted to do the kind thing and then go."

Guilt claws at me. "I didn't want to hurt her."

"You didn't," Mom says firmly. "Life did. Timing did.

And she told me—very clearly—that she didn't want you carrying the blame for choices she made with her eyes open."

That stops me. "She said that?"

"She did." Mom's gaze softens. "She said she'd been holding onto something that wasn't going to grow the way she hoped. And she didn't blame you for that. Not even a little."

My throat tightens. "It still feels . . . awful."

"I know." Mom steps closer, smoothing a curl behind my ear the way she used to when I was ten. "But listen to me: Ava isn't broken. She's disappointed, and she's grieving, and she's also stronger than you think."

She hesitates, then adds gently, "And she didn't leave alone."

My head lifts. "What?"

"Dylan was waiting outside," Mom says. "Just . . . to make sure she wasn't walking away from everything into nothing." She shrugs lightly. "Sometimes people find each other at strange moments. Doesn't mean anything dramatic. Just means she wasn't adrift."

I knew she'd left with Dylan, but I didn't understand until now that she wasn't leaving broken.

Mom squeezes my hand. "You don't need to spend another second punishing yourself for her path. That's hers to walk. Yours is here."

Her eyes drift toward the living room—toward Jake kneeling beside Luca, showing him how to adjust the telescope tripod.

"Your world is finally shifting into place," she whispers. "Don't look backward for permission to live it."

My eyes burn. "I don't know how to stop feeling responsible."

"Oh, sweetheart," she murmurs, pulling me into her arms,

"that's because you've always mistaken responsibility for love. They're not the same thing."

I let my forehead fall against her shoulder. "Then what is this?"

"Love," she says simply, "is choosing each other now."

And for the first time all day, my guilt loosens enough for breath to move.

38

YOU. HIM. US.

MIA

I step back into the living room, pulse steadier, guilt loosened, heart still a mess but at least beating in the right direction.

"Okay," I say, voice clearer. "Let's go."

Jake studies my face—sees the shift, doesn't question it.

"Come on, Lu," I say. "Den. Bring your ornament."

"Is this about my sled request?" he asks gravely. "Because Santa said he'd do his best."

"It's not about the sled," Jake says. His voice goes soft around the edges. "Promise."

"Hm." Luca eyes him like he's evaluating intel. "Okay. But I reserve the right to make a counter-argument."

Jake laughs under his breath. "Sounds fair."

The den is smaller. Less twinkle, more books. The noise from the living room drops to a muffled murmur—laughter, music, the clink of dishes. Out here, on the other side of the wall, my whole life feels like it's about to tilt.

Luca hops onto the couch, legs swinging. He sets the

ornament in his lap and pets it, like it might take offense otherwise.

"You're both making the weird face," he announces.

"What weird face?" I ask, offended.

"The 'I ate something spicy' face." He points. "That one, Mom."

Jake huffs out a startled laugh. It breaks some of the static in my chest.

I sit at one end of the couch. Jake sits at the other. There's space between us, but it feels like a line we're about to cross in a direction that actually matters.

"Okay," I start, then stall. My mouth goes dry.

Harper's voice rings in my head. *You don't have to be strong. Just brave.*

Jake's hand finds mine on the cushion between us. His fingers curl over my knuckles, steady pressure, quiet anchor.

"I'll start," he says. "If that's okay."

Relief floods me. "Yeah. Please."

Luca watches us, suspicious and curious and five.

"So," Jake begins, leaning forward a little, elbows on his knees, hands linked loosely. It's his debrief posture—calm, open, honest. "You know how some families work a little differently? Like how some kids have two houses. Or two moms and two dads. Or extra grandparents. Or a mom and a dad who didn't grow up together?"

"Like Amelia from school," Luca says immediately. "She has four grandmas. It's very complicated at snack time."

Jake smiles. "Exactly. People's families look all kinds of ways. But there's one thing that's always the same."

"What?" Luca asks.

"If a grown-up loves you and keeps showing up for you and would do anything to keep you safe," Jake says softly, "that makes them your family."

Luca considers this. "Like Nana and Grandpa."

"Yeah," Jake says. "Like them."

He glances at me. My throat is one giant knot.

"And sometimes," he continues, voice thinning, "people don't realize they're already family until a little later than they should have."

Luca tilts his head. "Like when you forget someone's birthday and then you say sorry and give them extra cake?"

"Kind of like that," Jake says. His eyes meet mine, bright with a truth that hurts and heals at the same time. "But bigger."

My heart is pounding so loud I'm surprised Luca can't hear it.

"Lu," I say, shifting closer. "You know how you asked about your dad before? And I told you some people take longer to get where they're meant to be?"

He nods slowly. "You said he was far away, but I was loved."

A tear slips before I can stop it. "I did."

"I was wrong about one part," I say, voice shaking. "He wasn't as far as I thought."

Luca frowns. "Is he here?"

Jake's hand tightens around mine.

I turn to him. It feels like stepping off the edge.

"Yes," I whisper. "He is."

Luca looks at me. Then at Jake. Then back at the ornament in his lap.

His eyes widen. "No way," he says.

My lungs seize.

Jake's voice is very gentle. "Yeah, buddy," he says. "Way."

Silence. One long, stretched second of it.

"You're my dad?" Luca whispers, like the words might break if he uses his normal volume.

"If you want me," Jake says, just as soft. "If that feels okay to you."

Luca stares at him. Then at me. Then at their joined hands between us.

"But—" His little brows knit. "How long? Like . . . since yesterday? Or since the motel? Or since I was a baby?"

The question cracks something inside me. I hear my own breath hitch.

Jake swallows. I see him choose his answer with care. "Since before you were born," he says. "I didn't know it yet. But that's when I became your dad. I just . . . didn't get to meet you until later."

Luca processes this with the full seriousness of a five-year-old processing the Marvel timeline.

"So you missed some stuff," he says finally. "My first Halloween. The dinosaur phase. When I learned 'Jingle Bells, Batman smells'."

A broken laugh escapes me.

"Yeah," Jake says roughly. "I missed a lot. That's on me. But if you'll let me, I'd like to be here for everything from now on. Good days. Bad days. Science fairs. Broken skate attempts. All of it."

He pauses. Breathes. "I want to be your dad, Luca. Not just your mom's friend. Not just the guy who takes you for cocoa and skates next to you. The real thing."

My eyes blur.

Luca looks down at the ornament and turns it carefully in his hands. The gold letters flash. "Did Santa know?" he asks.

Jake's mouth twists. "I think Santa might have had a hunch."

Luca squints. "Did Nana know?"

Mom's laugh carries faintly through the wall, as if on cue.

He looks back up at us. "I kinda already knew," he says suddenly.

It knocks the breath out of both of us. "You did?" I manage.

He shrugs, a tiny mirror of Jake's deflection. "You guys look at each other weird. And your laugh sounds like his. And Nana said you both said *Be Brave* the same weird way."

Jake chokes. "It was hot."

"So," Luca concludes, as if that settles it, "it just makes sense."

My shoulders shake with a half-sob, half-laugh I can't stop.

"Are you mad?" I ask, terrified.

He looks honestly perplexed. "Why would I be mad? This is the coolest twist ever."

Jake's eyes squeeze shut for a second, like he's trying not to lose it completely.

When he opens them, they're shining. "You sure you're okay with it?" he asks. "It's a lot of information for Christmas."

Luca thinks. "Does this mean you can come to career day?"

Jake lets out a helpless laugh. "If they'll let me."

"And teach me to fix stuff?" Luca adds. "And maybe we can share hot cocoa codes? And I can call you Dad?"

Jake swallows hard. "Yeah," he says, voice breaking. "Yeah, kiddo. I'd really like that."

Luca beams. Then, launches himself across the couch at Jake like a small, determined missile.

Jake oofs, catching him, arms wrapping around Luca's small body instinctively. He buries his face in Luca's hair for a second, shoulders shaking.

I look away because the moment feels too huge, too holy to witness straight on.

When I look back, Luca has his hands planted on either side of Jake's face, squishing his cheeks.

"You're my dad," he says, like he's trying it out. "For real."

"For real," Jake echoes, voice shredded.

He glances at me over Luca's shoulder. There's fear there —still. Regret. Guilt for the years they lost.

But there's also something else.

Peace.

We don't walk back into the living room right away.

We stay in the den until Luca has asked seventeen follow-up questions (Can dads get time-outs? Who decided my middle name? Does this mean we have to like the same sports team?), and Jake has answered every one like it matters.

At some point, Luca falls quiet, his head pillowed on Jake's thigh, fingers still curled around the ornament. His eyelids droop, full of sugar and revelations.

Jake's hand moves absently through Luca's curls, slow and steady.

I press my knuckles to my mouth. "He trusts you," I whisper.

Jake glances up. "Do you?" he asks.

It's not an accusation.

It's a risk.

"Yes," I say. My voice comes out rough but true. "More than I ever let myself admit."

His shoulders drop just a little. "Good," he says. "Because I'm terrified, but I've never been more sure of anything than I am about this."

"This?" I ask.

He looks down at Luca. Then at me.

"You," he says simply. "Him. Us."

Heat stings my eyes all over again. "That's three things," I say weakly.

"Yeah." A faint smile. "Turns out my math gets better when it's about you."

Luca snores softly. It smells like pine and sugar and possibility in here.

From the other room, someone turns the music up. Laughter rolls down the hall; the house vibrates with life.

I straighten, swiping under my eyes. "Ready to tell the rest of the world?" I ask.

"Not yet," Jake says. "But ready enough."

We share a look. Then we carry our son back into the noise.

39

NORTHLIGHT BLUFF

MIA

If anyone is surprised when Luca climbs straight into Jake's lap in front of the tree and announces, "This is my dad, actually," they hide it well.

Mom's hand flies to her mouth like she's catching joy itself. Dad blinks hard and clears his throat a few times. Cherie's cheeks are already wet. Darren's jaw clenches in that don't-cry, don't-cry way that never works.

Harper, of course, takes a picture. "About damn time," she says, voice suspiciously thick.

"Language," Mom warns automatically, dabbing at her eyes.

"*Darn* time," Harper amends, not sorry at all.

Houston slings an arm around the back of the couch, eyes crinkling. "Guess that solves the mystery of who Luca's side-eye belongs to."

"Genetics," I say. "Tragic, really."

Jake laughs, hand steady on Luca's back. He looks half dazed, half like his bones finally realize they live here.

Cherie crosses the room and sinks onto the coffee table in front of us, ignoring the protest it makes.

"Hey, sweet boy," she says to Luca, voice trembling. "You okay if I steal a hug from both of you?"

Luca nods, generous. "You're Grandma of the Year," he informs her. "That's important work."

She makes a sound that might be a laugh, might be a sob, and wraps her arms around them both—Jake and Luca, her son and her grandson, finally in the same frame.

I bite my lip so hard it hurts.

When she pulls back, she turns to me. Her hand finds mine and squeezes, her palm warm, familiar.

"You want to know when I knew?" she asks quietly, like we're picking up a conversation we started years ago.

I nod, not trusting my voice.

"The tree farm," she says. Her gaze goes a little hazy with memory. "We were getting ready to take photos, snow in his hair, and he looked straight at me like he'd already figured out the world. Just like Jake did. Same . . . way of taking in everything at once."

"You never asked," I whisper.

"Wasn't my question to ask," she says simply. "Just an answer I was willing to wait for."

I swallow hard. "Are you . . . mad?"

She shakes her head, eyes wet, smile small and fierce. "Honey, I'm holding my grandson and watching my son finally look like himself again. I don't have room for mad right now."

A sob catches in my chest. "I'm sorry," I say. "For the years. For the secrets. For—"

She cuts me off with a light flick to my wrist. "You did what you thought would keep everyone breathing. That's not something I fault you for. That's something I recognize."

My throat closes.

"You're here now," she says. "That's what matters."

Her thumb brushes my knuckles in the exact same pattern Jake's did earlier. "Besides," she adds, eyes softening even more, "you've always been his Mouse. The rest of us were just waiting for the story to catch up."

The words land in my chest and settle there, warm and true.

The living room erupts again—Harper yelling about frosting sabotage, Dad demanding someone hide the glitter—and it's suddenly too much. Too bright. Too loud. Emotion is still buzzing under my skin like electricity.

I slip into the kitchen, telling myself I just need water.

The quiet hits instantly. Soft. Cooler. The kind of quiet that lets the last hour settle somewhere deep.

And there, on the counter beside the fruit bowl, sits the Advent calendar.

I step closer, fingertips grazing the familiar felt edge. "Of course," I whisper. "You moved again."

A soft sound turns me. Mom leans in the doorway, dish towel over her shoulder, eyes gentled in the way that always makes me feel both seen and small.

"I didn't think you'd notice it this fast," she says.

"Did you move it?" I ask. "The calendar. It keeps . . . showing up."

She exhales—not guilty. Just honest. "I pulled it out of the attic the day you came home," she admits. "It was crushed in a bin with old stockings. It felt wrong, letting it gather dust when so much in you was waking back up."

I swallow. "So you filled the doors?"

"Some." She smiles sadly. "The drawing of Orion. The pinecone. Lucky was in the attic. I thought . . . maybe it would remind you of who you were before you left."

My eyes sting. "But Door 24," I say hoarsely. "Did you—"

"No." She steps closer. "That one was always between you and Jake."

She reaches out, smoothing a curl behind my ear like she used to when I was little.

"The calendar didn't move on its own," she says softly. "The people who love you kept shifting it closer until you finally opened the right door."

A tear slips free. "You knew," I whisper.

She smiles. "We all knew. Just not the part that needed to come from you."

Noise swells behind us—Jake laughing, Luca shrieking about rockets, Harper arguing with Houston over the definition of *burnt*.

Mom squeezes my hand. "Go on," she murmurs. "Your boys are waiting."

I nod, wipe my cheeks, and walk back into the light.

Later—after plates are scraped clean and Luca's half-slumped over his new rocket in a sugar coma—is when Jake nudges my elbow.

"Hey," he says. "I, uh . . . have something for him. For us."

"No more presents," I groan. "We're at capacity."

"Too bad," he says. "This one's grandfather-approved."

Darren perks up. "I plead the fifth."

Jake disappears down the hall and returns with a long, narrow box. Silver paper. Red twine. My heart does something ridiculous.

He crouches by Luca. "Hey, space ranger."

Luca lifts his head, hair wild. "Huh?"

"One more," Jake says, tapping the lid. "From me. And maybe from Santa, if you're not too full."

Luca perks up with miraculous speed. "I'm never too full. That's a myth."

Paper flies. The lid lifts.

He gasps. "A telescope," he breathes. "Like the big one at the Terrace."

"Smaller," Jake says. "Portable. For missions."

"Missions?" Luca's practically vibrating. "What kind of missions?"

"The kind where we go find Orion," Jake says. Then, his eyes flick to mine. "Properly. Not just from the parking lot."

Something flickers in my chest—memory and longing and a promise we never got to keep.

"You sure that's a good idea?" I ask, voice low.

"I'm sure it's the only one I've had all week that feels like it was already waiting for us," he says.

Luca holds the telescope like it's holy. "Can we go now?"

"After you put on real shoes," I say automatically.

"And three layers," Mom calls from the kitchen. "And someone text me when you get there."

"Yes, ma'am," Jake calls back, saluting with a cocoa mug.

The hill above town hasn't changed.

Frozen grass. The dark spine of trees. The whole of Frost Harbor sprawled below us—rooftops, steeples, the faint glow of the rink, the line of the river like a strip of black satin.

The sky is clear—sharp stars scattered in exact configurations.

The last time I stood here, I was sixteen and terrified of everything I wanted.

This time, I'm twenty-seven and still terrified—just of different things.

Jake plants the tripod in the snow, breath coming in short, visible bursts. "Okay," he says, stepping back. "Captain, you're up."

Luca squints into the eyepiece, tongue poking out. "I see . . . a blur. And another blur. And—wait—three tiny dots in a row. Like buttons."

"Good eye," Jake murmurs, and there's so much pride in his voice it makes my knees weak. "That's the belt."

"Orion!" Luca crows, nearly knocking the tripod. "Mom! Look, look, look."

"I see him," I say, even though I'm still looking at Jake's profile in the starlight.

His gaze shifts, finds mine. "Your turn, Mouse," he says softly. "Make a wish."

The words land differently now than they used to. Not as an escape. As an invitation.

I step closer, bending over the telescope. My fingers brush his on the barrel; he doesn't pull away.

The stars snap into focus—bright, distant, sharp. Three in a neat line. One shoulder. One knee. The same picture I've been carrying in my head since sixteen and pretending belonged to someone else.

Behind me, Luca's mitten finds my elbow. On my other side, Jake's palm rests light at my back.

We stand there like that—stitched together under a sky that has seen every version of us.

"What did you wish for?" Luca asks, bouncing a little.

I lower my eyes, look between them. *My boys. My once, my always, my North.*

"Nothing," I say, and for the first time, it's true.

I already got it.

DOOR 26

JUST TRUTH

MIA

The glitter massacre is almost contained when the floorboard sighs behind me.

I don't jump.

Not tonight.

Not after the day we had—the truth, the den, Luca curled into Jake like he'd been waiting his whole life to fit there, the ornament gleaming on the tree like a heartbeat.

Still, my pulse skitters as I turn.

Jake fills the doorway in red velvet pants, an open Santa coat, and the laziest, most devastating smirk I've ever seen. Firelight climbs his chest like it's found its favorite place to land.

"Ho," he says, voice lower than the fire behind him. "Ho. Holy . . . wow."

A startled laugh breaks out of me. "You're going to explain this."

He walks toward me—slow, measured steps that vibrate straight through the floorboards. "Found my dad's old Santa suit. Backup plan since I was twelve. In case the big guy got the flu."

He tugs the lapel. "Took a gamble, it still fits."

It fits too well.

"You forgot the belt," I say, breath tilting.

"Did I?" His tone is threaded with trouble. "Guess I got distracted."

I look away. I don't trust myself to look straight at him and not melt into a puddle on the tree skirt. "Santa's supposed to be jolly."

"Oh, I'm jolly," he says, stepping close enough for heat to roll off him and wrap around me. "You should see my mood tonight."

"Tonight?" My voice goes thin. "Because of . . . everything?"

His grin softens. "Because *my* family is asleep in this house."

My chest folds in on itself. "Jake—"

"And because," he adds, brushing a fleck of glitter from my cheek with his thumb, "you've been smiling at me all day like you finally stopped bracing for the worst."

I freeze, breath caught somewhere between wanting and fear.

"I'm still bracing a little," I admit.

His thumb sweeps slowly along my jaw. "Then let me give you something you don't have to brace for."

He doesn't grab.

He doesn't rush.

He just lowers his head until his forehead touches mine, a soft breath exchanging between us.

"Mouse," he murmurs. "Tell me to stop."

I don't.

His smile is barely there. "Yeah. I didn't think so."

Then he lifts me, not over his shoulder this time, not teasing or chaotic, just a steady, grounding scoop of arms under my knees and back that makes the world tilt in one long, controlled arc.

"Jake!" I gasp.

"What?" he asks innocently. "Santa does deliveries."

"Deliveries?"

"Mmhm." He nudges open the bedroom door with his foot. Candles flicker inside, stars crowding every surface. "Special orders only."

My breath stutters. "You lit all these?"

"After you put Luca down." He sets me carefully on the edge of the bed, kneeling between my knees. "I wanted . . . the right kind of quiet."

My heart trips. "There's a wrong kind?"

"For us?" His hand slides to my waist, warm and certain. "Yeah. Any kind that feels like running."

I swallow. Hard. Because tonight, for the first time, running doesn't even occur to me.

His gaze drops, not with hunger first—with reverence. "Mia," he says softly. "You've been carrying other people's fear for too damn long. Let me carry something back."

He reaches for the hem of my pajama top and pauses. "Can I?"

I nod.

He lifts the fabric slowly—not a reveal, but an unveiling—like he's tracing years, not inches. My breath sticks when the soft light hits the pale lines across my stomach.

I move to tug the shirt back down on instinct, but his hands close gently around my wrists.

"No," he whispers. "Not this time."

His thumb traces one of the faint silver marks. "These are mine to love," he says. "All of them."

My throat burns. "They're—"

"Proof," he cuts in. "Of what you survived. Proof of what you gave this world. Proof of him." His voice roughens. "Don't ever hide my son's story from me."

A tear slips before I can stop it. He kisses it from my cheek, slow and unhurried.

"Lie back," he murmurs.

I do.

He lowers himself over me, bracing on his elbows, his body warm and heavy in the best possible way. His mouth finds my throat, slow kisses trailing down my skin until he reaches the soft curve of my stomach.

He presses a kiss there. Then another.

Then one more.

"Thank you," he whispers against my skin.

"For what?" I choke out.

"For making him. For raising him. For not breaking under the weight of both of us."

My heart breaks open—not from pain, but from release. "You're going to ruin me," I breathe.

He lifts his head, eyes molten. "Mouse, I'm going to love you. You get to decide how that ruins you."

The kiss he gives me next is not tentative.

Not scared.

Not the hush of ghosts or what-ifs.

It's the kiss of someone who finally has permission to stay.

I arch into him, fingers sliding into his hair, every inch of me lighting up in places I thought had gone quiet.

"Jake—" His name escapes on a gasp as he shifts his hips. "God—"

He grins against my mouth, wicked and tender. "There she is."

He sinks into me slowly—not teasing, not torturing—just learning me again, inch by inch, breath by breath.

My hands shake against his back. His grip tightens on my thigh.

The world narrows to heat, to breath, to the rhythm we find together without trying.

When release hits, it feels like falling and landing at the same time.

After, he gathers me on top of him, my cheek on his chest, his palm sliding up and down my spine in slow, anchoring strokes.

"Mia?" he murmurs into my hair.

"Mm?"

"No more blank doors," he whispers. "If something scares you . . . tell me before it turns into a secret."

My breath catches. "Okay."

"Promise?"

I lift my head. His eyes find mine—soft, warm, completely unguarded.

"Promise," I say. "No more silence."

He exhales like it's the first full breath he's taken all day.

Then he kisses me again, slow, sleepy and sure, then pulls the blanket over both of us.

Outside, snow falls. Inside, for the first time, nothing feels like hiding.

Just home.

Just us.

Just truth.

BOOK TWO

FROST HARBOR SERIES

AVA

Airports used to calm me. The boards, the order, the illusion that movement equals progress.

Tonight, all it does is press on a bruise I can't quite locate.

The overhead announcements blur into a dull hum. Suitcases rattle past like loose thoughts. Someone's kid laughs too loud and too brightly, and it hits me right in the space where I've been pretending nothing is missing.

I grip my boarding pass harder than necessary.

Gate B12. One-way.

My reflection in the big glass wall is unsettling. Not because I look different, but because I look like *myself* for the first time in years. No ring. No borrowed future. No pretending I belong in a story that never fit.

Just me.

And Dylan, pacing behind me like he's afraid if he stops moving, he'll think too much.

He doesn't realize I'm watching him until he does. Then

he freezes, runs a hand through his hair, gives me that lopsided almost-grin that used to annoy me in high school.

"You don't have to come," I tell him. Again. For the third time tonight.

He huffs. "You said that in the driveway. And at the stop-light. And again when I bought your ticket because you were too busy panicking to remember your wallet."

Heat prickles my cheeks. "I wasn't panicking."

"Sure," he says. "And I'm not currently imagining the many ways this airport could burst into flames."

I fight the pull of a smile and look back at the window. Snow is falling in slow spirals across the tarmac, sparkling under the floodlights. Too beautiful for how hollow I feel.

"You should be home," I murmur.

"Home's . . . complicated," he says. "And you looked like you needed someone who wasn't afraid to stand close."

That one lands. Too clean. Too honest.

I swallow hard. "People are going to misunderstand. You being here."

"Let them," he says quietly, certain. "You deserve someone who shows up. Even if the rest of the world hasn't caught up yet."

The boarding line begins to inch forward.

I step up. Dylan follows.

My chest tightens—fear, relief, something between them. The idea of turning around and telling him to stay hits me like a wave. So does the idea of telling him to come closer.

Instead, I exhale. "You don't owe me anything, Dylan."

He leans in—not touching me, just close enough for his voice to land at the exact right depth.

"Maybe not," he says. "But some people you leave for a reason."

A beat.

"And some people . . . you leave *with*."

My breath stutters. I turn quickly so he won't see what that does to me. "Come on," I say, stepping onto the jet bridge. "We'll miss the flight."

Behind me, I hear him laugh—warm and a little wrecked.

I don't know what city we'll land in.

I don't know what we're walking toward.

I don't know if this is a mistake or the first time I've chosen myself in years.

But I do know this: *I didn't leave Frost Harbor alone.*

And maybe—just maybe—I'm finally stepping into a story that's mine.

ACKNOWLEDGMENTS

This book exists because of an entire constellation of people, and I want to shine a light on every single one of them.

To my editor — thank you for championing this story from page one, for your patience when I needed to rewrite (again), and for knowing exactly when to push and when to reassure. You made me braver.

To my friends and family, who celebrated every tiny milestone and pretended not to notice the chaos surrounding my writing schedule — thank you for loving me through deadlines, rewrites, and questionable snack choices.

To my early readers and cheerleaders — your messages, reactions, and late-night voice notes kept me going more than you know.

To the writing community that welcomed me without hesitation — your generosity, advice, and memes were a lifeline.

And to every reader holding this book now — You're the reason these characters get to breathe. Thank you for stepping into their world.

ABOUT THE AUTHOR

Calla Cross writes romantic suspense with attitude—glossy danger, high-heat tension, and enough twists to make you side-eye everyone. When she's not creating chaos on the page, she's usually reading, momming, or posting entirely too many bookish memes.

Come join her Facebook group, Calla's Crossroads, for sneak peeks, spoilers, and all the delightful chaos she doesn't put on Instagram.

ALSO BY Calla Cross

NorthRidge University series

Fighting Fate: Best Friends to Lovers

Fighting For Redemption: Enemies to Lovers

Second Chance Romance

A Second Chance in Blue Haven

Suspense Romance

Tell Me Something

Christmas Romance

Christmas Confessions

www.ingramcontent.com/pod-product-compliance
Lightning Source LLC
Chambersburg PA
CBHW050010120726
47903CB00006B/1708